WONDERFUL FOOL

SHUSAKU ENDO
WONDERFUL FOOL

TRANSLATED FROM THE JAPANESE AND
WITH AN INTRODUCTION BY FRANCIS MATHY

PETER OWEN
LONDON AND CHESTER SPRINGS

PETER OWEN PUBLISHERS
73 Kenway Road, London SW5 0RE

Peter Owen books are distributed in the USA by
Dufour Editions Inc., Chester Springs, PA 19425-0007

Translated from the Japanese *Obaka San*
First British Commonwealth edition 1974
English translation © Peter Owen Ltd 1974, 1995
This paperback edition 2000
Reprinted 2002

A catalogue record for this book is available from
the British Library

ISBN 0 7206 1080 X

Printed and bound in Great Britain by
Bookmarque Ltd, Croydon, Surrey

Introduction

This was the third of Shusaku Endo's novels to come out in English translation. *Silence*, published in Japan in 1966 and in English translation in 1969, was an historical novel treating of martyrs and apostates in seventeenth-century Japan. It won immediate critical acclaim both at home and abroad. Francis King, reviewing it in the *Sunday Telegraph*, praised it in glowing terms :

> It is a rare experience for a novel reviewer to have in his hands a book of which he can say without any qualifications : 'This is a masterpiece.' . . . Yet such are the universality and grandeur of its theme and such the brilliance of its execution, that a masterpiece is precisely what this story about the persecution of Christians in 17th-century Japan must be acclaimed as being.

Graham Greene named it one of the three finest novels he had read in 1969.

The plot of *The Sea and Poison*, published in Japan in 1957 and by Peter Owen in 1972, was based on an actual incident that took place in Japan towards the end of the war : several American prisoners were used as guinea pigs and killed in medical experiments conducted at a Japanese university. Endo imaginatively reconstructs the attitudes and feelings of the doctors, nurses, and medical students involved in the experiments.

The present novel was written in 1959 and thus falls chronologically between the other two. A light, humorous novel, it seems at first unrelated to either. Further consideration, however, reveals that the three novels have at least one very striking theme in common, the theme of what Endo frequently refers to as 'mudswamp Japan'.

In *Silence*, the 'mudswamp' is the symbol of Japan's inability to accept the Christian God. The apostate priest, Father Ferreira, tells another captured priest : 'This country is a mudswamp ... far more terrible than I ever could have imagined. The roots of whatever shoots are planted here rot and the leaves turn yellow and wither.' Later, when this second priest in turn apostatizes, a Japanese official tells him : 'Father, it was not by us that you were defeated, but by this mudswamp, Japan.' The same official tells Ferreira in *The Golden Country*, a play whose action parallels that of the novel, 'But the mudswamp too has its good points. If you will but give yourself up to its comfortable warmth. The teachings of Christ are like a flame. Like a flame they set a man on fire. But the tepid warmth of Japan will eventually nurture sleep.'

In *The Sea and Poison* the mudswamp has a moral dimension, rather than a religious, and symbolizes the moral apathy of the characters. The mudswamp is found at its most innocent level in the narrator, who accidentally stumbles onto the facts of the incident. He is a white-collar worker who asks nothing from life but one child, a little house in the suburbs, a modest job and good health – 'just an ordinary bit of happiness.' But this 'ordinary bit of happiness' is all that the doctors and nurses that took part in the experiments wanted. Endo implies that the only difference between these killers and the narrator and the millions like him is one of circumstances.

This theme of the 'mudswamp Japan' is developed still further in a number of other novels and short stories. *Yellow Man*, for example, begins with the following quotation from *Revelation* : 'I know your works; you are neither cold nor hot. Would that you were cold or hot! So, because you are lukewarm, and neither cold nor hot, I will spew you out of my mouth.' One of the characters says of himself, 'A yellow man like me has absolutely no experience of anything so profound and extreme as the consciousness of sin you white men have. All we experience is fatigue, a deep fatigue – a weariness murky as the colour of my skin, dank, heavily submerged.'

Outside his novels, Endo made the point still clearer in a series of essays in which he analysed what he termed 'the threefold insensitivity of the Japanese' – the insensitivity to God, the insensitivity to sin, the insensitivity to death. He also made it clear that this insensitivity is something he finds within himself, against which he himself must struggle.

It is no exaggeration to say that the starting point of all Endo's fiction is Paul's agonized plea in *Romans*: 'Wretched man that I am! Who will deliver me from this body of death?' The answer is also the same as Paul's. In a series of lighter novels, many of them very pleasantly humorous, Endo introduces a number of interesting characters that are obviously Christ-figures, symbolizing the love of Christ. These are never strong and heroic, for such strength and heroism would frighten away the other characters and the author himself; such strength and heroism would be impossible for them to relate to. (This is the reason also why Endo in his historical fiction neglects the martyrs to write with feeling and sympathy about the apostates.) The influence of these symbolic characters is subtle, but penetrating and, ultimately, decisive: everyone who enters into friendship with them is left somehow changed for the better.

The first of these characters to appear in print was Gaston Bonaparte, a descendant of Napoleon, the 'fool' of *Wonderful Fool*. Gaston descends upon a typical, modern Japanese family and after causing considerable consternation ends by changing them, by helping them to take at least a few short steps out of the mudswamp.

Far from the romantic ideal of a Frenchman the daughter, Tomoe, had imagined, Gaston is tall and ungainly, with the face of a horse, unsightly in dress and unrefined in manner. He seems to lack common sense and to cower before any slight threat of danger. His words and actions from the moment of his arrival convince Tomoe that he is a complete fool.

But Gaston has one great redeeming virtue : an over-powering, self-sacrificing love of people and animals. His loving trust in others forces all who come into contact with him to face up to themselves and challenges them to change. The son, Takamori, a young office worker with no purpose in life – a 'swamp dweller' – comes to realize that 'to abandon Gaston would be like abandoning the best part of myself.' After Gaston has departed, Takamori for the first time notices with concern the plight of the poor and suffering people about him.

Tomoe is a selfish, pragmatic career girl, lacking in sentimentality and well able to make her way in the world. But she too has her moment of insight :

A man with a simple love for others, trusting everyone; who, no matter how often he is deceived or betrayed, continues to keep his flame of love and trust from going out – such a man is bound to seem a fool in the world as it is today. But he is no ordinary fool. He is a wonderful fool !

The greatest change of all is effected in the professional killer, Endo, who has hardened himself to human emotion and is out to avenge himself on his brother's murderers. At the last moment, influenced by Gaston, he does not carry out his revenge.

In this novel Endo points to the way out of the mud-swamp. That way is love – self-sacrificing, trusting, gentle love. The denizens of the mudswamp must first be loved and then they themselves become capable of loving, capable also of meaningful action. Appropriately, the climactic scene of the novel takes place in a real swamp where Gaston saves Endo from being sucked down into the mire. That Shusaku Endo should have given his name to the character in the novel most in need of redemption is adequate proof that the theme of *Wonderful Fool* is one that concerns him deeply.

Readers may have difficulty with Gaston's sudden disappearance at the end, when the killer Endo sees a white egret fly up into the sky. Earlier in the novel Takamori likens Gaston to Princess Kaguya of the early Japanese tale, 'The Tale of the Bamboo Cutter'. Princess Kaguya is banished to earth from her moon kingdom for some fault and lives as the adopted daughter of a poor bamboo cutter and his wife, bringing them great happiness. When her guilt has been sufficiently expiated, she returns to the moon. Takamori playfully suggests that Gaston too may have come to them from the skies. By the use of this leit-motif Endo may wish to indicate the divine origin of a love for his fellow man such as Gaston displays, and to enrich his theme by putting it into the context of Japanese folklore. A further source of this imagery is the eighth-century chronicle *Kojiki* and other Japanese folk tales in which men are transformed into birds and fly away from this world of turmoil and travail.

The Japan of *Wonderful Fool* is quite different from the exotic Japan that appears in most of the Japanese novels that have found their way into translation, particularly those of Mishima and Kawabata. Endo is a keen observer of the contemporary scene and he is also a fine satirist. Whether the target of his criticism is the medical world (as in *The Sea and Poison*) or the literary and academic world (as in the untranslated *And You, Too*) or the world of the office worker in his selfish pursuit of 'an ordinary bit of happiness', Endo's stab goes deep. The humour and the interesting situations in which the satire is clothed, however, serve to take away much of the sting. All kinds of characters are subjected to Endo's scalpel : famous moralists leading double lives; former war criminals still clawing their way ahead in time of peace; university students whose actions are inconsistent with their ideals; the pickpockets, quacks of all kinds, call girls and call boys, conspiring bar 'madams', gangsters that prey upon people in the streets of Tokyo (Endo's Tokyo is not unlike Dickens's London). Endo's Christian faith gives him a firm standard of judgement, one of the requirements for effective satire.

Sophia University, Tokyo   Francis Mathy, S.J.

1 Descendant of Napoleon

It was a Sunday morning in late March. The first timid plum blossoms had been joined by whole clusters of their fellows and the swelling white buds of the magnolia trees in the garden were about to burst open. Takamori lay curled up in bed, turtle-style, enjoying its warmth. Then loud in his ears sounded the shrill voice of his younger sister, Tomoe, calling to him from below.

'If you stay in bed much longer, you'll go mouldy. It's ten o'clock.'

'I'm just getting up,' answered Takamori in a mournful voice, pushing his head out of the covers.

'That's what you said half an hour ago.'

'I'm getting dressed.'

That was a lie, of course. But Takamori knew from experience that he still had a few minutes before his sister mounted the staircase to his room and began peeling the blankets off his bed.

Every Sunday morning he was subject to three waves of assault. First, with ear-splitting volume, she would shout up at him from the first-floor hallway. Still half-asleep, he would not make out her words. This first attack could be withstood with a simple 'OK' or 'huh-huh'.

Next she would try intimidating him, as she was doing now, by stomping loudly on the staircase, and calling up again. But here too was still a margin of safety. He would answer, as now, that he was getting dressed.

This time she could not be put off so easily. He knew she was standing motionless on the staircase, ears pricked for any sound he might make.

'Come and see then,' he called to her in defiance.

'But I warn you, I haven't a stitch on. Still, if you don't mind. . . .'

When he considered himself safe, he stretched out arms and legs in a strong act of will and reached for a cigarette from the packet at his bedside. This leisurely lie-in, possible only on holidays, was what kept a working man like him going for the rest of the week.

Takamori, who worked six days a week at a bank in the Otemachi district of Tokyo, wished to enjoy at least on Sunday the luxury of a late sleep, but he had this nuisance of a sister to contend with. People speak of 'hen-pecked husbands', but whoever heard of a 'hen-pecked brother'? Still a bachelor, he could not easily imagine the terrors a future wife had in store for him, but he knew all too well the feeling of oppression brought on by an actually existing sister.

When his married fellow workers at the bank confided to him in the noon break the fear they had of their wives, he wondered how much of what they said was true, and how much was part of the age-old strategy of exaggeration through which husbands sought to mollify their wives and render them harmless. In the first place, however terrifying she might be at times, every wife had at the bottom of her heart a soft spot for her husband, hadn't she? In the end she would be moved to seek reconciliation with him. In this, at least, a sister was different.

In Takamori's experience a sister was from earliest childhood the self-appointed prefect and critic of her brother. Not his slightest lapse or defect escaped her vigilant eye. 'I'll tell Daddy of you!' she had threatened, her large black eyes gleaming, when as a middle-school student he had tried to steal away from his books and go out to play with his friends in the neighbourhood. And when he had gone up to the roof of the house to sneak his first cigarette, it was she who had discovered him. Not even the threat of physical violence could keep her in her place. Even as a child she almost never shed a tear, no matter what he did

to her. Only the usual refrain : 'I'll tell Daddy of you!'
When their father arrived home from the office, she did
just that, exaggerating the facts out of all proportion. In
short, it was always Takamori who paid.

If in the attempt to divert her threats he tried to get into
her good graces, it was even worse. Women seem to have
from birth a knack for taking advantage of men who are
nice to them. This woman at any rate – Takamori had
learned from experience – was not to be treated gently.

Takamori's first problem was his name. His grandfather,
a scholar of Chinese letters who had been born and raised
in Kagoshima, had decided that his first grandson should
grow up to be a great man like the most famous of
Kagoshima's sons, Takamori Saigō, and had insisted therefore on this name. But name alone does not create the
actuality : there was in Takamori not a trace of the large-
minded openheartedness of his famous namesake. Tomoe,
on the other hand, had all the characteristics of the historical Tomoe Gozen, who, it is written in *The Tale of
Heike,* could handle sword and bow so dexterously that
she was a match for a thousand warriors and fit to meet
either god or devil, and who was among the last seven to
ride in battle with her lord, Yoshinaka Kiso. She was
strong-minded, shrewd, and hated to lose in anything.
She had been raised, in short, in the manner of the
present-day Japanese girl.

Takamori thought his sister above average in good looks.
When she was not raging or pouting, she had some rather
nice points about her, but there was nothing in her of the
classical Japanese maiden of antiquity, whose eyes moist-
ened on looking at the stars and who would sigh over a
violet. Of course, Tomoe had not always been like this. As
a baby she would raise her pretty little hands – the colour
of maple leaves in autumn – to Takamori, who was six
years older than she, and follow him about the house on
unsteady legs, wanting always to be near him. But then
at a certain point she had suddenly changed into this

nuisance of a sister who looked down her nose at her brother.

'Ah! I wonder if all the men in the world are as spineless as you! If so, I'm never going to get married,' she was insolent enough to declare.

Takamori had finally learned that it was best not to answer her when she spoke in this fashion. No doubt she surpassed him in shrewdness and practical energy. Even from university days she had taken a calculating look ahead and had applied herself with vigour and diligence to the study of Italian, a language which almost no one else was studying, and to typing and shorthand. When she graduated there was a surplus of girls who knew English and French, but Italian was another matter, as she had foreseen. Her strategy paid off brilliantly when she was taken on by an Italian trading company that paid her the equivalent of a man's salary. She was in fact making more money than her brother, so that even in the matter of economic power, he could not hold up his head to her.

Girls of Tomoe's age are generally on the lookout for a suitable husband, but Tomoe, very much the realist and not to be diverted in her ambition by either stars or violets, showed little interest in men. If all men were such unreliable, impractical dreamers as her brother, she had no wish to marry, at least for the present. She made no secret of this and was openly contemptuous both of the men who worked with her in the office and of the friends of Takamori who came over to visit. Deep in her heart she probably cherished the image of a strong, gallant man who would someday appear to sweep her off her feet, but she was not so sentimental as to make any such revelation to her brother.

She spent little of the money she made, preferring to invest it and see it doubled, even tripled. While girls in the past had put their extra earnings in a piggy bank or at best a savings account, today they enjoyed the exhilaration of playing the stock market and accumulating profits. Every morning as she sat across from Takamori at breakfast before going to work, it was not the society column nor the cinema advertisements in the newspaper that she quickly scanned as she ate, nor even the serialized novel, but rather the more practical report on stock fluctuations.

As he watched her, Takamori thought to himself, She must have quite a pile by now, and he felt both envy and repulsion. What kind of man will she ever find to marry her? I'd just like to see his face.

Thankfully, ancient sayings abound in phrases that elevate men and put down women. 'Daughters and dwarfs are hard to raise.' 'Little sparrows, how can you possibly fathom the plans of the great geese?' As Tomoe sat with her face buried in the newspaper, Takamori struggled to recall these famous sayings, and his feeling of annoyance was somewhat relieved. But the fact was that there were often times when the great goose had to beg loans from the little sparrow, an embarrassing situation.

'After all, I am your brother,' he would plead, demeaning himself before her. (He could not forget that she was six years his junior.)

'Sentimental rot!' She struck him down with one blow. 'Didn't I lend you a thousand yen only the other day? No, I won't lend you another yen.'

'Then I'll just have to stick it out.'

She would eventually give in, but not necessarily out of praiseworthy love for her brother. 'All right. But I'll charge you ten per cent interest a week.'

'That's preposterous.'

' What's preposterous? If you don't like it, you can go begging elsewhere.' Imagine charging her own brother interest!

'Why don't you grow a little more ladylike?' he would occasionally lecture her in his pique. 'If you go on this way, you'll never find yourself a husband.'

'Do you think so? Then just watch me pick one out!'

'Be quiet a second and listen. For example . . .'

There had been an Italian film called *La Strada*. Tomoe undoubtedly had seen it. No movie could have been more instructive for her, thought Takamori. A man named Zambaloni was always being followed around by a woman named Gelsomina. However much he hit and kicked her, teased and abused her, she never left his side. Then finally she was abandoned by him in the mountains, as the desolate winter sun was setting. A woman with no clever plans for living her life, with no calculation of profit or loss. From the point of view of the modern Japanese girl what could be more ridiculous? Still it was this very spirit of long-suffering that had in the end transformed her into a beautiful saint. If a woman's heart is indeed superior to a man's, it is only in circumstances such as Gelsomina's. After finishing his account, he expected to see her moved to the point of tears.

'Listen,' he continued in a solemn tone. 'In life you've got to lose on occasion, to spend with extravagance. That's where you miss the boat.' He looked quickly into her face to see how she was taking this wisdom. She was laughing.

'That's nonsense. You're really old-fashioned. But it's very convenient for you men to think that way.' Her nose went up just a little higher than usual and her stiffened nostrils twitched victoriously, as with a laugh she dismissed Gelsomina's feminine psychology.

There was something wrong with her nose when she raised it like this, thought Takamori. She herself seemed to think it bore a resemblance to Sophia Loren's, but he couldn't see this. When she was a girl, she used to wrinkle it up and make faces at him. Now that she was grown up she no longer made such vulgar gestures, but her turned-up nose gave evidence all the same of the haughty arrogance of her attitude toward men, society and life in general.

That nose is going to collapse one of these days, thought Takamori. He wanted to give it a good tweak, but he knew that if he tried it, she would come flying at his nose in retaliation with twice or three times the violence he had used on her.

That was the reason why on this Sunday morning Takamori, curled up in his blankets like a caterpillar in its cocoon, answered his sister's shrill call in a voice that sounded as if it came from the bottom of an empty well.

After the second alarm had passed, Takamori smoked two cigarettes, one after the other. He was finishing the second when again he heard loud footsteps in the corridor below.

The real assault this time! He quickly ground out his cigarette and reached for his underwear. Strangely enough, she did not shout, but came quietly up the stairs. He hurried to get his undershirt over his head, but he didn't make it in time. The doors to his room were suddenly pulled open, letting in a bright morning sun. Tomoe, wearing an immaculate white sweater, stood looking down at him with piercing eyes, arms folded.

'Milord, congratulations on your engagement.' With some such incoherent words, she watched him struggling to get his undershirt buttoned. He was having trouble finding the buttons.

'You've got it on inside out, stupid.' She stood there with a sarcastic smile on her face, watching him do battle with the undershirt. 'You've got it on inside out,' she repeated. 'No wonder you can't find the buttons.'

'You don't have to tell me.' In his embarrassment he sought to avert her eyes by looking out of the window.

'Takamori.'

'Yes.'

'Are you getting married?'

Sitting cross-legged on the bed, he turned his head halfway to look at her. In her black eyes and arrogantly turned-up nose he thought he saw that she was making fun of him.

'Who is Hona Haruko?'

'Haruko? Damned if I know.'

'Are you telling me the truth?' Her voice was full of suspicion. She made a wry face and stared fixedly at him to observe the expression on his face.

But Takamori had no recollection of having heard the name. On this Sunday morning there was not a single girl he could think of who would be likely to telephone him.

'Are you implying that I've had something to do with a Hona Haruko?'

'I don't know, but . . .' and she laughed. 'A fat letter has just come for you from Haruko in Singapore.'

'Singapore!' Takamori stared at her blankly. He wondered if his sister, standing there bathed in the spring sun, had not begun to get a bit loony. Perhaps she had taken a loss on her stocks. He had never been to Singapore, and not even in his dreams had he had anything to do with a girl in such a far-off place.

'Show me the letter.'

'You don't expect to get it for nothing, do you? I'll hand it over in return for the money you owe me from last month.'

'You're joking! Besides, I don't know any such person.'

Even Tomoe could tell from the expression on his face that he wasn't lying. Still she continued to look at him with suspicion in her eyes. Finally, reaching into her sweater, she produced an envelope. Sure enough, it was postmarked Singapore. The address had been typed in Roman letters and there was his name, Takamori Higaki. Turning the envelope over to look at the return address, he found the name Hona Haruko written in characters, followed by other characters in parentheses which he could not make out. He was completely bewildered.

'What an atrocious scrawl,' he exclaimed, looking at the characters of the return address. The calligraphy was certainly horrible. It would be rather pleasant, he reflected, to get a charmingly written letter from a girl, even if it turned out to be a mistake. But this writing – it fitted no known school of calligraphy. What was the meaning of this terrible script? It was so bad that even the writing of an elementary school child would have looked good in comparison.

'Must be someone's idea of a joke. But it's a little early for that. April Fool's Day is still a couple of days off.'

'Open it, at least. See what it says.'

'You open it.'

'Why?'

'Why? Well . . . in the first place I really don't know anyone by the name of Haruko. You've been making all kinds of insinuations. I'm fed up with it. So you open the letter. Here. Right in front of me.'

'It's really all right for me to open it?' she asked. Curiosity, the special attribute of women, was getting the better of her. Her fingers with their red, manicured nails were already moving toward the envelope. 'Very well, then, if you say so.'

'Read it aloud. I have nothing to be afraid of. Girls today are full of suspicion and jealousy. It's a real problem.'

He watched her as she skilfully slit open the envelope and pulled out the letter. It was written on thin, transparent airmail paper and folded in four.

'What does it say?' Even Takamori's curiosity was aroused, as he looked over his sister's shoulder at the letter. The writing on the paper looked like rows of turtles stretched out in the noonday sun. The characters were so small and crowded that it was necessary to use a magnifying glass to make them out.

'Here I go.'

'Go ahead.'

' "Dear Takamori, I finally found the groin. . . ." What's this?' exclaimed Tomoe, blushing.

As a result of the drastic reduction of the number of Chinese characters in everyday use, young Japanese today make many mistakes in writing, often omitting characters altogether or substituting one for another. Even Takamori and Tomoe, whose grandfather had been a scholar of the

Chinese classics, were no exception. They also were poor in their knowledge of characters. But even they were taken aback at the number of mistakes in Haruko's letter.

If she had only omitted characters or interchanged them, it would not have been so bad. But there were places where the meaning, even after they had made out the characters, was still so obscure that their struggle to understand the text was not unlike that of an archaeologist trying to read the hieroglyphics of antiquity.

'I give up,' declared Tomoe at last.

'Let me have it.' This time Takamori, growing more and more curious, picked it up and began to puzzle it out.

'Ah, I understand.'

'What do you understand?'

'This isn't "groin". She's mistaken the character for "time" . . . "I have finally found the time." What a blunder!'

'What a blunder is right! That's terrible.'

Takamori sat cross-legged on the bed studying the letter. It was a quiet Sunday morning. Their home was in the residential district of Kyodo in Setagaya Ward, quite removed from the heart of the city. Each spring the birds returned to their garden, and they could be heard chirping now from the second-storey window. Except for the voice of the maid, Matchan, talking to someone at the kitchen door, the house was perfectly still.

The bright sun shone full in Takamori's face. Tomoe, watching her brother closely as he tried to puzzle out the letter, saw him become suddenly excited.

'What's the matter?'

Takamori lifted his eyes from the letter and said in a loud voice, 'Good heavens! This is terrible! That fellow from France is coming over.'

'What?'

'No joke. Not only that, but he's a descendant of Napoleon.'

A little bird that had been perched on the roof of the house flew off chirping. Matchan's voice could no longer be heard.

'What are you talking about?'

'No kidding. He's really coming over. He's already left Singapore! He's due to arrive at Yokohama in twenty days.'

'What in the world are you talking about?'

'You remember, don't you? . . . eight years ago when I was exchanging letters with some foreign pen pals?'

Tomoe had a vague recollection of it. Takamori, still in school, was writing to a number of boys in foreign countries, hoping to be able to learn a little English and at the same time add to his collection of foreign stamps.

'But who is Hona Haruko?'

'It's not Hona Haruko. Here, take a look!' Takamori showed her the letter and pointed to the last line of hideous characters that looked like a parade of turtles crossing the page.

' "My name, written in Japanese, becomes Honaharuko Gasuton." ' One stroke too many in his character for 'write' had transformed that word into 'noon', Tomoe quickly realized, but she did not immediately make out the 'Gasuton', so unlikely were the characters he had chosen to represent the sound.

'Gaston Bonaparte. His family name is Bonaparte and his given name is Gaston. Apparently he thinks that men's names also end in "ko".'

Takamori was not in a very good mood to begin with, after the previous exchange of words with his sister, and this was the last straw.

'He writes that he has studied Japanese for two years at a Far East language institute in Paris. Why should he want to come to Japan? But I remember that when we were corresponding with each other eight years ago, he was already very much interested in Japan. His uncle had spent some time in Kobe and on returning to France seems to have infected his nephew with the Japan fever.'

'Is he coming as a tourist? Or on business?'

'He doesn't say. I don't know why he's coming.'

Takamori looked at Tomoe and with mock seriousness proposed, 'Perhaps he's coming to look for a wife. Wasn't there an elderly South American millionaire who came over to Japan some years ago on such a mission? Tomoe, this may be your chance!'

'Don't be vulgar.'

'But he's a descendant of the great hero, Napoleon. I remember thinking it strange he should have such a family name, and when I asked him about it, he admitted the relationship.'

'Who was Napoleon anyway? He was the first Fascist, wasn't he?'

'But what are we going to do with him?'

'Well, at any rate, we'll have to talk this over with Mother. You can't take it on yourself to bring a complete stranger into the house – and a foreigner at that.'

A descendant of Napoleon coming to Japan! And planning to stay in their home! It was a thunderbolt out of the blue on this spring morning, come to disturb the calm of the Higaki family.

Tomoe's quick steps retreating down the staircase sounded like a machine-gun report. Her brother, hurriedly putting on his clothes, followed after her, dragging the sash of his kimono behind him.

'Mother, something awful has happened!'

Their mother, Shizu, was in the room overlooking the garden, carefully polishing the ebony table that had been one of their father's cherished possessions when he was alive.

'What's all the excitement about?' she asked as she looked up from behind her glasses at the face of Takamori, which for all the size of his body still had something of the child in it.

Six years had passed since her husband, who had been

a doctor and professor of a medical college, had died of a cerebral haemorrhage. Tomoe at that time was still in middle school, and Takamori had been on the point of graduating from college, somehow having managed to get through the four years without failing.

Now, as when he still lived, Shizu cleaned his study herself each day, wiping the shelves of his bookcases, removing the dust that settled on the books and polishing his ebony table. This alone she refused to entrust to the maid or even to Tomoe.

'Your sash,' she pointed out to Takamori.

'What?'

'Your sash isn't tied.'

Takamori wound the sash about him and tied it, as with great excitement he told his mother about the letter from Singapore. 'If you ask me, I think we ought to do our best to make him feel at home, Mother. After all, he's my pen pal from way back, and he's relying on me. Give him a chance to see how a Japanese family lives. He can eat pickled radish and *miso* soup* with us. I'm sure it will be all right.'

'This is so unexpected.'

'But Mother, "Even the hunter spares the bird that flies to him for refuge" ', pressed Takamori, pulling out of his memory bag an old saying of questionable application to the situation.

'That's all very well with birds, but how will we take care of him? In the first place, what about the toilet? We still don't have one that flushes. A foreigner is sure to find fault with a Japanese-style toilet.'

Shizu ordinarily gave in to her son and daughter on nearly everything, but even so, when it came to putting up a foreign guest in their house, she showed considerable reluctance.

'Besides,' she added, 'with a girl of Tomoe's age in the house . . .'

* A soup made of bean paste, very common in the Japanese diet.

'Mother, I can vouch for his character. After all, he's a descendant of Napoleon. He's not likely to take a second look at someone like Tomoe.'

2 Enter the Hero

Sitting in the office of Disanto Trading Company in the Marunouchi Building across the street from Tokyo Station, Tomoe found it unusually difficult to concentrate on her work. Ordinarily she was able to type seventy words a minute, but today her efficiency was down to forty or fifty.

'Signorina Higaki, is something wrong?' asked the boss, Mr Disanto, solicitously after he had found her several times looking absent-mindedly out of the window. 'Aren't you feeling well?'

'I'm all right,' she assured him as, flustered, she began to pound her keys again. But she could not keep it up. Her thoughts always returned to the events of the previous day.

In three weeks a young Frenchman would arrive in Yokohama. Most of the burden of getting ready for him would fall upon her mother, but she too would have to join in the preparations. Takamori, as might be expected, took the irresponsible attitude that the guest could eat pickled radish and *miso* soup like the family. He was of absolutely no help.

So I suppose it's up to me, she thought. Takamori is really useless in such situations.

Upset with her brother, she could not help being angry at herself too, for having agreed to take into their house a young foreigner they had never laid eyes on.

'Mr Osako,' Tomoe called over to a young man working in the office with her. 'I'd like to ask you something.'

'Yes, what is it?'

Takuhiko Osako, a man with gleaming rimless glasses, came to her desk, holding his handkerchief to his mouth. He had joined the company two years earlier than Tomoe

25

and was known to be a grandson of Baron Osako, a member of the pre-war nobility. He was as thin as an eel but so careful about his personal appearance that Tomoe wished her brother would take a few lessons in grooming from him. Whenever she passed on to him the documents she had finished typing, he received them with a feminine politeness that extended even to his choice of words. She held him inwardly in contempt, but this had not prevented her from going dancing with him on a number of occasions, since he was an acknowledged master of the dance.

'Mr Osako, since you're the grandson of a noble, you must know the answer to this.'

'Noble? Not at all . . .' He sounded just like a girl. 'But what is it?'

'Are there still descendants of Napoleon alive today?'

'I suppose there must be.'

'I wonder what they do to make a living?'

'I really don't know, I'm sure. But why this sudden interest in Napoleon?'

'Oh, nothing.'

She closed her eyes and tried to recall the bust of Napoleon in her history book. He wore a white waistcoat and had one hand tucked into it under a swelling chest.

I wonder if that's what he looks like, she speculated. Napoleon was a short, ugly man, they say.

Released for the noon break after three hours of work, the office employees of the Marunouchi area flocked onto the spacious lawns in front of the Imperial Palace for a few minutes of relaxation. One group, stretched out on the grass, which had just begun to turn green, were flicking through magazines. Some of the girls were playing volleyball, their cheerful voices accompanying the ball at each throw, while others watched them. At the edge of the moat, beneath the budding willow trees, a young man and his girl were looking down at the water and watching the swans skim gracefully over its surface.

'It was terriffic! The Lions were really hitting. First, Kinoshita hit one way out in right field. The pitcher panicked and before he could settle down, Wada and Aoki had also hit home runs. They gave him the old one-two-three . . . Hey, are you listening?'

With great excitement Iijima, who worked with Takamori, was telling him about the game between the Giants and the Lions he had seen the previous day, Sunday, at Korakuen Stadium. But Takamori, lying beside him with eyes fixed on one point of the clear blue sky, was only half-listening.

'What's the matter? Aren't you feeling well?'

'I'm all right.'

'You're not thinking of quitting our bachelors' club and getting married, are you?'

'No, nothing like that.'

Iijima, embracing his knees, looked over at the girls playing volleyball. The bright sun made him squint.

When spring came round each year, the young girls at the office began to look more than usually attractive to Takamori and his bachelor friends. As the weather grew warmer and they came to work, first without coats, then without suits, in short-sleeved dresses that displayed their white arms, they gave the impression of beautiful flowers come freshly to bloom. Ordinarily Takamori and Iijima, his friend from university days, spent their noon break ogling this flower and that. Today, however, it was different.

In Takamori's pocket was a note on Napoleon's family tree, which he had copied surreptitiously in company time from a biographical dictionary he had borrowed from the bank library. Napoleon's mother and father had had a flock of children. Napoleon had one older brother, Joseph, and three younger brothers and three younger sisters: eight children in all. Besides Joseph and Napoleon, there were Lucien, Louis, Jerome, and Elise, Pauline and Caroline.

This Gaston Bonaparte who was planning to arrive in

three weeks' time, from which of these was he descended? Was he a direct descendant of Napoleon or of one of Napoleon's brothers? There was no way of knowing.

'A foreigner? You don't say so!'

Shosuke, the fishmonger, stood at the kitchen door, tapping his stiff neck with the flat of his hand. Beside him was a placard on which were written the names of all the fish he had for sale that day.

'Then what'll you do? If he's a foreigner, you won't be able to speak to him in Japanese. I guess you'll have to learn a few words of English.'

'What are you talking about? I know enough English to get along.' In her displeasure, Matchan loudly rattled the dishes in the kitchen sink.

'Anyway, what's your order today?'

'What do you have?'

'How about some fresh *sawara*?'*

'How much is it?'

'Forty yen a slice.'

'That's pretty expensive.'

Matchan moved to the kitchen door and, hands on her hips, looked sternly at Shosuke.

'We're having a foreign guest. So I imagine we'll be ordering more meat. You'd better be careful and give us good service.'

'Is that a threat?'

Shosuke untied the towel wound around his head and wiped his sweating face with it.

'You're a tough customer.'

'But it stands to reason, doesn't it? Don't you know that foreigners eat nothing but meat?'

'All right, you win. I'll let you have it for thirty-five yen.' He licked his pencil and wrote the order in his book. 'How is it that a foreigner's staying with you?'

'Didn't I tell you? He's an old friend of Takamori's.'

* A kind of fish.

'Oh? Then I suppose it's natural for him to stay here. Come to think of it, there's a foreigner renting a room over at Mori's place . . . you know, near the police box. Isn't he teaching English or something?'

'Ours is completely different,' declared Matcham in a loud voice, put out at the implication. 'Ours is a descendant of Napoleon. Don't mention him in the same breath with Mori's man.'

'Napoleon?'

'You mean you don't even know Napoleon? What an ignoramus!'

'How'd you like to go to a film with me on Sunday?'

'I wouldn't. I won't go out with anyone till I'm ready to get married. If you've finished your business, then get out of here.'

The day in April when Gaston Bonaparte was due to land at Yokohama finally arrived.

'At last!' even Shizu was heard to sigh the night before his arrival. If she sounded as though her own child were returning from a long journey, that was because for the past week she had been feverishly preparing to receive the guest, repairing quilts, buying new sheets, thinking out a suitable menu.

'Tomoe, did you get some new pillow cases?'

'Yes, but Mother, I don't think you had to go that far. In the first place, we haven't the slightest idea why he's coming to Japan. Even if he is Takamori's pen pal, we surely can't be expected to put him up for the full length of his stay. I think it's a bad habit of the Japanese to go to such extremes in being nice to foreigners.'

'Perhaps, but since he's coming such a long way . . .'

'I wonder what sort of person he is, this Gaston.'

Turning off the radio, which was playing American western-style music, Tomoe tried to imagine what he looked like, as she had so often done in the past three weeks. But she could not come up with a satisfactory image. Unknown to her mother and brother, she had gone to Maruzen Bookshop in Nihonbashi to look for pictures of Napoleon. Maruzen had a number of books about him, but all the pictures she found were of an arrogant little man who looked more like one of the vultures kept in the Ueno Zoo. He certainly hasn't much appeal, she thought. She left the shop without buying a book.

Flicking through old film magazines, she came across pictures of Charles Boyer and Daniel Gelin in the role of Napoleon. She didn't dare expect Gaston to be as handsome as Gelin. She tried making a montage containing elements of Gelin and of the vulture, but in the end she was no closer to imagining what Gaston looked like than she had been in the beginning.

'What do you suppose has happened to Takamori?' Shizu asked, looking anxiously at the wall clock. It was already eleven o'clock, but Takamori was not home yet. As usual, he had probably stopped off at a bar with some of his friends from the office.

'He has absolutely no sense of responsibility. . . . Not home yet, and his guest due to arrive tomorrow!'

'He must be aware that tomorrow's the day.'

'Of course he is. He was going to go to the shipping company today for a boarding permit.'

People going to the port to greet arriving passengers are not ordinarily allowed on board ship. If they wish to do so, they must get a permit from the shipping company.

'I hope we have good weather tomorrow.'

'According to the radio it should be all right.'

It was past midnight when Takamori got home.

'The ship gets in at six in the morning. What'll you do if you're too tired to get up?' Tomoe needled her brother, but Takamori, nonchalant as ever, stood at the sink gargling and making a noise that could be heard all over the house.

'Don't worry,' he said at last. 'With customs and health inspection it'll be ten o'clock at least before they come ashore. There's no need to hurry.' A typically irresponsible answer, thought Tomoe.

Then it was the day of arrival, a Sunday. Shizu and Tomoe were already awake when the first grey light of morning crept through the window, and the sparrows on the roof began their song.

The *Vietnam* was scheduled to enter the harbour at six. Takamori had said that it would take until ten o'clock to get through customs and health inspection. But he was always so easygoing in these matters that they didn't know how far to accept his judgement. He was still sound asleep.

Seven o'clock. Tomoe could no longer restrain herself. She climbed up to the second floor and with great difficulty shook her brother awake. Rubbing his sleep-filled eyes, he reached for the cigarettes at his bedside, intending first to have a smoke. But Tomoe intercepted him, and grabbing him by the collar as she would a cat, succeeded in dragging him downstairs.

'What time do you suppose Gaston will reach the house?'

Takamori did not answer his mother. He sat gobbling up his breakfast, trying to keep from yawning.

'Hey, Tomoe,' he broke out suddenly, 'you'll take care of the fare to Yokohama, won't you?'

Eight o'clock. Tomoe changed into a blue jersey suit with narrow white stripes and put on a snow-white hat.

'That's really nice.' Takamori's flattery was transparently aimed at getting his sister to pay their fare to Yokohama.

Tomoe set out a shirt for him, handed him a tie, got him into his suit, then practically pushed him out of the house. By this time it was well past eight-thirty.

From Kyodo they took a bus to Shibuya, where they boarded the Toyoko line for Yokohama, a ride of about forty minutes.

Tomoe looked nervously at her watch. 'I wonder if we'll be on time. It'll be ten-thirty by the time we get there.'

As the train drew near to Yokohama, the harbour and its ships came into distant view. The sea was blue and the sky was clear.

'Which ship is it, do you suppose?'

'You can't see it from here. Foreign ships dock at the American Pier.'

'How long does it take to get to the pier from the station?'

'Let's see. About half an hour by bus, I imagine. They're awfully slow. I don't have any money, so I don't mind if we walk it.'

Today of all days she had no desire to quarrel with him. Disagreeable though it was, she hailed a taxi in front of the station. Settling himself comfortably inside, Takamori remarked, 'After all, a taxi is the most convenient, isn't it?'

As they neared the port, an off-sea breeze, smelling of salt, blew in from the east. The cab turned at the newly-built Silk Centre and headed for the American Pier, where the foreign ships docked.

'This is terrible! The passengers have already landed,' exclaimed Tomoe, jumping out of the cab. But on closer inspection the green ship Tomoe had taken for the *Vietnam* was a Dutch tanker, the *Jepsen-Marx*. Behind it an eight or nine-ton Japanese freighter, the *Santosu-maru*, with the flag of the rising sun hanging limply from its flagpole, was taking on cargo. There were only the two ships.

'Are you sure this is the right pier?'

'Yes, positive. That's what they told me at the company yesterday.'

Tomoe had been to Yokohama two or three times to see off friends of university days who were going to America for further study. The ships had always left from this pier, so it couldn't be a mistake. Still, she felt anxious.

'There's no *Vietnam* here.'

'Look over there!' Takamori pointed to the farthest end of the wharf where the murky sea began. Forty or fifty

men and women stood there looking out to sea. Strains of
band music were carried by the wind to where Takamori
and Tomoe were standing.

'Is that where the *Vietnam* is due to land?' Tomoe asked
a passing porter, just to make sure.

'Yes, miss.'

'It's quite late in getting in, isn't it?'

'Health inspection seems to have taken a long time.'

As they walked towards the group of people at the end
of the pier who had come to greet the incoming passengers,
they heard once again the sound of brass instruments, and
when they got closer they saw that it was the police band
in their dark blue uniforms adorned with white braid. They
were standing in two columns and playing the Colonel
Bogie March.

'Quite a crowd!' Even Takamori seemed surprised. Then
something at the front of the group caught his eye. 'Tomoe,
look . . . over there!'

A young lady, evidently an actress, dressed very fashion-
ably and holding a bouquet of flowers, was having her
picture taken by cameramen. Around her were four or
five men who might very well have been newspaper
reporters.

'You don't suppose they've come to welcome Gaston, do
you?'

'Don't be an idiot.' All the same, even Tomoe's heart
began to beat faster.

'Well, why not? After all, he *is* a descendant of Napoleon.
It wouldn't be strange for newspaper reporters and a brass
band to come out to welcome him.'

Tomoe thought that highly unlikely. Still, there was
something in what Takamori said. For the millionth time
she asked herself, What will he be like?

Suddenly from behind the distant breakwater, like the
yawn of a giant, came the sound of a ship's horn.

'It's coming in!'

The 15,000-ton, freshly-painted, white French freighter,

the *Vietnam*, guided by two pilot boats, moved slowly into the harbour. Above the chimneys of the boats seagulls glided gracefully, barely fluttering their white wings.

The band, which had been taking a break, burst into action again, playing the Colonel Bogie March at greater volume than before.

Finally the ship was close enough to make out clearly the faces of the passengers lined along the deck rail like little birds. Mixed in with foreign tourists were a few Japanese youths, who leaned over the rail waving their hats at those on the dock. In a corner clustered together were several nuns looking down at the wharf. A red-haired sailor hung out from a porthole near the waterline. On every face was an expression of joy.

When the ship silently touched the dock, those on hand to welcome the passengers, still waving their hands, moved into action. The only mournful voice was that of the seagulls, who continued to perform their ballet above the pilot boats, which were no longer needed.

'Dekochan!'

'Look this way!' The voices of a group of young girls standing near Takamori exploded shrilly.

The newspaper reporters with their cameras rushed to board the ship. Only then did it dawn on Takamori that all this excitement was for the famous film star Hideko Takamine (familiarly known to her many fans as Dekochan), who was returning to Japan on this ship with her husband. The lady standing at the middle of the deck rail, waving her hand slightly and smiling sweetly, was none other than Hideko Takamine, whose face he remembered having seen in the cinema.

'It's Deko. Dekochan's on board,' he exclaimed, nudging Tomoe.

Tomoe turned her face aside and did not respond. All these people then, including the newspaper reporters and the actress with the bouquet of flowers, had not come to meet Gaston but a famous film star. She had known all along, of course, that it would be something like this. Still, she could not help feeling somewhat disappointed.

'I wonder where Gaston is.'

'We don't even know what he looks like,' answered Takamori, his eyes not leaving the actress at the deck rail.

When a large truck with a crane moved in to set up the gangway, the people on the dock began to run in that direction. Passengers, luggage in hand, prepared to disembark. Jostled along by the people around them, Takamori and Tomoe also took their places at the foot of the gangway.

First off was a sick passenger, who, accompanied by two nurses, was gently carried down in a stretcher. He was followed by a tall, elderly, ruddy-faced foreigner, who hurried down, waving his hands. Because of his age, they knew that *he* was not Gaston. Next was a Japanese student, wearing a brand-new suit. His family took possession of him immediately, shouting 'Kenchan, over here!' and he went off with them to enjoy the pleasure of reunion. Then came the Catholic nuns, a Japanese gentleman, a foreign couple. . . .

For twenty minutes they kept coming, as Takamori and Tomoe with a growing feeling of frustration watched at the foot of the gangway. The newspaper reporters and the actress with the bouquet had gone up to meet Hideko and her husband. All the other passengers seemed to have disembarked. No young foreigner they might suppose to be Gaston was anywhere in sight.

The police band had packed its instruments and departed. The welcoming and the welcomed, with their handshakes and embraces, had also disappeared. The wharf was now a deserted span of white. One lone seagull flew with mournful voice above the waves.

'Let's go aboard and look for him,' suggested Tomoe.

'Shall we?' Even Takamori felt depressed. 'He couldn't have passed us, could he?'

The two climbed the gangway, showed their boarding permit to the Japanese watchman at the entrance, and boarded the ship. The inside was like a hotel, with sparkling chandeliers on the ceiling and colourful murals on the walls. Foreign passengers and officers of the ship, dressed in dark blue uniforms, were conversing in French that rolled smoothly off their tongue.

The floors were so richly carpeted that Tomoe felt her high heels sink deeply into the nap.

'Tomoe,' said Takamori, wiping the sweat off his forehead, 'I have to go to the toilet. I'm afraid I can't hold it much longer.'

'For goodness sake. . . . You've picked a fine place.'

It wasn't enough that they couldn't find Gaston. Takamori too had to behave like a child. Tomoe walked up boldly to the front desk of the salon and accosted a middle-aged clerk with the face of the late French film actor, Louis Jouvet.

'*Parla lei Italiano?*' She asked him if he spoke Italian.

'*Si, si, signorina.*'

The man gave her a warm smile and bent slightly toward her in a gesture that reminded her all the more of Louis Jouvet.

'I wonder if you would kindly check the passenger list for me. I'm looking for a Gaston Bonaparte.'

'*Aspetta, signorina.*'

'*Tante grazie.*'

When she turned around, Takamori was inspecting the mural on the wall, apparently embarrassed at her boldness.

It took the clerk a long time to work down the passenger list. Then he banged the folder shut and with a slightly sarcastic smile raised four fingers. '*Quarta classe.*' Fourth class.

Never having travelled on a foreign ship, Tomoe and Takamori were not even aware that such a class existed.

'Where is fourth class?'

The clerk called a blue-eyed sailor standing over in a corner and whispered something to him, not taking his eyes off Tomoe and her brother. The sailor too shrugged his shoulders derisively.

They were led by the sailor through a corridor honey-combed with first-class cabins and onto a wide deck where under a blinding sun a crane was noisily pulling boxes of cargo out of a net and piling them up.

'Over here!' The sailor pointed to an opening at their feet. It was a square-shaped entrance to the ship's hold. A perpendicular metal staircase disappeared into the darkness below.

Tomoe gasped. So this was fourth class!

'Gaston Bonaparte!' The sailor squatted and called down into the hold. A head suddenly popped up from below as if it had been awaiting the summons. It was not Gaston Bonaparte, however, but the ship's cook, who had a white apron around his waist and a meat cleaver in his hand.

A very fat man with a protruding stomach, he kept stroking his nose, which resembled a red dumpling, the result perhaps of too much wine. He looked at Tomoe and Takamori and, shaking his head, asked, '*Vous cherchez Gaston, n'est-c pas?*'

'Yes, yes.'

Takamori did not understand a word of French, but hearing Gaston's name answered 'yes'.

The man seemed to be inviting them to climb down the metal ladder into the ship's hold.

'Are you going down?' asked Tomoe who, for all her courage, was suddenly hesitant. Even from the opening she could smell in the hot, stuffy hold the odour of oil and paint, mixed with the kind of stench associated with pig pens and cow barns. Seeing the two of them hesitate, the cook spoke to them again in rapid French.

'Yes, yes,' said Takamori. He took tight hold of the ladder and began his descent.

French passenger ships, unlike Japanese, have no third class. There are many grades of first class, but the cabins are like luxurious hotel rooms. The price of these is staggering. In the second class, also called tourist class, two or three passengers share a cabin. On a voyage from Yokohama to Marseilles, these cost somewhat over 150,000 yen.

Most people don't know that there is also a way of getting to France on 50,000 yen. That is by travelling fourth class in the ship's hold. Here there is of course no cabin service or other personal attention, and passengers serve themselves at meals. Tiers of canvas bunks, looking like silkworm trays, are set up in hold space not needed for cargo. In these are generally to be found half-naked Chinese coolies boarding ship in Singapore or Hong-Kong and bound for jobs in other parts of the world. There is a constant turnover, as old ones leave and new ones come on at every port.

Takamori and Tomoe, of course, did not know this as they plunged down into the foul-smelling bowels of the ship.

'Takamori, what a stench!'

'I wonder what it is?'

Though it was broad day, the hold was dark and deathly still. Tiny electric bulbs without shades, suspended here and there, made little impression on the dark. Away in a corner under a solitary porthole were a number of canvas bunks. In the rays of light streaming in through the porthole dust particles could be seen dancing in the air. On one of the bunks sat a very tall man with a duffel bag on his knees, looking disconsolate.

'Gaston Bonaparte?' called Takamori, when he was still some distance away.

The man jumped up. Standing at full height, he looked like a Sumo-wrestler. 'Oui . . . yes, yes, yes,' he answered.

Tomoe gasped. 'Horse!' It was all she could do to keep from pronouncing the word that came spontaneously to her lips when she saw the man rise and come towards them.

Silhouetted against the light that entered the dark hold through the porthole, the man seemed to be trembling with joy as he extended his hand to Takamori. His face was so sunburned that he could easily have passed for an Oriental, and it was very long – a horseface indeed!

It was not only his face. His nose too was long. And when he opened his huge mouth to laugh, displaying the gums of his teeth, the impression of 'horse' was all the stronger.

Since she was after all young and romantic, Tomoe for all her cynicism had secretly conjured up a dream image of this young Frenchman who was to stay with them for a time. It did not seem too much to ask that this descendant of Napoleon, if not exactly another Charles Boyer, should at least be elegant, fairly good-looking, and radiate a kind of manly charm. But on each count Gaston rated zero.

He had the face of a simpleton in which not a glimpse of intelligence could be discerned. If one were forced to compare him to a foreign film actor, it was the monstrous potato face of the Mexican comedian, Fernandel, that came to mind. It was absolutely impossible for Tomoe to find in him anything that could ever cause her heart to skip a beat.

'This is my sister.' Even Takamori seemed shocked, as he turned and introduced her.

'Do you understand my Japanese?' asked Gaston, with deep concern.

'Yes, of course, we understand.'

Clumsily Gaston extended a hoof-like hand to Tomoe and shook her hand vigorously. This awkward handshake reminded her all the more of a horse. She had all she could do to keep from laughing bitterly as the intuition flashed upon her, 'We've been taken in. We've been royally taken in!'

Disillusion, disappointment, chagrin – all of these and more pressed in upon her. The rosy dreams she had secretly been harbouring for three weeks, all collapsed. Her cheeks twitched in something between resentment and anger. It was all Takamori's fault, everything. . . .

What fools we Japanese are! Here we come all the way to Yokohama to welcome to Japan a tramp with the body of a horse. Not only that, we even arrange to take him into our own home. Just look how he's dressed. It's bad enough that his trousers are out at the knees. But they don't even fit him; they're six inches too short.

'What *shall* we do?' Tomoe asked her brother in a low, quick whisper that Gaston could not catch. If left to her, they would quickly get rid of him.

But Takamori, laughing, merely answered, 'Don't you know? First we go through customs and then we find a taxi. I'm relying on you for the fare, you know.'

Then and there she would have liked to give him a good, swift kick in the rear.

'Gaston.'

'Yes.'

'Do you understand my Japanese?'

'Yes. Yes.'

'Then let's get out of here. Where's your luggage?'

Gaston pointed to the duffel bag on the bunk.

'Is that all?'

Gaston nodded.

In addition to the smell of paint and oil, there was something else, much worse. Tomoe put her handkerchief to her nose and turned to look behind her. There she saw a toilet with the door wide open, letting out the offensive smell.

Many years ago she had seen a film called *Slave Ship*. Two or three hundred African slaves had been chained together and pushed into just such a hold as this.

'Did you enjoy the trip, Gaston?'

Gaston did not understand Takamori the first time, but

when he repeated the words more slowly, he caught the meaning.

'Yes, it was very nice.'

They climbed back up the ladder, careful not to miss their footing. Gaston accustomed to the ladder, managed it as dexterously as a large monkey, skilfully manoeuvring his long legs on the rungs. First to reach the deck, he stood looking down at them with his long face.

'Beautiful!' He seemed to mean that he thought Tomoe beautiful. With great familiarity he offered her his hand.

Tomoe was put out, but she could not very well refuse his gesture altogether. So she handed him instead her handbag. He opened his large mouth and smiled with great joy.

When they emerged on the upper deck, the sun was bright to their eyes, which had adjusted to the darkness below. The fat cook and the sailor who had shown them the way down were standing there with folded arms. When they saw Gaston and Tomoe together they whistled and made some teasing remark to Gaston in French. Gaston smiled again.

Without knowing the language, Tomoe had a pretty good idea what they were saying. This fellow doesn't even have any manners, she thought. With an air of disdain she turned away to look at the blue sea and pretended to ignore the existence of both Gaston and the whistlers.

The dock under the midday sun was completely deserted. Both the ship passengers and those who had come to welcome them had long since gone. When they stepped off the gangway, Gaston pulled a map of Tokyo out of his pocket.

'Please show me a good inn,' he said.

'Inn?'

'Yes, inn . . . hotel.'

'Gaston, you'll be staying with us,' explained Takamori.

Gaston did not grasp his meaning at first. Takamori repeated what he had said, and this time he understood.

His long face began to crumple as if he were about to cry. He looked long at Takamori, then extended his hand and said, 'Thank you . . . you're very kind.'

3 Enigma

The Higakis had had a week to get acquainted with their incongruous visitor. During that time Gaston had drawn to himself the astonished eyes of all the members of the household, with the exception of Takamori. Tomoe, in particular, was upset. Her nose, that barometer of her feelings, was livid with rage, and she glared at Takamori as if to put all the blame on him.

To tell the truth, her anger was not entirely unjustified. Their misadventures with Gaston had begun the very day of his arrival. After leaving the ship Tomoe had agreed to a taxi, though she was not happy at having to pay a second time the high fare between the port and Yokohama Station. Inside the taxi Gaston was like a three-year-old child. He sat glued to the window, fascinated with the sights of springtime Yokohama. Takamori pointed out to him the landmarks of the city as they passed, but he remained with face pressed to the window, too absorbed in what he saw to answer. Occasionally he opened his large mouth and laughed to himself, the same simpleton's laugh that had offended Tomoe when he had first greeted them on the ship. Tomoe could understand that having arrived at last in the Japan of his dreams, he should be moved by what he saw in the streets of Yokohama, so different from those of his native city. All the same, that laugh was too much.

With an idiotic smile on his horselike face, Gaston turned to Tomoe and pointed out a group of children playing samurai with wooden sticks.

'Children *san* !'

The taxi turned a corner and startled a mongrel cur

with leg raised against the side of a lamp-post. The mongrel scurried away.

'Dog *san*,' said Gaston, apparently thinking that the term of respect 'san' could be applied to dogs as well as people.

What could she do but shake her head, ' yes'?

'Dog *san* . . . dangerous.'

'Yes, it's dangerous for dog *san*.' It was easier to humour him than to point out his mistake. Gaston seemed to be fond of dogs. He kept his eyes on the mongrel until it was completely out of sight.

All this was nothing compared to what happened next. It was a little after twelve when they reached Yokohama Station.

'Tomoe, let's get something light to eat before getting on the train,' suggested Takamori, still relying on his sister's capital resources. 'How about some *sushi*?* After all, *sushi* is the number-one Japanese dish.' Gaston must have understood his words, because his face lit up and he shook his head vigorously in approval.

The eyes of everyone in the *sushi* shop – waiters and guests alike – were on them as they took their place at the counter. Tomoe looked off to the side as if she were a perfect stranger to the other two. Gaston listened to Takamori's explanation of how to eat *sushi*, and then suddenly reached into his duffel bag and pulled out a piece of white cloth with long strings.

'A sailor on a Japanese ship in Marseilles, Tanaka *san*, gave this to me,' he said proudly in a loud voice. Then with the eyes of everyone in the shop fixed on him, Gaston proceeded leisurely to tie the strings around his neck. 'To eat *sushi*, I must use my Japanese napkin.' And he laughed innocently.

Tomoe and Takamori were the only ones in the shop

* Rice cakes covered with raw fish or rolled in seaweed. Some Japanese restaurants serve only this.

that did not explode with laughter. What Gaston had tied around his neck was a Japanese *fundoshi*, the loincloth that some Japanese men still wear in place of undershorts.

In the train going to Shibuya, Takamori with a wry smile questioned Gaston about the *fundoshi*. The story that came out was this. Two days before boarding the *Vietnam*, Gaston had noticed that there was a ship flying the Japanese flag in dock. On closer investigation it turned out to be the Japanese freighter, the *Akashiro-maru*. Just to hear the name of the ship was enough to excite him, and so naturally he set out to inspect it.

A young sailor by the name of Tanaka graciously showed him about the ship, then took him to his cabin and served him pickled plums, seaweed and Japanese cakes. From the porthole of the cabin fluttered a long white cloth with strings attached to either end. Freshly laundered, it had been hung there to dry.

'What's that?' asked Gaston, with his insatiable curiosity about everything Japanese.

The young sailor, too embarrassed to tell him the truth and yet having to give him some explanation, finally stuttered, 'That . . . is a Japanese napkin.' There was, in fact, some resemblance between the *fundoshi* and a Western napkin.

Wishing to have a remembrance of his visit to the ship, Gaston had proposed an exchange: he would give Tanaka his necktie in return for Tanaka's 'napkin'. Thus driven into a corner, Tanaka could not but agree to the exchange, though he probably did so with a feeling of guilt and inwardly begging Gaston's forgiveness for the deceit.

When all the circumstances were understood, it was clear that Gaston was nowhere at fault. He had been innocent enough to believe what Tanaka told him, and at the *sushi* shop in Yokohama, he had made that unfortunate gesture out of an innocent desire to express to Takamori and Tomoe his joy at being in Japan.

But one must put oneself in Tomoe's place. In a shop full of people to become suddenly involved in the open display of such a vulgar object (the Japanese will not even pronounce the word '*fundoshi*' in polite company) and then to have the whole place convulsed with laughter at their expense – that was too much. Tomoe's thoughts at that moment had been hot enough to set the shop on fire.

'Even if he is a foreigner,' she thought, 'he's a fool . . . an utter fool. In all seriousness, I wonder if there isn't something missing upstairs.'

All the way home on the train and then on the bus, she stood silent with face averted, refusing to talk to Gaston, of course, and even to Takamori.

'Be reasonable. It couldn't be helped. After all, it's his first day in Japan.' Takamori, hanging on to the strap next to hers, tried unsuccessfully to intercede for Gaston. 'If you were to go abroad, you'd probably do something just as bad.' But Tomoe kept her lips pursed and refused to answer.

As for Gaston, he sat with his duffel bag on his knees looking out of the window, entranced as before with the springtime scenery of Yokohama and Tokyo.

When they reached home, both Shizu and Matchan stared in dismay at the Frenchman. Tomoe left it to the other two women to entertain him and went immediately to her room and stayed there. Scattered over her desk were the film magazines in which she had searched for pictures of actors who had played Napoleon. The melancholy countenance of Daniel Gelin, staring up at her from one of the magazines, served to increase her wrath.

'And this is your room. . . .' She heard Takamori in the corridor showing Gaston about the house. 'Please make yourself completely at home.'

'This is no joke!' she wanted to shout at the top of her voice.

Thinking that after his long trip Gaston would be tired

and would want to take a nap, they had shown him to his room and prepared his bed for him. At three o'clock Tomoe, her wrath having somewhat subsided, went down to the kitchen to ask Matchan to prepare tea and cakes for the guest.

'Tomoe *san*.' Matchan had something on her mind.

'Yes.'

'Is he really related to Napoleon?'

'It seems so. Why?'

'He left the house a short time ago in his night clothes.'

When Matchan was cleaning the front entrance of the house about half an hour earlier, Gaston, who was supposed to be resting, suddenly made his appearance, dressed in the summer kimono Takamori had lent him in place of night clothes.

'My shoes . . .' He started looking for his shoes. Matchan brought him his huge clodhoppers, which were worn out and badly in need of repair, and presented them to him.

'Thank you.' He quickly put them on and left the house.

'Oh no! What next? Why didn't you stop him?'

Detecting the note of reproach in Tomoe's voice, Matchan became sullen. 'How was I to know? I thought he was only going to take a turn around the garden.'

Kimono and shoes! What a combination! How embarrassing if the neighbours should see him. And yet, how was Gaston to know that the Japanese never wear shoes with a kimono?

'I'll go and look for him. Please call Takamori.' Tomoe asked Matchan to summon Takamori, who was taking a nap on the second floor.

'What's the matter?'

'Everything's the matter! You had to invite that fool into our home!'

When Takamori had heard her out, he burst out laughing. 'Oh, this is wonderful!'

Tomoe rushed into the street, but Gaston was nowhere

in sight. If he should wander into the shopping area, she thought, it would be a repetition of the scene in the *sushi* shop. They would be the laughing stock of the neighbourhood. As if she didn't already have her hands full with Takamori, now this imbecile from abroad had dropped down on them and was even more of a problem than her brother.

She stopped a group of little boys with running noses who were playing in the street. 'You didn't happen to see a foreigner pass by here, did you?'

'An American wearing a kimono?'

'He's not an American. But, yes, that's the one. Where did he go?'

Just then she caught sight of Gaston ambling towards her in a leisurely manner. He cut a ridiculous figure with his huge Sumo-wrestler's body wrapped in a kimono much too short for him and those awful clodhoppers on his feet. He was followed by a mangy, half-starved mongrel that walked with a limp. When he saw Tomoe, the now-familiar idiot grin came over his horseface.

'Poor dog *san*. He's starved. Won't you give him something to eat?' The nerve of the man!

Then it was evening and Gaston's welcoming party. The dinner table around which they squatted was decked out with all kinds of special dishes. The guest of honour had changed back into the clothes he had been wearing when he disembarked. He sat straight up on his cushion, his knees pulled up awkwardly in front of him. Takamori tried to get him to sit cross-legged, but his legs were too long and he was not accustomed to the position.

'Oh, *non, non*. I can't!'

Seeing all the unusual dishes ranged in front of him, Gaston was as excited as a child and began to point to them and count, 'One, two, three, four, many many dishes.'

Tomoe, seeing his innocent delight, was almost ready

to forget her grievances against him. 'Is this the first time you've eaten Japanese food, Gaston?'

'I had Japanese food once in Paris.'

There was a Japanese restaurant in Paris, The Peony, run by a Japanese who married a French girl. Gaston had been there once with friends.

'What did you have to eat?' asked Shizu. She looked apprehensively at Takamori, afraid that Gaston might not understand her Japanese.

'Mother, don't use such difficult words.' Shizu had used the most polite form of the verb 'to eat'. 'If you use simple words and pause between phrases, he'll understand you.' Takamori's advice was meant for them all.

'Gaston, from now on we'll call you Gas. Gaston's too difficult.'

'Yes. I understand.'

'Gas, what did you have to eat at The Peony?'

'*Sukeyaki.*'

'Not *sukeyaki*. The word is *sukiyaki*.'*

For some time Matchan had been standing in a corner of the room, unable to take her eyes off Gaston. Tomoe tried to signal her to stop staring, but she was so absorbed in what she saw that she even forgot to take proper care of the table.

Gaston was indeed a sight to behold. His chopsticks would descend awkwardly upon a morsel of food in one of the dishes before him, take hold of it and carry it precariously in the direction of his mouth. Then the horseface co-operatively met the chopsticks halfway, the mouth swung open, and plop! – the food disappeared inside. Slices of raw fish, spinach – everything was devoured in this fashion. There was nothing in his style of eating to distinguish him from the hippopotamus Tomoe had once seen in a Disney film.

---

* A kind of stew made of thinly-sliced pieces of beef and a variety of vegetables.

'Gas, you're a descendant of Napoleon, aren't you?' Takamori finally managed to ask him.

Gaston's line was descended from the child that was born to Napoleon and Maria Walewska.

He seems to be telling the truth, thought Tomoe, observing Gaston's face. This horseface with table manners no better than a hippopotamus! I can't believe that Gaston could possibly have as his ancestor that courageous hero who managed the perilous crossing of the Alps and went on to conquer Italy. She was suddenly struck with the suspicion that he might be a fake.

She knew nothing of Mendel's laws of heredity nor of Lysenko's, but it seemed strange to her that the first and last member of a family line could be so unlike in every respect. If they were really related, then what a tragedy!

Looks aside, even in his personal appearance and demeanour it was as hard to find a trace of Napoleon in him as it would be to find a fish in a tree. If the world had remained unchanged since Napoleon's time, his descendant today would be called Count Gaston de Bonaparte. Tomoe tried to imagine him at the Versailles Palace with its scintillating chandeliers, reverently kissing the hands of elegantly robed noble ladies and waltzing them around the ballroom floor.

Preposterous! Even to associate this horseface with the graceful waltz was to explode all romantic dream and expectation. Her suspicion returned. What if behind that idiotic look he were really plotting something against them? With this in mind, she turned a stealthy eye on him. He had stopped eating and was looking vacantly towards the window.

'Gaston, won't you have something more to eat?'

He did not answer.

'Gaston.'

This time he turned to Tomoe and smiled sadly.

'What's the matter, Gas?' asked Takamori in a concerned tone of voice, putting down the whisky bottle from which he had been pouring himself another drink.

'Dog *san*,' answered Gaston, pointing to his plate, 'wants to eat.'

'Dog *san*?'

Gaston's meaning suddenly flashed upon Tomoe as she recalled the figure of Gaston in his kimono and old boots leading back to the house that emaciated, dirty mongrel.

'Ah yes, that stray mongrel.'

The old dog was always about the neighbourhood. Sometimes it got into the kitchen or upset the garbage pail, calling down Matchan's wrath.

Gaston rose and opened the window. The dog could be heard coughing outside. Apparently dogs got asthma just like men. Gaston took food from his own plate and threw it to the dog, while Tomoe and Matchan looked away in disgust.

'From today dog *san* your friend. Like me, your friend,' declared Gaston, looking around at the others with a happy smile on his face.

That night after Gaston had gone to his room, Tomoe sighed wearily. She felt completely exhausted in body and spirit.

'Now I hope you're satisfied . . . bringing that fool into our home,' she said to Takamori with deep resentment.

He shook his head and answered, 'It's still too early to tell whether he's a fool or not. He may surprise you.'

'If not a fool, then a fake who's trying to put something over on us.'

Takamori, who after all was responsible for Gaston's coming to them, made an eloquent defence of him, but he was unable to convince his sister. Gaston's horseface and slowness of movement she could attribute to Providence and agree that there was nothing much to be done about them. But after listening to what he had to say and observing his actions, she was forced to conclude that he had the mental age of a small child.

'All that's only on the surface. This applies not only to France, but also to Japan. See what an unsavoury lot our

own self-styled intellectuals and men of culture are.'
Takamori spoke with conviction.

'No matter what you say, there's still the matter of
degree. Like going out this afternoon in his kimono and
boots. . . . That shows lack of common sense, even if he
doesn't know our Japanese customs.'

'That's a good point. He may be a man as deep as the
ocean, who doesn't get hung up on all these trivialities.
At any rate, Tomoe, you never did have much of an eye
for discerning the worth of a man. Even with me, you've
never been able to realize that I'm a man among men.'

A man among men? Someone like Takamori who slept
to all hours of the morning? Who constantly tapped his
sister for spending-money?

If he wanted another opinion on the subject, she thought,
just listen to that clatter in the kitchen! Matchan
was taking out her bad temper on the dishes. Women have
a delicate sensibility. When Matchan got out of sorts, she
let the dishes know how she felt.

'I don't see how Napoleon's relatives can very well
lord it over anyone with such a specimen in the family,'
Tomoe said crossly. 'They have lost face completely. Why
did he come to Japan anyway?'

'I asked him about that, but he didn't give a very satisfactory answer. He's an enigma, isn't he?'

The next morning Takamori and Tomoe got ready to go
to work.

'Gas, what are your plans for today? How would you
like to take a look around Tokyo?'

Gaston walked with them to the Kyodo station. In his
hand was a tourist map of Tokyo on which Takamori had
carefully marked the sights to be seen. He got off with them
at Tokyo Station.

'After you've seen the Diet* and the Ministry buildings,

---

* The Japanese Parliament.

go on to Tokyo Tower. It's even taller than the Eiffel Tower, you know.'

'Oh? Taller than the Eiffel Tower?'

Gawking curiously at everything about him, Gaston disappeared into the morning crowd.

'Just look at him,' remarked Takamori, watching Gaston's retreating figure. 'He's fully capable of managing the streets of Tokyo by himself. There's nothing stupid about him.'

'I wonder if he'll be all right.'

'Of course he will.'

But when Takamori and Tomoe reached home that evening and asked Gaston, who had returned before them, what he had seen that day, it turned out that he had seen nothing. The itinerary that Takamori had gone to the trouble of mapping out for him – the Japanese Diet, the Ministry buildings, Tokyo Tower, and even the Nichigeki Burlesque,* which he had been careful to tell him about when Tomoe was not listening – all these he had ignored.

'Then what *did* you see, Gaston?'

'A temple,' and he smiled a little sadly. 'I saw many many children and doves.'

He had passed along Marunouchi and the Ginza† without stopping to look at anything and had entered the grounds of a temple, where he had spent the day watching the children and the doves. Why in the world had he crossed the wide ocean and come to Japan? This man was truly an enigma.

Then an incident took place that gave them an insight into the kind of man that Gaston was. On Sunday Takamori proposed taking him on a night tour of Tokyo.

'Where will you take him? The Ginza?' Tomoe asked.

'No, not to the Ginza. I'll show him the real Tokyo, which even you don't know, Tomoe,' Takamori answered,

* A theatre.
† The most famous (and most expensive) shopping district of Tokyo.

laughing. 'Just the two of us will go, Gas.'

But then, remembering the problem of money, Takamori quickly reconsidered and invited Tomoe to accompany them after all. 'On second thoughts, Tomoe, it might be an education for you to come along.' He tried to make the invitation sound very casual.

'Are you planning to show Gaston the seamy side of Japan?'

'Don't be stupid. But you can come along and keep an eye on us, if you like.'

After they had finished dinner, Takamori and Tomoe left the house with Gaston, who had a happy look on his face. He was still wearing the suit that was several sizes too small for him. They took the Odakayū line to Shinjuku.

This was Gaston's first view of Shinjuku. It was Takamori's boast that he was so well-acquainted with this part of the city that he knew even where the rats had their holes.

'Rat holes are all right, but just don't take him to the kind of places that are a disgrace to Japan.'

'You don't have to tell me that.'

But they had no sooner left Shinjuku Station and started down the street with Gaston sandwiched between them than the very thing Tomoe feared happened.

Gaston, greatly excited, was staring all around him. He reacted to everything – the lights of the tiny bars lining the street like a string of matchboxes, the enticing smell of barbecued chicken, the voices of barkers inviting them to step inside their shops, the sound of clicking balls at the pachinko parlour.*

'Takamori *san*, this is big surprise.'

'I thought you'd like it. This is the Casbah of Tokyo, Gas. Listen, how'd you like to have a drink?'

---

* pachinko: a kind of pinball machine, set up vertically rather than, as in the West, horizontally. Japanese cities and towns abound in shops ('parlours') with rows of pachinko machines and nothing else.

At these words, Tomoe pulled at her brother's coat and voiced her disapproval. While she was still arguing with him, a young man with his hands in the pockets of his jacket, approached Gaston and, with a leering smile, whispered to him familiarly in a low voice.

Tomoe turned and saw the man, but she had no idea what he was. Takamori, catching sight of him at the same moment, called out quickly to Gaston, 'Gas, Gas.'

'Just a second,' Gaston replied. They saw him laughing and talking with the young man, whose hands were still in his pockets. 'This fellow wants to show me some beautiful pictures of Japan.'

'Never mind, Gas. Come along.' Takamori pulled him along by the arm as he spoke. 'Don't be taken in by this lout.'

Only after a quick explanation from Takamori, did Tomoe realize what was going on, that the fellow was trying to sell Gaston some dirty pictures.

Gaston still did not understand, but Takamori and Tomoe pulled him along with them. They had walked only a few steps when the man came up to them again.

'Watch who you're calling names, mate. You looking for a fight?' he challenged Takamori in a low voice.

Tomoe, frightened, got behind her brother and clung to him tightly. Strong as she was, at such a time she still looked to her brother for protection.

'Don't try to run away, lady.'

'We're not running away,' said Takamori in a hoarse voice, as he shielded Tomoe, 'but I wonder if you realize who this foreigner is?'

'What?'

'Take a good look. Don't you remember him? Haven't you seen his picture in the papers? . . . You still don't recognize him? That's the Brazilian boxing champion, Mr Gaston. He's scheduled to go into the ring next week with Yonekura. This lady and I are on the staff of the *Daily*

Herald.' Then Takamori called Gaston, who was looking into a pachinko parlour, completely oblivious of the drama that was being enacted about him.

'Mister Gaston, please.'

'Yes, yes.'

'Please, Gaston.'

'Yes, yes.'

'*Knock out this thug.*' Takamori spoke in English, which neither Gaston nor the young man understood. For a moment the latter stood hesitating, his eyes fixed on Takamori and Tomoe. But when Gaston finally pulled himself away from the pachinko parlour and began to walk towards him, the man took several steps backwards and disappeared down the alley which lay between the pachinko parlour and a bar.

When it was all over, Tomoe began to tremble violently, and her heart to pound. 'Takamori!'

Takamori was wiping the sweat off his forehead. 'We've got to get away from here, Tomoe.' They began to walk quickly, pushing Gaston along. The faces of the people on the street, most of whom had had a few drinks, took on a strange expression when they saw Gaston.

Even when they reached the crossing in front of Musashino Hall, Tomoe was still trembling. 'You really pulled us out of that one, Takamori. That was a good story!'

Takamori, seeing that his stock had risen in his sister's eyes, began to boast. 'I could have taken care of ten like him.'

'Let's stop and rest somewhere. My heart's still pounding.'

They were standing in front of the coffee shop, Couillon. From inside they could hear the sweet strains of a French song. This shop specialized in a kind of ersatz French atmosphere; it was known for its 'Paris mood'.

'I'm sure you'll like it, Gaston.'

'This place is terrible,' protested Takamori, with a look

of disgust. 'It's a hangout for all the French culture set.
They give me a pain.'

But since there was no other suitable place in sight, they
went in. Inside it was as dark as in an aquarium. Even in
the daytime all outside light was shut off with thick cur-
tains, so that the dim light of the lamps hanging on the
gold-coloured walls gave the faces of the young customers
sitting under them the sallow look of fish in a fishbowl.

In fact, as he looked around him now, Takamori thought
that the faces themselves, even apart from the lighting,
had a fishlike quality. The eyes of that arty young man
with knitted eyebrows, for example, who seemed to be
pondering some deep philosophical problem, were exactly
like those of a grey mullet. And that girl sitting with a rapt
expression on her face as she listened to the saccharine
chanson being sung was like a killifish, such as you buy
ten for a penny. The middle-aged man talking to her in
a hushed voice was as repulsive as a pollack.

Takamori had never understood what people saw in
coffee shops of this kind. He was not the type to sigh
deeply over his bitter coffee as he listened to a *chanson*
about 'the soul of a poet'.

The Couillon attracted a peculiar breed of young
Japanese enamoured of all things French. Just as the
young 'Russians' of Tokyo, dressed as they imagined
Russian workers dressed, gathered together at certain bars
to sing Russian folk songs, so these Francophiles flocked to
coffee shops like the Couillon, berets on their heads and
French books tucked under their arms, to sigh over French
chansons. Takamori, ill at ease in such a place, felt much
more at home in the neighbouring bars.

But since Tomoe was footing the bill and they had just
had that unpleasant adventure, he saw no alternative but
to follow her and Gaston into the shop.

No sooner had they sat down than Tomoe caught sight
of Osako, the man from her office, at a nearby table. She
called over to him. Surprised to see her, he put down the

coffee cup he held daintily in his hand and approached their table. He was foppishly dressed and the impression of an eel was as strong as ever.

'Takamori, I'd like you to meet Mr Osako, who works in my office. He's a grandson of Baron Osako.'

'So you're Takamori. Tomoe has told me so much about you.' He sounded just like a woman.

'And this is . . .' Tomoe hesitated a moment. 'Gaston Bonaparte. He's come over from France and is staying with us.'

At the word 'France' Osako's face suddenly grew tense. But not only he. The young men and women sitting behind their table all turned and looked at them.

'I wonder if you would be so kind as to allow me to join you.'

'Please do,' answered Takamori, stroking his face in irritation. He realized that everyone in the shop was listening in on their conversation. He felt itchy all over.

With no further ceremony Osako pulled up a chair and began to address himself immediately to Gaston. 'It's a great privilege to be able to speak with a real Frenchman.'

'Yes, yes.' Gaston extended his large hand and shook hands with Osako.

'Everyone who comes to this coffee shop is a lover of French art.'

Just then Takamori chanced to look in the direction of the door. There, standing in front of the shop, was the fellow in the jacket who had tried to sell Gaston dirty pictures. And he was not alone. With him was a man of sturdy build with a flashy sports coat thrown over his shoulders. He might very well have been an ex-boxer. Occasionally they pressed their faces to the glass door to get a better view of Takamori's table.

Frantically Takamori looked around the room for sign of a back exit. His heart sank when he saw that there was none. They would have to run the gauntlet at the front door.

'Are you pleased with Tokyo? It's a very dirty city, isn't it? Paris, now, is a wonderful city . . . the art centre of the world . . . the chestnut trees and the River Seine. Tokyo is such an awful place. It can't begin to compare with Paris, can it?'

Osako, addressing himself to Gaston and Tomoe, continued to criticize Tokyo and Japan in this tone. Contempt for the country in which they were born and the city in which they live is one of the characteristics of these Francophiles. It was impossible to tell if Gaston was following the conversation or not. He was staring wide-eyed at Osako with his mouth half open.

Even Takamori, for all his denseness in these matters, understood that Osako was not really talking to Gaston at all, but to his sister, Tomoe.

'Besides, the Japanese today are aping American culture in everything. Aping American culture. . . . Gaston, do you understand the word "ape"?'

'Ape?' Gaston's voice sounded sleepy.

Whenever Takamori ran into anyone like Osako in a bar or coffee shop, he made it a point to get away as soon as possible. It wasn't that he thought everything such people said was mistaken. In the first place, he was not very good at this kind of abstract thinking. But somehow it didn't seem right that Osako, in front of a foreigner and a girl like .Tomoe, should show contempt for his own people, and his own city.

But he could not leave. The thugs at the door still had their eyes on them. It was clear that they were lying in wait.

'Ape!' Osako, not knowing what was going through Takamori's mind, spoke in a shrill voice. 'Tomoe, how do you say "ape" in French?'

'I'm sure I don't know.'

'Ape . . . that is, monkey.' Osako turned to Gaston and did an imitation of an ape.

'Ah! Ape!' Gaston said in a loud voice and shook his head. 'You're an ape. I understand.'

Tomoe burst out laughing. Osako, annoyed, began to stir his tea vigorously with his spoon. He had nothing more to say.

Perhaps Gaston sensed that his words had offended his companion. He turned glumly toward Takamori and regarded him with a sad face. Tomoe, embarrassed, proposed that they leave. Not waiting for a response, she took hold of her handbag and rose.

'I'll be on my way too.' Osako also got up.

Takamori glanced again at the door. The man in the jacket, seeing him look in that direction, quickly hid himself in the shadows.

Osako and Tomoe, unaware of the danger before them, stood at the table side by side. Takamori tried to conceal himself behind Gaston.

'Tomoe, let me pay for this,' offered Osako.

'No, certainly not.'

They both reached for the bill. It was of no concern to Takamori which of the two paid, since his own wallet would not be affected. He stole another look at the door from his place of concealment behind Gaston's shoulders. There was no one there now. The men were probably hidden.

'Tomoe, just a second.' Takamori, flustered, caught his sister just as she was about to precede the others to the door. It would be terrible if she stepped outside and were suddenly attacked.

'Is something wrong, Takamori?' Perhaps because of Osako's presence, her speech sounded somewhat affected.

'I have something important to say to you.'

Tomoe looked at him suspiciously, allowing Osako and Gaston to step ahead of her.

'After you, *monsieur*.' With a smile Osako opened the door and took Gaston familiarly by the arm.

'What is it?' Tomoe looked up at Takamori.

'Just wait here a second.'

'What's the trouble?'

Just as Takamori expected, as soon as Osako and Gaston reached the street, two thugs suddenly appeared, one on either side of them.

'Oh, that same man!' exclaimed Tomoe, taking hold of Takamori's arm.

'Exactly!'

'What shall we do?'

The second man, who might have been a prizefighter, turned and looked back at Takamori and Tomoe. Osako, his face pale and contorted, also looked towards them. The thug whispered a few words to him and began to walk off, and Osako followed, his scared face still turned in their direction. Gaston followed, smiling amiably.

'I'll telephone the police,' said Tomoe.

'That's no good. We have no idea where they're taking him.'

Tomoe was silent for a moment. A white anger rose to her cheeks and her nose began to twitch. Takamori knew from long experience that no mere threat of violence would ever stop her when she got this way.

'I'm going with them,' she said with decision. 'Come along. We won't let them get away with it.' Then when Takamori did not answer immediately, she added, 'You're afraid, aren't you? Coward!'

'All right, then, let's go.' Even Takamori, who was after all a man, did not want his sister to think him a coward. Besides, there were three of them, and only two of the enemy. But what good would that sissy Osako be? But there was Gaston. When he understood the situation, surely he would rise to the occasion.

The two thugs watched Takamori and Tomoe approach.

'All right, lay off.' Takamori *sounded* tough, at least.

Osako seemed to take new courage. In his high-pitched feminine voice he implored them not to use violence.

Another two thugs they hadn't noticed before appeared suddenly out of nowhere and stationed themselves to right and left of Takamori and Tomoe. One of them looked like an idiot. His mouth was half open and he was playing with a little toy in his hand.

The people who passed them had no inkling of their plight. A little further down the street they would come to a row of cheap bars that were known to be the dens of these Shinjuku toughs. There was a dark corner behind Shinjuku Station where the constantly passing trains drowned all other sounds and where there was always the strong smell of stale urine. Takamori realized that this was where they were being manoeuvred.

Suddenly Tomoe stopped abruptly and called out to two students who were just passing them. 'Please help us! These thugs are molesting us!'

The students looked at her with a puzzled expression which soon gave way to fright when the man with the flashy sports coat, who was evidently the leader, took up a threatening position before them.

'Excuse us, boys,' the leader said in a low voice with a smile on his face. 'My girl friend's had a bit too much to drink.'

The two students were so frightened that they stood stock still, unable to move. In the same low voice, but much sharper this time, the leader gave them a word of advice. 'Don't you think you'd better move on?'

Aspiring intellectuals are never of any help in such situations. It did not take much calculation for the students to realize that they would not profit from getting embroiled in this matter, and, their faces stiff with fear, they quickly slunk away.

Even the leader, watching them go, was moved to comment, 'Cowardly bastards . . . no guts.'

Choosing that very moment when the thugs were off guard, Osako, who was being watched by the first fellow in the jacket, made a break for it, screaming in a soprano voice as grating as scratches on metal.

'That bastard!' exclaimed Osako's guard, but by the time he had lurched forward to stop him, Osako was well away. Bumping into people, running into girls that were in his path, straight as an arrow, without shame or regard for appearances, Osako ran on until he disappeared from view.

The people on the street finally understood the situation. They stopped for a moment and looked at them. But they were no different from the students. Not one raised a finger to help them.

'Gas, Tomoe, *now*!' shouted Takamori, as he threw the full weight of his body against the moron with the toy who was guarding Tomoe, grabbed her hand, and started to run. They thrust their way into the crowd. Tomoe was feeling faint. She remembered nothing of the next few minutes, but when she reached full consciousness again, she saw that Gaston was not with them. Her hand was still in Takamori's, but they were standing now on the main street, which with all its neon lights was almost as bright as day.

Tomoe stopped to rest against a lamp-post. Her face was drained of all blood and she was panting. There was a police box directly in front of Shinjuku Station. Takamori led his sister, who still could not speak, to this box and, without wasting any time on explanations, said urgently, 'Please come with us. A friend from abroad has been cornered by toughs.'

'Where,' asked the policeman in a matter-of-fact voice. For him this was merely routine.

In the meantime what about Gaston? When he saw Osako run off screaming and then heard Takamori call to him and Tomoe, and saw them also run off, he understood at last what kind of men these were. Robot-like he began to lumber toward the crowd of Japanese watching from a safe distance with eyes which reflected both fear and curiosity.

'Ho! Wait a minute!' the thug with the toy shouted to him. 'Are you going to buy these pictures?'

Gaston was silent.

'Will you buy these pictures or won't you?'

Gaston stopped and with a smile on his long face shook his head. 'My friends. . . .'

'I don't give a damn about your friends. I'm talking to *you*. . . . Hey, you got a screw loose, or something?'

The leader walked slowly towards him and the watching people shuffled backwards. The man fixed his pale eyes on Gaston and looked him over slowly from head to foot. Then with a fierce expression he turned to his henchmen.

'What the hell are you talking about? This ain't no boxing champion. Look at the bastard's hands. Those hands ain't never been in the ring. OK, Nishino, take care of him.'

Nishino, the thug who had first approached Gaston and his friends, came up to him with his hands still in his pockets.

Thugs also have their scale of values. There's much more glory in roughing up a famous wrestler, for example, than in bullying a high school student. Nishino's social status in the gang was bound to rise a step by beating up this enormous fellow with the body of a cow. And as a further bonus, the man was a foreigner.

'You damned Americans! Walking all over Japan as if you owned the country!' Nishino pulled two white-bandaged hands out of his pockets and took a *karate* stance.

'Farewell, everybody,' Gaston cried out with a smile that seemed glued on his face. 'Farewell!'

Nishino jumped up into the air and came at him with both hands and both legs, hitting him in the stomach and at the knees. With a loud wail Gaston's huge body folded in two.

'Oh, *non, non*. . . . *Tu m'as fait mal*.'

'Blue-eyed bastard!'

In the excess of pain Gaston seemed to have forgotten all his Japanese. He stood bent in two moaning in great agony. Nishino went at him a second time and then a third. The crowd watched the spectacle with mixed emotions. They felt both a painful sympathy for Gaston and a tingling pleasure – the kind of pleasure the Japanese experienced long ago when the little Japanese wrestler, Rikidozan, defeated the much larger Sharp brothers. No one tried to help the foreigner.

Finally Gaston slowly lifted his arm and looked long at Nishino's face. The spectators thought, 'Now he's angry and will return the attack.' But instead of rising to the full stature of his huge body and rushing at his assailant, Gaston merely used the arm to cover his long potato face. For some time he stood there not moving, with his face covered. The crowd waited in silence with bated breath for this strange foreigner to move. Nishino, who was prepared to launch his next attack, along with the other thugs, looked at him in amazement.

'Oh, *non, non.*' Gaston removed his arm from his face. Tears, like pearls, were streaming from his eyes. 'Oh, *non, non.* You mustn't. . . . Why do you try to hurt me?'

Cows, it is said, will shed tears when beaten unjustly. On Gaston's face was the same dark melancholy to be found in the face of a cow maltreated by its master.

'Look! He's just a big cry baby!' said one of the thugs derisively, the one with the toy and the face of an idiot.

'We're . . . all . . . friends,' Gaston appealed to them in broken words. 'All . . . friends! . . . Why? Why? Why? Why? . . .' He repeated the word again and again.

The Japanese watching the scene were unable to meet the look of appeal he turned on them and they began to scatter in all directions. The leader of the gang, too, his coat thrown over his shoulders, suddenly turned round and walked off. For some reason or other, both the assailants and the spectators felt something like shame well up in their hearts.

After everyone had gone, Gaston remained standing in exactly the same position, on exactly the same spot. It was here that Takamori and the policeman found him.

'Gas!' Takamori shouted and grasped his hand. The shy smile of a little boy came over Gaston's face. Takamori saw that his trousers had been torn and were stained with blood.

They returned to the police box and, an hour later, after they had answered all the policeman's questions, they headed for home.

'Does it hurt, Gas?'

'No, it's all right.'

Takamori said almost nothing all the way home. His conscience was bothering him. Why had he left Gaston behind and run away?

Tomoe, looking out at the neon lights that passed by the cab window, was thinking: To cry like that . . . a big man like him. Doesn't he have any self-respect? To let them beat him up without even trying to defend himself . . . with that huge body of his, too! Still, for the first time she felt a tenderness toward this man, the kind of tenderness a mother might feel toward a crippled child.

I should never have taken Gaston to Shinjuku at night, thought Takamori. For all his easy-going irresponsibility, he now felt deeply responsible and apologetic for Gaston's misadventure.

'Gas, don't feel too badly about what happened. All the Japanese are not like the ones you met tonight.'

Gaston, looking straight ahead, shook his head. He seemed lost in his own thoughts. Takamori could understand how he felt. To come all the way across the world to the Japan of his dreams and then on almost his first day in the country to be hit and kicked by Japanese!

'Tomoe, this was a real disaster, wasn't it?'

Tomoe, sensing her brother's dejection, tried to raise his spirits. 'Cheer up. It's all over. When I get home I'll bake a cake for you and Gaston.'

By the time they reached home Gaston was his usual smiling, amiable self. He put a finger to his lips and said to the other two, 'Let's not say anything to your mother or Matchan. Let's keep it a secret. We'll tell them I fell and tore my trousers. OK?'

Takamori and Tomoe understood that Gaston did not want to give their mother and Matchan cause for anxiety on his behalf. Tomoe thought : He may be a coward and lacking in self-respect, but he certainly has a good heart. She felt she had finally come to understand his good qualities, and looked at him now with new eyes.

Tomoe's chocolate cake, baked to help them forget the events of the evening, was a great hit with Gaston. Joyfully he shovelled it into his huge mouth which, despite her new-found regard for him, still reminded Tomoe of the mouth of a hippopotamus.

Then suddenly Gaston's expression became very serious as he stopped eating and turned to Takamori.

'I have something important to discuss with you.'

'What is it, Gas?'

Gaston hesitated. He looked around at Shizu and Tomoe, as if finding it hard to speak in their presence. Takamori understood at once and said, 'Gas, shall we go up to the second floor?'

'Yes, yes.'

Preceded by Takamori, Gaston climbed slowly up the stairs. Tomoe, left behind in the dining-room, turned on the radio and waited for them to return. She was put out that Gaston, who had suddenly become so serious, had not invited her, too. Besides, she was curious about what he had to say.

The radio was playing one of her favourite pieces, 'Taboo'. Takamori and Gaston still did not come down. Shall I go up and eavesdrop? she thought. She was, after all, a woman, and like most women had a fondness for learning the secrets of others.

Finally she heard her brother's footsteps on the staircase. Turning toward him, she saw that his expression was very grave, which was quite unusual for him.

'What is it, Takamori?' she asked in a low voice, her eyes sparkling.

'Gas says he's going to leave us,' Takamori answered, his hands tucked into his sash.

4   All Alone

'He says he's going to leave us?'

'Yes.' Takamori blinked his eyes to hold back the tears.

'Then he's not happy with us. After all we've done to entertain him! I think that's mean.'

'No, it's not that.'

'The shock of what happened in Shinjuku must have been too great. He's probably disillusioned with Japan.' Tomoe thought privately that although Takamori and she were to blame, their guest might have had a little more courage and fought back. After all, there are millions of Japanese and rotten fruit can be found on any tree. To meet a few bad Japanese and get so upset about it – that's not manly. Tomoe's nose twitched with displeasure.

'That's what I thought it was too, at first. But Gaston says that that's not the reason he's leaving.'

'No? Then what is it?'

'He wants to get to know many Japanese, he says. He wants to have a chance to meet all kinds.'

Takamori sat down next to his sister. He wrapped his arms around his legs and rested his chin on his knees. For some time he stared at one spot on the floor, lost in thought.

'Gas is certainly a strange man, isn't he?' Takamori broke his meditation to remark. 'He's really an odd one. He's not like the run of travellers and tourists. He's not at all interested in seeing Tokyo Tower or the Great Buddha of Kamakura. All he's done since he arrived is walk around and make friends with dogs and children. He really fascinates me, but I haven't the slightest idea what he has in mind.'

'But he must have had a reason for coming to Japan.'

'I've asked him, but he seems shy about telling me what it is. Still, I'm sure he has some definite purpose in mind. There's something he's come to accomplish.'

'He could hardly be a smuggler, could he? Or a spy sent to ferret out the secrets of the Self-Defence Force? It's nothing like that, is it?'

The newspapers frequently carried accounts of foreigners arrested for smuggling. Drawn to Tokyo by the international character of the city, they came to Japan from such ports as Hong Kong and Singapore. This was frequently a subject of conversation at the Disanto Trading Company, where Tomoe worked.

'Are you crazy? Takamori looked up at the ceiling and, thinking of Gaston upstairs, sighed. He recalled Basho's famous haiku about man's isolation in autumn and adapted it to their present circumstances:

> It is deep spring
> My neighbour –
> How does he live, I wonder.

They heard the stairs creak under Gaston's heavy footstep. Then a moment later Gaston opened the door of the room and shyly poked his horseface into the room. 'Excuse me.'

'Gas, come and sit with us.'

Gaston entered the room. Looking a little sadly at Tomoe, he clumsily bent his knees and sat down.

'Tomoe *san*. I spoke to your brother. Really, thanks for your kindness. But I say to Tomoe *san, au revoir.*'

Takamori and Tomoe both urged him to stay on with them. Gaston listened politely with head hung low, and then answered, 'Thank you, thank you, but I. . . .' He repeated this again and again like a parrot and could get no further.

'Gas, you say you want to meet a lot of Japanese. But

you can do that and still remain with us,' Takamori
pointed out as an argument against his leaving.

'That's true, Gaston,' Tomoe said, joining forces with
her brother. 'What kind of people would you like to meet?
We'll do anything in the world for you that we can. Won't
we, Takamori?'

Gaston's hands rested awkwardly on his long knees.
Takamori and Tomoe had never seen him like this before.
Usually so quick to shake his head up and down in the
familiar sign of agreement, tonight he held it obstinately
still.

Takamori finally gave up. 'Then it can't be helped.
Tomoe, we'll have to let Gas do as he thinks best. . . . But
Gas, please come back to us whenever you feel like it. As
long as you're in Japan, you have a home here.' He spoke
with deep feeling.

When it was all decided, Gaston got up. He went to his
room and brought down four small packages wrapped in
French newspapers. One he gave to Takamori and another
to Tomoe.

'Here, Takamori *san*. Here, Tomoe *san*.'

The other two packages he asked them to give to their
mother, who had already gone to bed, and to Matchan.

'Gaston,' exclaimed a surprised Tomoe, 'you're not thinking of leaving tonight, are you?'

'Yes, tonight . . . now.'

That was unthinkable!

'Gas, that's impossible! In the first place, you haven't
got a place to spend the night, have you?'

'Don't worry. Don't worry. On the ship I even slept on
the deck.' His whole face broke out in a smile.

'I'll call Mother and Matchan,' said Tomoe.

Shizu, when she learned of Gaston's decision, hurried to
him and also did all she could to get him to reconsider.
But whatever he had in mind, he would not be persuaded.

'I'm a coward. Maybe tomorrow my spirit no good. Will
want to be at Takamori's house again. But tonight, my

mind is made up.' Looking at Takamori and Tomoe, he apologized profusely for troubling them like this.

'Takamori, at least you might arrange to get him a place to stay,' suggested Shizu, deeply concerned.

But Takamori saw that Gaston's decision to set out on his own was unshakeable. 'No, I think it best now to let him go as he wishes.'

Gaston, with his duffel bag in his hands, stood at the door of the house with all the members of the family lined up to say goodbye. It had been so sudden and unexpected that Matchan was too stunned to remember to put out his shoes and had to be reminded. She just stood there staring at him.

Gaston waved even at Matchan. 'Matchan, goodbye. Thank you.' Looking as if he might cry, he expressed his thanks to each in turn.

'Goodbye, Gas. Be sure to come back now.'

When he had reached the darkness of the street, his huge body turned to them again and he waved his hand awkwardly. As he walked away, he was joined by a companion.

'It's that dog!' cried Tomoe. The old mongrel that Gaston had befriended had suddenly appeared from no-where and began to limp along behind him.

'I just don't understand,' muttered Tomoe. 'I just don't understand.'

The stars were twinkling. Some of them had a sharp brilliance and others only a gentle dimness. Looking up at the night sky, silvery with glimmering clouds of stars, Gaston felt as if he had sprouted wings and was being called up to them.

From childhood Gaston had liked to look at the stars. On the deck of the ship coming to Japan he had spent most of the night looking up at the sky. There had been the stars in the milk-coloured sky of the Mediterranean in early morning, the small stars shining in the dark African night, and the stars over the Indian Ocean, as infinite in number as those that could be seen tonight.

The stars never change. But he . . . he had come this long way to Japan. And tonight he was once more alone.

Where would he go? He had nowhere to go. He had no place to sleep tonight. But this was the way of life he had chosen for himself.

'Dog *san*,' he called to the old mongrel crouched at his feet. 'Dog *san* too has nowhere to sleep, same as me.' When he began to walk, the dog staggered along behind him, coughing all the while.

'*Non, non*, dog *san*. Goodbye.' But the dog just lifted his head and stared at him. There was something pathetic in those eyes. They seemed to beg Gaston not to go away without him. Gaston squatted down and stroked his head. Looking into the dog's sad eyes he felt that he understood what they were trying to say. The dog had no master to take care of it; it was ugly and old and had this bad cough. It was completely alone in the world just as he was. He himself, of course, was still young and had a large, healthy body. But he was a coward, a simpleton, who had gone from one failure to the next. The old dog had undoubtedly been pelted with rocks, and chased by everyone. From the time he was a child Gaston too had always been laughed at and made fun of by his brothers and friends.

In Gaston's native region of Savoy, large men who are thought to be somewhat simple are called poplars. That is because the wood of the poplar tree is not good for anything but matchsticks. It does not make good lumber, and it cannot be used for pillars or beams. And so Gaston's friends had nicknamed him 'poplar'.

But Gaston had always wanted to trust people. Not everyone in the world, he thought, was born clever and strong like Napoleon. The earth is not just for the clever and the strong. It must be possible even for weak and pitiful creatures – like himself and this old dog – to make some contribution in their lifetime. Among this multitude

of stars, too, there were some like themselves . . . not only
confidently shining stars casting a strong light, but less
brilliant ones. Even a weakling like himself, if he were
wholly alive, if he made full use of the life that was in
him, should be able to snatch for himself a fragment of
the beauty of the stars.

'All right, then, come along, dog *san*.' Gaston stood up
and started to walk. The dog, still coughing, followed along
behind.

The foxes have their holes and the birds of the air their
nests. With his eyes on the stars, which sparkled like jewels
in the night sky, Gaston turned a corner and started
walking east. He could not take a bus, since the dog would
not be allowed on, and his slender means did not permit
him the luxury of a taxi. Gaston, who had so little he could
boast of, did take a certain pride in his ability to walk
long distances. But the most important problem now was
to find a place to sleep for the night. As he had explained
to Takamori, on the *Vietnam* he had spent many a
night on the open deck. A bench in a railway station or
the steps of a church would serve him equally well; there
he would be able to await the coming of day.

It was good to be alone again. He felt apologetic to
Takamori and Tomoe for feeling like this, since they had
been so kind to him, a perfect stranger, but nevertheless
he experienced a great joy in this solitude and freedom,
which he had not known for a long time. He had often
dreamed of walking the exotic streets of Tokyo like this,
without giving trouble to anyone. But what a huge city it
was!

He found himself on a bustling street bright with neon
lights. Consulting his map, he decided that this must be
Shibuya, but when he stopped to investigate he found that
it was Sangenchaya, still on the outskirts of Tokyo. Compared to Paris, which could be crossed from east to west
in two hours, Tokyo was like a vast desert, difficult to come

to terms with. Although it was ten o'clock at night, there was as much noise and activity here as in Montparnasse in broad daylight. So many people in so little space!

Rows of wooden houses, built so close together that they resembled a giant honeycomb; men in wooden clogs; mothers carrying their children on their backs; noodle sellers; pachinko parlours – he was awed by everything he saw. Takamori had told him, 'Tokyo has many people. The population problem is the cancer of Japan.' Gaston understood now what he meant.

'Shibuya – where?' he asked the girl who tended a tobacco shop in the centre of Sangenchaya.

The girl, who looked very like Matchan, answered, 'Over there,' and pointed to the east.

'Is there an inn?'

'Inn?'

'Yes, hotel.'

Why was it that she looked at Gaston with sarcasm and contempt and merely laughed, without answering his question?

Gaston and the dog set out again towards the east. They passed Sanjuku, Ohashi. Gaston held in his hand the map Takamori had given him and memorized the names of the sections of the city through which he passed. He had already walked two hours since leaving Kyodo.

'Dog *san*, tired, aren't you?' Gaston called to the dog, who was sniffing around a pile of rubbish. Even his own legs were now very tired.

The foxes have their holes and the birds of the air their nests. Man too must have a place to rest.

Reaching the top of a slope, Gaston was startled at what he saw. All about him, wherever he looked, were hotels and inns. Buildings with HOTEL written in red neon lights, Japanese inns with lanterns at the gate and names like Kōonkaku, Sekireisō, Hotel Spring, Sampei Inn. Neither in France nor in any other country had Gaston ever seen such a concentration of hotels. This was certainly another indication of the warm hospitality with which Japan treated its foreign guests! Japan is really a very kind country, he thought with warm admiration.

Stopping in front of a building with a neon sign on which the words HILLTOP HOTEL flashed on and off, Gaston found additional reason for admiring the excellent service Japan provided for its tourist visitors. Below the name of the hotel was written

Full night : 800 yen
One hour : 400 yen

Even the famous Paris hotel, the Ritz, was not so considerate of its guests. A hotel guest is never so ill at ease as when he is afraid his room may cost more than he has anticipated. What greater service, then, than to let him know beforehand the actual cost of the room. And to carry that kindness still further by indicating the cost of stopping for a brief rest.

In great admiration of this way of doing things, Gaston, followed by the dog, opened the door to the hotel and walked in. It was quite unlike any hotel he had ever seen : there was neither lobby nor front desk. He had to call twice before he heard footsteps coming down the long corridor.

A girl dressed in a Japanese kimono came hurrying down the corridor to greet him. Her lips were painted a bright red. When she saw Gaston, she stopped, dismayed.

'Do you have a sleeping room? 800 yen?' Gaston added '800 yen' as he recalled the straitened conditon of his wallet.

The girl did not reply.

'Do you have a sleeping room?' he asked again.

'Are you alone?' she asked, surveying him suspiciously from head to foot.

'Yes, alone. . . . No, this dog is with me, but he'll sleep outside.'

The maid turned and called in a loud voice to someone

inside, 'Tanida *san,* will you come here a second?' She disappeared, but Gaston could hear her talking in a low voice.

'It's an odd foreigner. He says he wants a single. What shall we do?'

'A single?' The voice that answered her was a man's. 'Yes, a single.'

'This is a problem. Is he an American?'

'I don't know.'

'Well . . . all right. It can't be helped. Show him to Marguerite.'

Gaston could judge by the tone of their conversation that he was not a welcome guest. Why don't they want to put up a single guest? he wondered. Why don't Japanese hotels like to rent rooms to single guests? *'C'est ça. C'est ça!'* Gaston now realized that the Hilltop Hotel had not been set up to give service to foreign tourists. It must have some other solemn purpose. This was no place for him. He turned around and was about to walk out of the door when the girl returned.

'Please come in,' she said, setting out a pair of slippers for him. He was too cowardly to refuse her invitation.

'Dog *san* too . . .'

'This fellow has a dog,' she called again to Tanida, making a wry face. 'He says he has a dog with him.'

At that moment the front door opened and a man and woman came in. The man was middle-aged and had a face that resembled General Tojo's. When the woman saw Gaston, she quickly concealed the lower portion of her face with her shawl and hid herself behind the man. The receptionist greeted the couple in a respectful manner markedly different from her attitude to Gaston.

She led him down the corridor, which was shrouded in an eerie silence. From somewhere he could hear the sound of running water. Because of his height and the low ceilings, he had to draw in his neck like a turtle. Looking at the names of the rooms he noticed that they were all named after flowers – Rose, Cherry, Hyacinth, and so on, and that in front of each door were two pairs of slippers. In this hotel Gaston was the only simpleton, lumbering innocently down the corridors in search of a single room. He couldn't understand why they were all dark and why this strange silence prevailed.

When the girl came to the room called Marguerite, she put the key in the lock and opened the door. The room had a strange smell, which was not that of plaster or paint. The body odours of the man and woman who had only just vacated it still lingered.

'Mr Foreigner, here we receive all money in advance,' explained the girl, and she repeated the word 'money' in both Japanese and English, to make sure he understood.

There are probably couples unethical enough to sneak away in the night without paying their bill when they have finished their business. To make this impossible, hotels of this kind require the guests to pay in advance. Gaston, surprised, paid her the money. She threw him another look of contempt and disappeared down the corridor.

Gaston sat down cautiously on the edge of the bed. Tomorrow he would have to look around for some other place, a place where he could really sleep.

'Mitchan, Mitchan,' suddenly he heard a man's voice on the other side of the wall. 'I have to go to the toilet.'

'Be quiet and let me sleep.'

'I'm getting up.'

'You're keeping me awake. . . . If you must go, you can use the washstand.'

Gaston was stunned. He held his breath and listened. What he heard was unmistakably the sound of trickling water. Apparently the man was doing as 'Mitchan' had told him and was urinating in the washstand in the corner of the room.

Shocked, Gaston jumped up from bed. He was incensed that the man should be relieving himself in the very washstand where other guests would wash their faces. He coughed loudly so that he would be heard next door.

The trickling sound stopped abruptly, but then he heard the sound of water flowing from the tap. The man had turned on the tap to drown out the other sound as he continued his business.

Gaston had done a good bit of travelling and seen many things, but this was so shocking to him that he lost all desire to wash his face and hands, and he sat on his bed dejected. Still, having walked all the way from Kyodo to Shibuya, he was so tired that his eyes began to close.

'Takamori *san*, Tomoe *san*, *bonne nuit*.'

Before going to bed, he had to go to the toilet. He stepped cautiously into the corridor and there a strange sight met his eyes.

A Japanese woman had opened the window at the end of the corridor and was about to jump out. It was the woman that had come in with the man who looked like General Tojo. Seeing Gaston, she began to back away in fear. She had with her a bulky cloth bundle, but Gaston could not imagine what it contained. Around her neck was a soiled bandage. She was short and emaciated. Gaston found the faces of Japanese women as expressionless as Noh masks, and this woman was no exception. He could not fathom what she had in mind.

For some time the woman looked with eyes full of fear at this monstrous foreigner, so like a horse. Then finally she spoke.

'What are you?' There was both anger and desperation in her voice.

Gaston couldn't imagine why she should be angry with him. He flashed his usual gentle smile at her.

This must have given her courage, because her next words were, 'I hate *Ame-kō*.' *Ame-kō* was the term of opprobrium used for Americans. 'Get out of my way!'

Just then from a room across the corridor near the staircase, a man shouted in a loud voice, 'Hey! Somebody! Come quick!'

The woman, startled by the shout, looked all around her like a cornered rat and then grabbing her bundle started down the corridor. But when she saw the light go on in the maid's room, she turned her frightened face to Gaston and shouted, 'Where's your room? Quick! Take me to your room.'

Before Gaston could say anything, she spotted his door, which he had left slightly ajar, and quickly darted inside for concealment, Gaston following her.

'Please, help me! Please!' She repeated her request several times, as she heard voices in the corridor approaching the door. Gaston looked down blankly at her desperate, contorted face.

'Help me, help me!' she repeated. She folded her hands before him in petition, as before the Buddha. Her fingers were as long and thin as needles.

In the corridor the maid and the man who had shouted could be heard talking loudly. Gaston heard both of them use the word '*shōben*'. He knew this word meant 'to urinate', and he gathered from the conversation between the two that this had been her offence. So that was it! A big smile came over his face and he shook his head understandingly. Like the man next door, the woman had had to go to the toilet but, unable to control herself, she had wet the bed. This for a woman must occasion great shame. He sadly recalled that as a child he too had wet his bed and been despised for it by his brothers. Gaston felt that he could now understand the woman's contorted face and look of desperation.

'Over there.' He put his finger to his lips to warn her to be quiet, and pointed to his window. The woman pulled up her skirts, revealing short, fat legs shaped like a Japanese radish, and climbed on to the window sill with the dexterity of a monkey. The cloth bundle tucked to her side, she jumped down. Gaston heard a cry of pain; she must have hurt herself in falling. The cry echoed through the darkness.

The two in the corridor also heard the cry. Gaston's door burst open and General Tojo and the maid came rushing in. When they saw that the woman had already escaped, General Tojo turned to Gaston in great anger.

'Why the hell did you let that woman get away?'

'*Shōben* . . . you do it too. You wrong to get angry because she make *shōben*', said Gaston with a very serious face.

At these words General Tojo went into a frenzy. His face became flaming red with anger.

'Get out of here.'

Although it was two o'clock in the morning, Gaston was thrown out of the hotel by the scruff of his neck as if he were a cat.

How hard and how presumptuous it was for a simpleton like him to come to the help of others. Before leaving the hotel he had been roundly excoriated by General Tojo.

'Why do you stick your nose in other people's business, when you don't understand Japanese?' The word *shōben*, Gaston learned for the first time, had two meanings. Unfortunately he knew only the one that was in his dictionary, the physiological meaning. General Tojo, with angry gestures and curses, explained to him the other: when a prostitute steals her client's wallet and, on the pretext of going to the toilet, escapes with it in the night – this, too, is called *shōben* and is written with the same characters as the other.

General Tojo turned to the manager of the hotel. 'That whore took my clothes. I don't care if this ass is a foreigner. He's got to pay for my clothes. It's your responsibility to make him.'

Gaston could not follow his Japanese. But he had no difficulty in understanding what the man wanted. The manager of the hotel finally succeeded in getting Gaston off the hook, but he then asked him to leave the hotel.

'I'm sorry, Mr Foreigner, but I'll have to ask you to go.

At a hotel like ours we can't afford to have guests who
don't know their way around.' He reluctantly returned
Gaston's 800 yen. 'Chizuko, throw out that mongrel dog,
too. He's keeping everyone awake with his coughing.' And
so Gaston and the dog were thrown out of the hotel
together.

The stars were still twinkling in the night sky. The old
dog stuck faithfully to Gaston's long shadow. Along the
street were other hotels still open for business – Kuroyurisō,
Kōonkaku, Aoba Hotel – but Gaston lacked the courage
to enter any of them.

With so many hotels in Tokyo, there was nowhere
Gaston could find a quiet place to sleep. Even he could
not fail to see the contradiction in his beloved Japan that
this implied.

He kept walking towards the east. Now that it was after
two in the morning, all the shops were closed and only an
occasional lamp-post stood like an old man casting a feeble
light. Almost no one was to be seen on the street.

No matter what I do it ends in failure, reflected
Gaston. He was painfully aware of his shortcomings. It
was not only tonight. Whatever he did always ended in this
fashion. The same ill fortune that had caused him to be
thrown out of the hotel for helping a woman in need had
hounded him from childhood. How could someone like
himself ever do anything good or beautiful for others?

Shibuya at two in the morning is deathly still. The coffee
bars, cinemas and shops are all closed and shuttered. This
was the first time that Gaston had ever been to Shibuya,
but he realized at once that this was a far more bustling
section of town than Sangenchaya, which he had passed
earlier.

In the back alleys he could hear voices singing loudly,
probably those of men returning from bars where they had
spent the night drinking. To the ears of a foreigner like
Gaston, their songs had a kind of Oriental melancholy.

They resembled the sad Arabian songs he had heard in Aden.

He felt depressed. His legs were tired from walking. In fact, he was tired all over. But he was more worried about the old dog than he was about himself. The poor dog had had a long day. He stopped and looked about him to see if there might not be a place still open. But the only lights on the street were those of the lamp-posts and the ones shining in the display windows of shops that had long closed for the night.

Then he heard someone call to him in a low voice. 'Hey, fellow, the night's still young. How about coming along?'

The voice came from a dark opening between a cinema and the neighbouring shop. As he looked, there emerged ghost-like from the opening, which might have been the entrance into a cave, the face of a woman. It was the woman with the bandage around her neck.

'Good heavens!' she cried in surprise. 'The *Ame-kō* from the hotel.'

Gaston blinked his eyes sadly. Although it was because of this woman that he had been kicked out of the hotel in the middle of the night, he did not feel any resentment toward her. Simple Gaston was constitutionally incapable of harbouring resentment or hatred towards anyone. Even when a child, no matter what trick his companions played on him or how cruelly they treated him, he was of such a temperament that he could not hate his persecutors. To hate was for him the most odious of tasks. Instead, he was quickly moved to trust in the goodwill and friendship of others, or at least to want to trust in them. And so there was in his face now no sign that he resented or, in fact, even remembered the incident at the hotel.

'What happened? Weren't you staying at that inn? Thanks to you, I got away. But I hit my behind when I fell. It's still a little sore.' She pointed to her hip with a laugh that displayed the red gums of her teeth. 'But what happened to you?'

'The hotel people made me leave.' His usual smile covered his face, as he rubbed his eyes in weariness.

'Oh? You were kicked out?' The woman looked up at Gaston's face in surprise. In her look there was still an element of caution. 'But if we keep standing here, a policeman's liable to come along. Let's go inside.'

Gaston took two or three steps and then, as if he had just thought of it, said, 'Food. . . .'

'What?'

'Food . . . for the dog . . . me', and he pointed sadly to his stomach. The woman stood a while assessing him, and then as if he had passed the test, she invited him to come along with her. She disappeared into the cavelike crevice with the speed of a wharf rat. Gaston had heard that cities of the East, such as are described in the Arabian Nights, abound in labyrinthine passages full of conundrum and mystery, but he had never expected to find such a passage in Tokyo. Making himself as small as he could, he followed the woman, who had disappeared into the darkness.

'What are you doing?' He heard the woman call from somewhere below his feet. 'Here, there's a staircase.'

His eyes, finally adjusted to the dark, made out a stone staircase just in front of him. The high wall of the cinema rose to one side of it. This was an emergency exit for escape in case of fire or earthquake.

When he reached the bottom of the stairs, the woman turned on her flashlight. Gaston wiped the sweat off his forehead with his huge hand. On the floor at his feet was the cloth bundle he remembered from before.

'Don't make any noise,' the woman warned him in a low voice, and turned off the flashlight. 'I'll go and get you something to eat.' She climbed back up the staircase, as rapidly as before, and disappeared into the dark.

With his heart in his mouth Gaston crouched on the cement floor, his arms around his legs, and waited in silence, hardly daring to breathe. The old dog gently licked his hands.

Gaston looked up at the sky and saw that it was still studded with a vast multitude of twinkling stars. It was like a dream to be here where he was – in a distant country waiting for a woman whom he had never met until tonight to bring him food. Then he recalled Takamori and Tomoe. What does Tomoe *san* think of me, he wondered. He smiled as he thought of her small turned-up nose. Brother and sister must be wondering why he crossed the seas and came to distant Japan. But he couldn't tell them his purpose, at least not yet. Perhaps some day he might be able to explain. But first he would have to meet many many more Japanese and make a decision.

'Is he alone?'

'He's got a dog with him.'

He heard the woman's voice above the stairs. This time she seemed to have two or three other women with her. The beams of a flashlight lit up the staircase, and Gaston saw white legs ending in muddy shoes and beaten-up clogs on the steps.

'Are you crazy? Bringing an *Ame-kō* down here.'

'It's all right. This fellow's all right.'

The voices suddenly stopped. Three women flashed their light on Gaston, who was still squatting on his heels. It was as if they were scrutinizing an abandoned cat.

5   The Hermit of the East

'Is this the fellow?' asked one of the women in a high, squeaky voice, shining her flashlight into Gaston's face, making him squint. She was incongruously dressed in a faded sweater, a man's trousers, and high-heeled red shoes. The third woman, fat and round like an egg, wore a threadbare suit and had on wooden clogs. The latter squatted beside Gaston, smiling up at him. Her soiled bloomers could be seen between her fat legs, causing Gaston to turn his eyes away in confusion.

'This fellow hasn't broken out of the pen by any chance, has he?' Gaston looked to her as if he might be an escaped convict. The first woman reassured her.

It is not to be marvelled at that in their eyes Gaston looked as if he might be a jail-breaker such as they had seen in American crime pictures. Besides, a number of foreigners wanted by the police on suspicion of drug and smuggling offences were known to be wandering about loose in Tokyo.

'Look at that build, Kimie. Wouldn't he be a good thing to have around?'

They were speaking a back-alley Japanese that Gaston had not been taught in language school. He could hardly understand a word they said, but he knew all the same what they were talking about. What disturbed him more than their conversation was that the egg-shaped woman squatting beside him was running her fingers up and down his thigh.

Gaston, always the gentleman, suddenly realized that he had his hat on. He hurriedly removed it and excused himself for his bad manners. 'Pardon me.'

'Oh, he speaks Japanese!' exclaimed the woman in the red shoes in surprise. The woman called Kimie began to laugh in a high voice.

'Don't make so much noise,' cautioned the first woman, the one with the bandaged neck who had taken Gaston under her wing. She spread out a newspaper in front of him and placed on it a cracked plate with food. He identified the round, yellow objects as egg yolks, but what were these things that looked like mouldy crusts of bread jabbed onto a slender stick?

'That's *o-den*. Haven't you ever eaten *o-den*?'*

'How could he have? He's a foreigner,' said Kimie. She watched as Gaston, with a sad smile, took one of the egg yolks and plopped it into his mouth. 'Oh, he's eaten it!'

'So he has.' The three women observed him with as much interest as they would watch a monkey at the zoo trying to shave himself with an electric razor.

Gaston gave a piece of *o-den* to the dog crouching at his side.

'Is this your dog? Does he have a name?'

'Yes. Napoleon.' Gaston didn't know why he had said the dog's name was Napoleon, but then and there he decided to name him after his illustrious ancestor.

'Me . . . dog . . . no place to sleep,' he said, smiling weakly.

'He says he ain't got a place to kip.'

The women went into consultation. They sounded like chirping sparrows.

This rather simple man who had fallen into their hands was like a kind of pet that had to be cared for. He was interesting and he aroused their curiosity. The only foreigners they had met until now were swaggering Americans, to whom Gaston, with his humble and good heart, was a striking contrast.

'Don't you have any money?'

* Hotchpotch.

Gaston pulled out his wallet and showed it to them. When he had changed his money into yen at Yokohama Customs, the middle-aged man in charge had asked in English, unbelievingly, 'Is that all?' It amounted to a mere three thousand yen. Gaston had in addition, of course, his return ticket home. But there was nothing else in his wallet.

'If he has three thousand yen, he can get lodgings anywhere, can't he?' the woman in the red shoes pointed out plaintively.

'Don't be stupid. What'll he do tomorrow? He's got to eat tomorrow too.' The woman with the bandage was not only the eldest of the three, but was, it seemed, the most intelligent. She turned to Gaston. 'Put that away and take good care of it.' She took the wallet from his hands and tucked it into his pocket, just as a mother will do with a child departing on a school excursion.

Gaston could not understand why these prostitutes were so kind to him. The very woman who had robbed her client at the Hilltop Hotel of everything he had on him, including his clothes, was now transformed into this gentle, warmhearted person.

'How about Dachi's place?'

'That crook! He'd con this guy out of his three thousand yen by morning.'

'Then how about *sensei*?'* the fat woman, Kimie, suggested.

'Now that's an idea.' The three were silent for a moment in thought. 'How about it? Would you like to go to *sensei*'s place?'

'Yes, *sensei*'s place.'

'He's a funny old man, but if we ask him, he'll let you stay overnight. He may even have some work for you.'

Having made a unanimous decision, the women stood up and escorted Gaston and Napoleon up the staircase

* A term of high respect used both when addressing the person and in speaking about him.

much as if he were a samurai lord. There was no one on the street.

'Please take this.' Gaston pulled a note out of his wallet and tried to hand it to one of the women.

'What's that for?'

'Money for the food.'

'Don't be a fool. Didn't you save me from getting caught tonight? I guess I can stand you a little *o-den* at least.'

Gaston didn't know where they were walking. They crossed the railroad tracks and came to a narrow stream whose water was a foul black and smelled of sewage. Lined up along the stream was a row of cheap bars that looked rickety enough to be a film set. At this time of morning none of them were open.

The women, who, of course, were at home here, did not have to consider which path to take, and kept up a continual stream of chatter as they threaded their way through a labyrinth of interweaving alleys that had Gaston completely confused. Whether they turned left or right, all the alleys looked the same to him, and it even seemed as if they might be going round and round in a circle. But they finally came to a stop in front of a bar, which, like all the others, was closed for the night.

They did not go to the front door but went around to the side of the building, where Gaston saw a narrow staircase going up to the second floor. It was barely large enough for him to pass.

'Wait here a second,' the woman with the bandage told him. She went on ahead up the stairs, followed by the other two. The sound of their footsteps on the wooden staircase echoed through the silent night.

'*Sensei*!' he heard them call. They were trying to wake up someone inside. A light came on in a second-storey window. Except for Napoleon's quiet whining, not another sound was to be heard in the still night. Gaston wondered what time it was. To tell the truth, he was afraid. What kind of man was this *sensei* he was about to meet? He was fearful of what kind of treatment he, an unknown foreigner, might receive at the hands of the Japanese. These women had been kind enough to him, it was true, but after his experience in Shinjuku he realized that his Japanese was so poor that unless he took care, he might again mistake the situation.

Still, he was determined that whatever kind of man he found here, he would not be suspicious of him. He would trust him. Even if he were deceived, he would try to keep on trusting. This was one of the tasks he had set himself to accomplish in Japan. He had left behind him across the seas the world in which suspicion and doubt were rampant, the culture and learning which refused to enter deeply into the heart of the other and to recognize his good will. He was firmly convinced that what was most necessary in the world today was trust in men. Simple Gaston had taken it upon himself to maintain an unwavering trust in men as the first step in his enterprise.

'Hey, you!' one of the women called to him from the top of the staircase.

'Right. I'll come up.'

Just as he thought, the staircase was so narrow that he could barely squeeze through. The ceiling was low and he bumped his head a couple of times. Finally, to protect his head he brought his hands up to his forehead.

There was a damp smell in the small room at the top of the stairs. On a threadbare quilt with the cotton stuffing sticking out sat an old man as thin as a stick. He was leaning against the wall with his legs stretched out in front of him. He had on trousers, but in place of a shirt he wore a woman's red sweater.

'Then we'll be running along home,' said one of the women. The old man did not answer. He poured a black liquid from the tea kettle into his cup and drank it with slurping sounds. Even after the woman had gone, he said nothing, but kept on drinking with his eyes fixed on Gaston, studying him closely.

Finally he spoke 'You're not American, are you? Where
do you come from? . . . No, you needn't answer. I'll
figure it out. Bring your face a little closer.'

Gaston did as he was told and placed his long horseface immediately in front of the *sensei*, and the old man
looked at it with great intensity for a time.

'This is interesting!'

'Yes. Yes.'

'That point above the nose should indicate that you
have a great hero in your family tree.' Gaston started to
answer, but the old man stopped him. 'I'm a diviner. I
want to read the face of the man who is to spend the
night with me. . . . Yes, you must have a great ancestor.'

Gaston could understand only about half of what the
old man said, but filling in the blanks with his imagination, he guessed what he was saying. 'Napoleon,' he
explained in a low voice.

The teacup fell with a clatter from the old man's hands
onto the reddish-brown mat. 'Napoleon! That explains
it. Then I wasn't wrong. So you see, I am able to tell a
person's character from his face. . . . I forgot to introduce
myself. My name is Chotei Kawaii. I'm an Oriental
diviner.'

'My name is Gas.' Gaston presented the name that
Takamori had affectionately given him.

'Gas? Gas? Not the gas that comes out here, I hope,'
said the man without smiling, pointing to his emaciated
rump. 'It's an interesting name, but your face is really
unusual.'

'Yes. Yes.'

'You have a physiognomy such as one seldom sees these
days.' Then lowering his voice, the old man asked, 'You
have some great enterprise in mind, haven't you?'

'Enterprise?'

'Something you plan to do. I can see it between your
eyebrows. Why did you come to Japan?'

Gaston did not understand the old man's Japanese well

enough to be able to answer. And the old man on his part withdrew the question immediately. 'No, it's rude of me to ask. Let's go to sleep now. We can talk to-morrow.' He stretched himself full length on the quilt as if he had already forgotten everything that had been said.

'There are some blankets on the shelf over there. Take as many as you like.' He had hardly finished speaking before he began to snore.

Gaston turned out the light and covered himself with a blanket. The old man next to him did not move at all in his sleep. Gaston felt something crawling up his legs, making them itch. Probably fleas. What in the world was this man, wondered Gaston. Was he a hermit such as he had seen in old Eastern paintings?

When Gaston awoke the following morning, the hermit was already up and starting a fire in the cooking stove. He was still wearing the woman's red sweater.

'If you're awake, you can go out and wash.'

Gaston did as he was told. He went down the narrow staircase. At its foot he found Napoleon lying with his chin resting on his paws. The dog looked up at him wistfully.

A woman, perhaps a waitress from one of the bars, was standing in front of the public toilet across the street, but seeing Gaston she was startled and walked off. The water tap for washing was immediately to the side of the toilet.

When Gaston returned to the room, the old man put some fried sardines on a plate. 'I wonder if you are able to eat anything like this,' he said. But to Gaston, who was famished, sardines had never tasted so good. He did not forget to heap up the sardine heads at the side of his plate for Napoleon.

'What's that for?' asked the old man, putting down his chopsticks.

'This is for dog *san*.' Gaston, embarrassed, told the old man he had brought a dog along with him.

'So you like dogs, do you?' The old man once again made a close study of Gaston's face. 'You're quite an unusual Westerner, aren't you?'

'Yes. Yes.'

'People think me rather strange, too. Believe it or not, I was once a school principal.' His face had a melancholy look as he spoke. 'Now I live in a place like this and make my living telling fortunes. I also write the women's love letters for them and listen to their complaints. I'm pretty much disgusted with today's Japan. Tell me, how does Japan look to you, a foreigner?'

Gaston only smiled his sad smile, his usual response to questions he did not understand.

'Even an old man like me, living in this hole in the wall, can tell you what is missing in Japan today . . . trust – trust in people. The politicians and intellectuals are more suspicious than foxes and badgers. The politicians have a distrust of all ideals, and the intellectuals, a distrust of man himself. This is a sad state of affairs.'

He poured himself a cup of the black medicine-like tea and continued talking with growing vehemence. 'The only ones who still trust each other are people like us. Those women who brought you over last night, for example . . . They may sell their bodies and steal whatever they can, but deep down they're good and trusting . . . even to a foolish degree. They have a warmth of feeling for others and are pure of heart. These are qualities you won't find in the politicians and men of education.'

Gaston sat with his hands on his knees, nodding his head, though he understood less than half of what the old man, his breath reeking of sardines, was saying so vehemently.

'Purity of heart . . . young Japanese have no use for it. They think it's something superfluous, of no use whatsoever in getting on in the world. That's the tragedy of a poor country. We're not poor in material things. It's in the spirit that Japan is poor.' As he said this, his withered body shook in patriotic indignation.

He apologized to Gaston for being carried away and asked, 'But, Mister Gas, what are your plans?'

Gaston smiled faintly and answered, 'I have no place to stay. I'll just keep on walking with my dog.'

'Is that so?' The old man folded his arms and stood for a moment in thought. 'If that's the case, how about staying here with me? I've taken a great liking to that long face of yours. It's the first time I've ever had a foreigner living with me, but this too is probably *karma* from my last existence.'

'I don't have any money. I'd like to work if I can find a job.'

'That should be no problem. Being a foreigner you can probably get a job as a sandwich man.'

'Sandwich man?'

'Yes. There are many restaurants here in Shibuya. You could walk around with placards advertising a restaurant on your shoulders. That's what we Japanese call a sandwich man. Or, you could become a diviner like me and tell people's fortunes. A Western fortune-teller! Now, that ought to go down well.'

'But I don't know anything about fortune-telling.'

'There's nothing to it. It might look odd if you were to use the divining rods as I do, but you could try cards.'

'But that would be deceiving people.'

'Not at all. You give courage and new strength to the troubled people who come to you. That's the purpose of my divining.' Then the old man, lowering his voice, proceeded to justify his occupation. 'To a certain extent, of course, it's necessary to tell lies, but it's to a good end. I'll start breaking you in tonight.'

The old man began then and there to teach Gaston certain basic principles essential to the art of divination.

The first step was to learn to read palms. That was how

the diviner got his client to trust him. From the very beginning it was important to have his confidence.

'You must speak to a woman in a different way from that in which you speak to a man. For example, in the case of a woman who seems to be a housewife, you look intently at her hand and with great solicitude say something like this : "You have had much bad luck. . . . The trouble is that you have too warm a heart. So you are always being taken advantage of.' If you tell her this, you may be sure that she will never disagree with you. Mister Gas, do you understand?'

When Gaston did not answer, the old man smiled proudly, showing his yellowed teeth.

'One of the conclusions of my study of people is that there's not a single Japanese woman who doesn't believe that she always gets the thin end of the wedge. They've all got that firmly planted in their heads.'

The old man went on to explain a number of other techniques of palm-reading. 'Now, if the client is a young girl, a different technique must be used. The easiest way to win her confidence is by saying, "Ho! This is really extraordinary! I've never seen a line like this before. You must be extremely sensitive. You are a very complex person!" You'll never make a mistake in taking this tack, since every young city girl is convinced that she has greater sensitivity than the average person and a very complex personality. You can carry that line one step further and tell her, "Your great sensitivity has often been the source of great suffering." Japanese girls have a predilection for the word "suffer". They like to think of themselves as tragic figures. Eight out of ten will nod their heads in agreement when you tell them this.

'Occasionally a student who has been drinking, or a woman from one of the bars will be perverse enough to deny that she is a tragic figure and will say that life for her is a comedy. But even then, you can get them where you want them by saying, "Your face may smile, but in your heart you weep. You can't fool me. I can see what a truly sensitive and complicated person you are." At any rate, if you can win their confidence in this way by reading their palms, they will listen with attention to anything you tell them after that.'

In this way the old man emphasized to Gaston that divining was basically the art of winning the client's heart. 'You, too, when you were young . . . no, excuse me, you're still young . . . have had the experience of trying to win over a girl. Palm-reading is much the same art.'

Gaston blinked his eyes. He could just about understand what the old man in his unfamiliar Japanese was saying, but all his life girls had shown nothing but contempt for him because of his long horseface; never once had he ever been loved. Moreover, coward that he was, he couldn't conceive of taking the offensive and working to win a woman's love.

But what troubled him more than this was how to go about refusing the old man's proposal, made with such good will. In the first place, with his poor Japanese how could he ever achieve such a degree of eloquence?

It was evening. The shadows of night gradually crept into their second-storey room.

'Shall we be off? Now I'll show you the real Japan!'

The old man took off his old red sweater and trousers and dressed himself in the *hakama* and *haori** he wore to ply his trade. When they left the house, the bars along the street were already lit. The waitresses standing at their doors greeted the old man and then, catching sight of Gaston, manifested surprise. Napoleon appeared from nowhere and fell in behind them with his usual unsteady gait.

'He's staying with me. . . . Don't be a fool. He's not an American. He's a Frenchman . . . a Frenchman,' the old man explained to them proudly.

---

* *hakama*: a divided skirt for men's formal wear. *haori*: a coat worn with the *hakama*.

But when they got on to the main street he looked some-what sadly at Gaston and explained to him the not so pleasant side of his work. 'Tokyo's divided into zones – all of Japan is – and each zone is in the grip of a racketeer who sells us protection. You're a foreigner, but if you're going to help me, I suppose we ought to pass by and introduce you.'

Gaston was finding it hard to follow what the old man said. Japanese itself was difficult enough, and the old man used many words Gaston had never even heard before. At first, not wishing to hurt the old fellow's feelings, soft-hearted Gaston kept nodding his head as if he understood, but he finally gave this up. The old man did not notice the look of incomprehension on Gaston's face and went on talking.

'And above the small racketeer, there are the big boys. A year ago the Hoshino gang had a tight hold on every-thing. But there was a big incident last year and the Hoshinos have had to lie low ever since. As long as they were in charge, it was one thing after another. They didn't hesitate even to kill. . . .'

'Kill?' Gaston seized upon the one word he understood and repeated it.

'Yes, kill. They had a specialist in killing by the name of Endo. I ought to know. I was his teacher.' The diviner, who had once been a school principal, stopped and looked sadly at Gaston. Excited by the recollection, he began to speak all the faster.

'Many years ago when I was teaching at an elementary school in Chiba, a boy transferred to our school from Tokyo. All our boys had shaved heads, which was usual for elementary school boys at that time. But this one had long hair. He had a fine character and was good in his studies. He even won a place at university. I lost touch with him for about twenty years but then quite accident-ally I ran into him again. I had become a diviner and he . . . he had become a gangster. The war may have been

D

responsible, but he'd lost all faith in men, all faith in the world . . . he'd become a complete nihilist. Since he was a college graduate and had distinguished himself in the army as a sharp-shooter, it didn't take him long to work his way up in the Hoshino gang.'

The old man continued to talk in a low voice, but Gaston was no longer listening He was completely taken up with the sights around him – the colourfully lit shops on both sides of the street, the glaring neon façades of the cinemas, the beautiful wares on display in the shop windows, and the mob of people milling around him. From the mouth of Shibuya station issued a massive wave of people, returning home after the day's work. They were sucked into the flowing stream on the street, to be succeeded by yet another wave. In Paris, in Singapore, in Hong-Kong, as here in Tokyo, there lived an uncountable number of people . . . living with no other purpose but to hang on to life as long as possible.

Near the station other fortune tellers, young and old, and dressed like Chotei, were waiting patiently for customers in the feeble circle of light cast by the candle in each stall.

If Gaston had reached the station some ten minutes earlier, he might have caught sight of Takamori in one of the waves of people. But Chotei's chatter had prevented their reunion. On his way home from the bank, Takamori had stopped off with his friend, Iijima, at a small eating place called Otafuku, where at this very moment he was drinking beer and stuffing peanuts into his mouth.

'Takamori *san*, you've run up quite a bill. I wish you would pay it today.' But the waitress's harsh words did not bother him, accustomed as he was to Tomoe's grumbling.

Trains zoomed by above Gaston's head, making a terrible noise. Each time one passed, a few drops of some kind of black liquid dripped down to the pavement. Napoleon was sniffing and scratching away at a rubbish container.

In the shadows, which were but faintly dispersed by the candle, the old man had his face drawn up to that of a hunchbacked middle-aged woman, very poorly dressed, and he was whispering to her in a low voice. The woman would now and then look down at her palms and nod her head slightly in agreement. Undoubtedly the old man was putting into practice the advice he had given Gaston on winning the confidence of his client.

'You haven't had an easy life. Because you are willing to put yourself out for others, your good nature is always being imposed upon.'

In two hours there had been only two customers. The first had been a couple that looked as if they might be engaged, and now this woman. After each guest departed, Chotei dropped his hundred-yen fee into a huge alligator-skin purse.

'Mr Gas. Can you eat *shina-soba*?'

'*Shina-soba*?'

'Yes. That's noodles served Chinese style. It's very good, believe me.'

About half past nine the old man stopped a passing *soba* cart and treated Gaston to his evening meal. Tonight's *shina-soba*, just as last night's *o-den*, seemed very exotic Eastern food to Gaston, and with his voracious appetite it could not but taste delicious. He ate half of it and gave the other half to Napoleon, not without regret.

Between nine-thirty and ten-thirty there was not a single customer. Gaston sat ten metres away in the shadow of the railway underpass. Occasionally the old man called to him, 'It's all right to just sit there and wait, but wouldn't you like to try your hand at a little fortune telling with cards?'

Gaston felt a deep sympathy for this old man and for the hunch-backed woman who had held out her palm for him to read. She had a very sad face. Did she perhaps have a sick child on her hands? Had she reached a dead end in her life and didn't know which way to turn? Beyond the underpass he could see a million stars twinkling in the sky just as the night before.

There are as many people on earth as there are stars in the sky! Gaston, having travelled so far to Japan, was keenly aware of this. He understood too that there were as many misfortunes and hardships and causes for grief scattered about the earth as there were stars in the sky. To all these unfortunate people Gaston wished to be of help. Dull-witted and clumsy as he was, he wanted to do something for them. But he was only a foreigner and could do nothing but walk these streets with Napoleon in tow.

Eleven-thirty. The crowds on the streets had thinned out considerably. Another train passed overhead, causing the understructure to shake. Another few drops of black liquid fell to the pavement below.

'I wonder why business is so dead tonight? It's really glum.' The old man asked Gaston to take over while he went to relieve himself. He had no sooner left the stall than there stepped out from the shadows of the railway underpass a tall man with the collar of his raincoat turned up. He seemed to be ill, since he had his hand to his mouth and was coughing.

He stopped suddenly as his eye was drawn to the candle and to Gaston standing beside it. He had a dark, sinister face. His expression was more than sinister; there was the shadow of black misfortune discernible in it. His cheeks were sagging and he seemed to have a fever. His eyes had a fierce gleam.

He planted himself in front of Gaston and asked in a hoarse voice, 'Who the hell are you?' When Gaston did not answer, he asked again, 'Where did you come from?'

Under the man's piercing stare, Gaston shrank back against the wall behind the stall. He was overcome by the same fear as when he had been attacked by the thugs in Shinjuku.

'I . . . I'm a foreigner,' he stammered.

The man looked Gaston up and down, but did not take his hands out of his raincoat pockets. Then all at once his body bent in two under the fury of a violent coughing spell. Gaston stood there staring at him.

'What happened to *sensei*?' the man asked, when he had stopped coughing.

'He went for *shobin*.'

'*Shobin*?'

'No. *Shoben*,' Gaston answered in a tremulous voice. He was so frightened that the Japanese words would not come out right. The man pulled a white handkerchief out of his pocket and slowly spat into it and wiped his mouth. From somewhere Gaston heard chimes announce the hour: eleven forty-five. The echo of the chimes went out in waves across the black roofs of the buildings and the sky full of twinkling stars.

'What are you doing here in his stall?'

'I have nowhere to stay . . . *sensei* kind . . . I slept in *sensei*'s house.'

'A tramp! How long've you been staying with him?'

Gaston answered that he had been with him only the one night. As he spoke, he prayed that the old man would quickly appear. But he heard no footsteps from the direction of the underpass, which was as dark as a cave. All that was to be heard was the grating sound of another train passing overhead.

'Then you met *sensei* last night for the first time?' Over the man's face, lit only by the feeble light of the candle, came a faint smile. 'Give me a hand, foreigner.'

When Gaston did not answer, he continued, 'I need your help. I have a puncture and have to change the tyre.'

Gaston's Japanese was not good enough for him to realize that the man's form of address had suddenly become very polite.

'Help me. I'll pay you for it.'

Gaston's timid heart was instinctively on its guard against the man. If he went with him, anything might happen. It was this knowledge that made him shrink back. But then the man had another violent coughing attack.

That man is ill, thought Gaston. You're still suspicious of people, he told himself, as he looked at the man, who seemed to be in much pain. Why did I come all the way to Japan? Is it still impossible for me to trust people?

'I'll go with you.' And Gaston walked off behind him.

They went through the underpass and turned left into a dark alley. On the left of the alley a grey cement wall, the colour of an animal's belly, stretched ahead for a long distance. Parked beside the wall was a black car, which could barely be made out in the dark.

'The front tyre,' the man told Gaston in a hoarse voice. 'Foreigner, take the tools out of the car.'

Gaston, doing as he was told, pushed his long body through the half-open door into the dark car. There was the smell of perfume inside.

'In the back, under the back seat. There's a black bag, isn't there?' the man asked, standing outside without taking his hands out of his pockets.

Gaston felt around and found something wrapped in a black cloth between the back seat and the back window. 'Is this it?' he asked.

'Yes, that's it. Don't break it.' The man slid himself into the car. 'Easy does it. Hand it to me.'

The man had implied that it was something breakable, but the object wrapped in the black cloth felt heavy in Gaston's hand. It seemed to be made of brass or iron.

'Sit down!' said a voice directly over his head. Only then did he notice that there was another man stretched out on the front seat.

'Endo, you've really picked up an odd one.' The man in the front seat spoke in a low voice to the man in the rain-coat.

'What happened to the old diviner?'

'I'll explain later. Start the car.'

The man in the front seat closed the car door and

without asking Gaston's leave started the engine. The car
began to throb dully and then to move.

'I don't . . .'

'I don't . . .' The man called Endo imitated Gaston.
'We're taking you along with us.'

'Dog *san*!'

'What?'

'Napoleon *san* . . .' Gaston looked back and in the weak
light cast by a street lamp he saw that the emaciated mutt
was running as fast as it could after the car. Gaston pressed
his face to the window. 'Aaaa, Napoleon *san*. . . .'

But Napoleon was too old and sick. He could not see
where he was going and ran into the lamp-posts. Finally
he had to give up the chase, and just stood there. As Gaston
watched, he became a speck in the dark and then
vanished.

For the first time in his life Gaston felt anger rise from
the pit of his stomach like a black clot of blood. The dog
had been the first to be helped by him after his arrival in
Japan. More than just a dog, he had been his companion
for these two days, sharing his life. In that ugly dog's eyes
he had seen reflected the very sadness that he himself felt.
Without him how could the dog keep on living?

'I'm getting out!' Gaston pressed down on the shoulder
of Endo, who was sitting beside him. His weight was so
heavy that Endo's face winced in pain. The black bundle
fell to the floor and an object tumbled out of it. It was
a Colt pistol.

6 Night in Sanya

The man in the raincoat did not try to stop Gaston or to recover the pistol. Before he could shake off Gaston's heavy hand, bearing down full-strength on his shoulder, he was overcome by another fit of coughing. He put his fist to his mouth and coughed violently.

Had Gaston taken advantage of this opportunity, he could have retrieved the pistol lying at their feet. But when he saw Endo's body shaking in great pain and the sad gleam – as of an animal that has been brought to bay – that flashed momentarily into his eyes, soft-hearted Gaston was foolish enough to withdraw his hand.

Endo wiped his mouth with a white handkerchief, then unfolded the handkerchief and examined it in the light of his cigarette lighter. Red blood like skeins of silk was mixed in with the spittle. Endo stared down at the blood.

This man is sick, thought Gaston. He turned his back to the side window and remembered with compassion Endo's sadly contorted body of a moment before and the strange light he had seen flit in and out of his dark eyes. His anger had left him entirely. When Endo leisurely stooped down and recovered the pistol, Gaston was unable to stop him.

Meanwhile the driver had been throwing sharp glances at the back seat as he drove. If Gaston had tried to pin Endo down, he would have stopped the car immediately.

'Are you all right, Endo?'

'Yeah.'

'Don't you have any more medicine? It's because you didn't take your medicine that you get like that. . . .'

They've got good medicine even for TB now. You don't seem to want to get well.'

'What difference does it make if I get well or not?' Endo answered in a hoarse voice. 'A killer like me won't get much of a crack at a long life anyway.'

Then he turned toward Gaston and, half smiling, raised the hand that held the pistol. He kept it pointed at Gaston for a time, taking pleasure in watching the long horseface of the foreigner contract in fear. He put his finger on the trigger and slowly pulled.

Nothing happened. There was only a click, no discharge.

'Don't try to get away, foreigner. . . . There'll be bullets in it next time. *You speak English*?' Endo asked in English. When Gaston did not answer, he repeated his question. '*I say, you speak English*?' Gaston shook his head weakly.

'I . . . I . . . Frenchman.'

'*Tiens!*' Strange to say, the man in the raincoat expressed his astonishment in French. '*Tu es Français? Mon Dieu!*' He had a slight accent, but his French was understandable.

'Endo, you speak French?' asked the driver in a low voice, as he drove the car around a curve. They were on the broad avenue going from Komaba to Meguro.

'I studied it a long time ago.'

'What do you intend to do with this French bastard?'

'We can use him in the place of the old man. In fact, being a foreigner, he'll be especially useful in the get-away,' Endo answered as he pushed bullets into the chamber of the pistol in the palm of his hand. The shops along the street, seen from the car window, were just a blur of lights. No one walking on the pavements could have guessed that Gaston was in the car trembling with fright.

He had only intended to have one drink and then head for home, but as usual he was unable to break away. So he made the rounds with his colleague, Iijima, to Otafuku, Hiroshichan's, Hotta, and other bars. Before he knew it, the chimes of the Tokyū Department Store in Shibuya were announcing midnight. To his mind's eye came the image of the disapproving face of his sister.

Until a short time ago, whenever he was late in getting home he had been able to sneak into the house through the kitchen door, which Matchan, out of consideration for him, had been kind enough to leave unlatched. But two months earlier a thief had broken into the house of the Iwamis nearby, and since then Tomoe herself had made certain that every door in the house, including the kitchen door and even the front gate, was safely secured by ten o'clock. The fence was low enough to climb over, but the only way of getting into the house now was by ringing the doorbell. And of course it was always Tomoe who came to open up for him.

'You're lucky to be living in a flat,' he said to Iijima.

'Don't be ridiculous. I don't have a wife to take care of me when I get back.'

'At least you don't have a shrew of a sister picking on you.'

After he had broken away from Iijima, Takamori walked slowly in the direction of the station to board his bus for home, thinking all the time what excuse he would make tonight. There was a company party and I had to stick around to take care of the bigwigs . . . I ran into an old friend from university days. . . . He could think of many more. The trouble was that he had already used them all. She would not be deceived.

Then there was the gift strategy. He could buy a hundred yen's worth of bananas and thrust them at her as soon as she opened the door. He would bounce into the house announcing, 'Plenty of Vitamin C . . . full of nourishment . . . a little token of brotherly affection.' This occasionally worked, but tonight he had drunk so much that he did not even have a hundred yen in his pockets. He had only his bus pass and an empty wallet.

Suddenly he saw something that brought him to a quick

stop – an old emaciated, limping dog that he recognized at once, a mangy cur whose bony rump stuck out like a shingle. 'That's the dog Gaston befriended!'

Takamori had just been telling Iijima about Gaston as they drank together. He had only been with them a week, but they had come to feel as if he had tumbled down on them from some far-off blue sky. With a heart such as one seldom encounters in this egotistical world. Of sterling character and unfailing amiability.

'Only to know that there are still men like that in the world has been enough to give me a new view of life,' Takamori had just been explaining to Iijima.

The stray dog that Gaston had cared for limped past him and disappeared around a corner of the dark street.

'Then Gaston must have been in Shibuya!' Takamori forgot all about the excuse for Tomoe and began running after the dog. At the corner where the dog had disappeared, he saw an old diviner getting ready to close up shop for the night.

Slender threads of rain began to hit the car windows at an angle, and, trickling down, made them look as if they were cracked.

'Endo, it's started to rain.'

Endo remained with his face pressed to the window and did not answer.

'Shall we go on to Sanya?'

'What's that?'

'Shall we go on to Sanya . . . or shall we drop in at Michiko's?' Endo did not answer, and he continued, 'Michiko's is probably being watched. I know you want to see her, but it's pretty dangerous.'

'Yeah.'

'I think it's safer to lose ourselves in Sanya for the night.'

'You're probably right. I leave it to you.'

Endo stuck the pistol in his pocket and put a cigarette

in his mouth. Turning to Gaston, he asked, 'Do you smoke, foreigner?'

Gaston shook his head despondently. In the red flame of Endo's lighter was revealed for a brief moment the huge body of Gaston huddled in the corner like a bear and the profile of his face half-buried in his arms. Dull witted as he was, Gaston seemed to have realized the position he was in.

Gaston closed his eyes and behind his eyelids marched a procession of images. The women who had given him something to eat. The old diviner with a body like a dried tree. The black liquid that trickled down every time a train passed. And then the pitiful image of Napoleon, with his strange gait, running after the car.

The night streets, wet with the rain, were a shining black. Several cars passed them. Gaston stole a glance at the dashboard. The needle of the phosphorescent speedometer was pointing to forty kilometres.

'We're in for it, Endo!' cried out the driver suddenly. 'The police are making a road check.'

Up ahead on the road, which looked like a black river, could be seen four or five men with lanterns.

'Police?'

'Looks like it.'

'Don't move,' said Endo in a low but sharp voice to Gaston, who had begun to change his position. He put his hand in his raincoat pocket. Gaston felt a hard object pressed against his ribs. '*Ne bouge pas* . . . I won't hesitate to shoot. I mean it.'

Supporting his head with his huge hands, Gaston looked up at Endo in a silent appeal for mercy.

'I . . . I want to go back.'

'Now, foreigner, laugh and pretend to be talking to me . . . especially when they look into the car. Do you understand? Laugh!'

'I want to go back!'

'All right. But laugh! *Parle n'importe quoi.*' Endo had

a faint smile on his lips, but he kept the hand that held the pistol pressed close against Gaston's ribs.

A young policeman carrying a lantern in his right hand approached. The driver obediently put his foot on the brake and brought the car to a stop.

'*Sacre flic . . . va au diable, n'est-ce pas, monsieur?*' With laughing face Endo made the pretence of conversing with Gaston. Spouting out a string of incoherent French words, he tried to give the impression of a pleasant conversation.

If he were to escape, now was the time. Gaston stared intensely at the policeman, who had a rather boyish face under his policeman's cap. Since the pistol was still shoved into his ribs, he could not say anything, but he tried to communicate his desperation with his eyes. Unfortunately, the more serious he became, the more comic was the expression on his long horseface.

'*Fils de putain de crapaud.*'

'Excuse me.' The policeman tapped on the window of the car with his fingertips. 'We're making a spot check of all vehicles.'

'*Quel pet rance.*' Endo kept up the pretence, not forgetting to smile. When Gaston opened the window, the Colt went still deeper into his side. '*Caca merde pipi.*'

'Oh, a foreigner,' said the policeman, his manner immediately becoming reserved.

'Here!' Gaston desperately thrust a white cloth into the policeman's hands. The stunned policeman unfolded it and two long strings fell down dangling. It was the loincloth that had earlier landed Gaston in trouble.

Endo, smiling wryly, apologized to the policeman. 'This foreigner has had a little too much to drink. He's a real comedian. . . . All right if we go, officer?'

'Fine. Go ahead,' signalled the young policeman, still dumbfounded. The car began to move again through the drizzle. The yellow lanterns were soon far behind them.

'Did you ever see anything like it!' exclaimed the

driver, turning round. 'This fellow's not quite all there, is he?'

'Perhaps not, but it's because of him that we got through. Foreigner, do you always do crazy things like that?'

At that very moment Takamori was getting a report of Gaston's activities from Chotei, the diviner.

'He disappeared while I was having a pee. All his stuff's here still.'

Sure enough, Gaston's only possession, the old duffel bag, was lying there on the floor.

'I waited an hour for him, but he never came back.'

'Where do you suppose he's disappeared to?'

'That's what I don't know.'

'Can't you find him with your divining rods? Won't they tell you where he is?'

'No, I'm afraid not,' answered the old man sheepishly, in a low voice.

The rain grew heavier and heavier. They drove on for another hour. To Gaston, arms still wound about his drooping head, the rhythmic vibration of the car sounded like human speech. Sometimes it was the voice of Tomoe, sometimes of Takamori. You've got to get away, Gas. You've got to get away. Then suddenly it became the old diviner's sharp voice of appeal. No, it wasn't Chotei's voice, but the voice of another, the whispering of another person whose face he could not make out. You still have no trust? . . . Weren't you the one who was going to trust everybody? Behind his closed eyelids rose again the image of the stars twinkling in the night sky, and then of Napoleon staggering after him until he could go no further.'

'We're here, Endo.'

Endo put up the collar of his raincoat and opened the car door.

'Get out, foreigner.'

The rain fell on Gaston's face and neck. He resigned himself to his fate as he exposed his elephant-like body to the black rain of this unfamiliar country. The driver turned on the car radio. A singer was crooning a sentimental ballad.

> Gentle one, don't be cruel
> Lover, don't be heartless

'Then I'll be on my way.' The driver closed the door and waved his hand. Endo nodded in response, then moved close to Gaston and motioned for him to follow.

Through the rain came an almost animal smell. Before them was a long string of houses that looked like animal pens, and beside them, umbrellas over their heads, stood prostitutes waiting for customers.

'Where are we going? Here?' Gaston asked Endo in surprise.

'This is Sanya. Sanya. We're still in Tokyo, but the arm of the police doesn't reach this far,' Endo answered sullenly, putting his hands to his face to keep off the rain. 'So you'd better resign yourself. . . .'

Looking around him, Gaston saw that all the houses were really inns, but very different from those in Shibuya. They were all dirty and run-down and in the cracked window of each was a sign that read 'One night – 40 yen'. It was unbelievable that one could get a night's lodging so cheaply. Endo stepped into one of the houses.

'Do you have a private room – A room for two?'

'If you want covers, it'll cost you 300 yen.' The man answered from within so that they could not see his face.

'Fine.' Endo pushed three hundred-yen notes through an aperture in the door.

'Go up to the second floor. It's the second door to the right. Better take your shoes up with you or they'll be stolen.'

Gaston, preceded by Endo, walked up the narrow

staircase. The animal smell he had noticed before was everywhere, in the room they entered as well as in the corridor. Floor mats brown with age, walls on which previous occupants had scribbled, blankets piled up in a corner – there was nothing else in the tiny room. It looked to Gaston like a chamber of hell. True, Chotei's roost had been in greater disorder than this, but at least it had had the feeling of being lived in.

'Don't leave your shoes in the corridor,' warned Endo. 'And you'd better roll up your clothes and sleep with them under your head. Or else they'll be stolen from you in the night, foreigner.'

Endo leaned against the wall and, coughing hoarsely, began to polish his pistol with his handkerchief.

'Shall we go to bed?'

After they had fixed their beds on the mats, Endo took off his coat, shirt, and trousers, and did as he had instructed Gaston to do. He folded them and put them under his pillow. Then he lay down. Fully dressed, he had seemed to be a tall, thin man. Now in his undershirt he proved to be well-built. He did not have the kind of body one would expect of a man who coughed up blood. He put the Colt pistol at the exact centre of his bed, showing the customary caution of a man who lives by the gun. Should an enemy surprise him in his sleep, this was the best position for it. It could be got at most quickly.

'Foreigner, aren't you going to bed? It's two in the morning,' said Endo in a low voice. 'Let me warn you. I'm a light sleeper. I'll hear you if you try to leave the room.'

Gaston smiled sadly. He was still trembling from fear and anxiety, but something in him told him that he must stay here.

Switching off the 30-watt light, Gaston crawled into bed. His long legs stuck out considerably from the bed covers. Worse than that, the covers were permeated by a strange smell, not the smell of sweat or ordinary body odour. And not only the bed covers, but also the walls and the ceiling. All exuded this strange stench.

Gaston closed his eyes and listened to the rain beating upon the window panes. From somewhere he heard the shrill laughter of a woman, sad and strained. The rain became more insistent and sounded like snapping beans. Endo began to cough again, and this sound too had something sad in it.

'Sick?' Gaston asked in a low voice. When Endo did not answer, he asked again, 'Are you sick?'

'I've got TB. How do you say that in French? I've forgotten. It's been a long time since I studied French.'

'*Tuberculose.*'

'Is that it? *Tuberculose?* That's a terrible word.'

He turned around in bed and faced Gaston. 'You . . . Are you really a tramp? Why did you come to Japan?'

Gaston did not answer.

'You don't want to say? Then don't. It's no business of mine anyway.'

'Your work?'

'Work?' Endo laughed a low, hoarse laugh. 'I suppose you could call killing people for money my "work".'

'Killing people?'

Noticing the throb of fear in Gaston's voice, Endo lightly tapped the foreigner's bed covers with his fingers.

'You don't have to be afraid. If you don't try anything, I won't kill you. There's something I want you to help me with.'

'What's that?'

'I'm going to kill a man. It's not for money this time.' Endo said no more. He began to cough again. The sound of coughing blended with that of the rain and seemed to go on endlessly.

Gaston, of course, had no way of knowing it, but this Sanya had the reputation of being the black jungle – the Casbah – of Tokyo. Cheap wooden houses, euphemistically called 'inns', lined the streets. There were about one hundred and fifty of them.

As Gaston had learned with surprise, one could get a night's lodging here for as little as forty yen (dormitory style); and for the maximum of three hundred yen one could get a private room. In some of the inns, called one-hundred-yen-inns, it was possible to get a bunk for a hundred yen. The bunks were piled up in tiers like silk-worm trays. In the common dormitories were crowded a motley assortment of men, but the three-hundred-yen rooms were often occupied by families.

The families who lived here were for the most part those of working men who hired themselves out for the day, of vagrants, of pimps and of ex-convicts. One group of working men, though hired only for the day, went regularly to the same job; while another group waited on the street each morning for a truck to come round and carry them to wherever they were needed for that day. The pimps lived off the income of the women who worked for them. But most of the pimps of Sanya were of a different breed from those in other parts of Tokyo. There were in Sanya a number of families who had come to Tokyo from the country to make their fortunes and had fallen upon hard times. They rented one of the three-hundred-yen rooms and managed somehow to accommodate themselves to it. Three hundred yen a day amounted to nine thousand yen a month. It would seem that at that rate they could have found something better elsewhere. But since these people were paid for their work each day, they never had nine thousand yen in their hands at one time. There was no other way but to pay their three hundred yen a day and crowd together – wife, husband, and children – into the one bare room.

Now in some of these families the husband – with the consent of his wife, of course – played the pimp and had his wife stand out in the street to solicit customers and lead them to her room. In the meanwhile the poor husband

and children had to go outside and wait patiently for the business to end.

From about eight o'clock at night there were dozens of women standing in the dark alleys between the inns. Since the passing of the anti-prostitution law there is probably no other place in Tokyo where so many women can be seen lining the streets ready for business. In the old days, their clientele was almost exclusively composed of the day labourers who lived in the district, but of late, customers from other parts of town, deprived by the law of a convenient outlet for their lust, come crawling like ants to Sanya. By midnight the number of prostitutes in the alleys has increased greatly. Since the women in Sanya are not organized under a boss, anyone is able to 'work' here. There is a story of a woman who got into a fight with her husband and, leaving the house in a huff, went to see a movie in Asakusa. Then, having used up all her money, she found a customer there and returned home the following morning.

Even the police, except in the case of murder or other serious crime, close their eyes to this kind of prostitution, unless they happen to stumble on the scene. But prostitution is not all that goes on here. In these pen-like inns, extortion, theft, and other such crimes flourish unchecked.

On rainy days Sanya is especially dangerous. That is because on those days the workers living in the inns do not go out to work and are in a particularly vicious mood. The night Endo and Gaston stopped there was just such a danger-filled rainy night.

'Killing people.' Endo had off-handedly spoken these fearful words. Gaston could not get them out of his mind.

He closed his eyes and tried to sleep, but sleep would not visit him. The sound of the black rain beating down on the roof remained in his ears. Something was crawling up his legs . . . a flea? a louse? I must be dreaming, I must be having a terrible nightmare, he told himself. He was still living in Tomoe's house. It was because of the heavy weight of the Japanese quilt on his chest that he was having this frightening dream. No, he was really in Chotei's tiny room. See, the man breathing heavily next to him was the hermit of the East, that emaciated, withered stick of a man.

But the man breathing next to him was neither Chotei nor Takamori. He was a killer who lay with a Colt pistol within easy reach. Gaston would doze off for a time and then open his eyes again and steal a glance at the figure beside him.

The light of morning began to dawn on Sanya.

'Where are you going?'

Though Gaston had made only a slight rustle in getting out of bed, Endo jumped up and shouted at him. Then, understanding, he nodded. 'Oh, to the toilet. You'd better not try any funny business.'

'*Non. Non.* I . . .'

'No use trying to escape. There's only one way out of this building. I can hear your footsteps from here. Just try it and see what happens. I'll know immediately if you head towards the door.'

Gaston nodded and stepped quietly into the corridor. Endo had not lied. There was only one staircase to the first floor. Moreover, the toilet, judging from the smell, was at the end of the corridor opposite it.

Gaston blinked his eyes as he walked. He rubbed his horseface with his huge hands and wiped away the tears.

On both sides of the corridor were a number of sliding panels whose paper had been torn. From the rents in the panels of one room could be heard a man's heavy snoring. That same animal smell was everywhere here too. Then suddenly Gaston heard a low voice call out to him.

'Hey! Hey!'

Gaston stopped and looked behind him, but he saw no one.

'Hey! Hey!'

This time he realized that the voice was coming from the tear of a panel directly in front of him.

'Who?'

'It's me. Remember? Shibuya?'

Then he recognized the voice. It was the woman who had made *shoben*. It was the voice of the woman who had given him *o-den* to eat.

'Oh, you!'

'Not so loud.'

'Are you making *shoben* here too?'

'Lower your voice. . . . Why did you leave the *sensei*'s place? I caught a glance of you last night and got quite a shock.'

Gaston was silent.

'Do you know who that man is you're with? That's Endo of the Hoshino gang. He's got TB. He's a man without blood or tears. He kills men, and he's bound to get his too one of these days. You'd better get out of here fast.'

Gaston still did not speak.

'Beat it! Scram! You mustn't waste a minute. Escape any way you can. Leave the house and run out to the main street where you can flag a taxi. You still have the three thousand yen, haven't you?'

The woman remembered Gaston's wallet.

'Get in the taxi and tell the driver "Shibuya". When you get there go to the *sensei*'s place at once and tell him you were caught by Endo.'

'Yes.'

Gaston nodded. Just then the woman must have had a premonition because she stopped talking abruptly. Gaston heard someone clear his throat behind him. Turning around, he saw Endo standing there, dressed in trousers and white shirt.

'Foreigner. . . .'

'Yes.' Startled, Gaston, who had been stooping down to catch the woman's words, straightened up in consternation.

'What's the matter?' asked Endo, in a gentle voice as he yawned sleepily. 'Weren't you on your way to the toilet?'

'Yes . . . toilet. . . .'

'Then go along. *Va au shotte.*'

Behind the panel the woman could be heard moving. It was the sound of a frightened human being looking for a way of escape.

'Go along,' Endo repeated.

Gaston had no choice but to do as he was told. The ceiling of the toilet was low, the urinals were cracked and stained a dark brown. The door, which was half off its hinges, would not close.

Just as he was trying to get the door to close, Gaston heard the sound of someone being slapped, followed by a woman's scream. It came from the room of the woman who had called out to him.

'I . . . didn't do anything.'

Then the woman's scream turned into a pain-filled moan. In Sanya such scenes are common. The other rooms on the floor remained still. Gaston dashed out of the toilet and in two or three bounds reached the panel from which the voice had come. Once more he heard the sound of someone being slapped.

What met Gaston's eyes when he opened the panels to the room was Endo standing with his belt in his hand and, sprawled on the floor in front of him, a woman covering her face with one arm. When she removed the arm and raised her head, Gaston saw that red blood was trickling down from her mouth to her chin.

Seeing Gaston, Endo smiled wryly. 'Have you finished your business?' he asked softly.

'You . . .' Gaston shouted. 'That woman is very kind. Why do you hit her? . . . You're bad! Very bad!'

'Bad, eh? Perhaps,' answered Endo in a low voice, putting on his belt.

'Bad. You're bad. . . . This poor woman . . . Pitiful.'

'Foreigner, I'm a man who does as he likes. I have no pity for anyone.'

'Why not?'

'Because I don't consider any man worth pity any longer.

I've rid myself of that sentimental rubbish. That's why I'm in the killing business.'

'Why don't you trust people?'

' I don't trust them because I've been made not to trust them.'

7 The Trap

The day was a national holiday. Even when told that it was ten o'clock, Takamori remained curled up in bed in his usual turtle style with the quilt drawn over his head. As he lay there, half asleep half-awake, in an indescribably euphoric state, he heard the stairs creak ever so slightly, and reached out automatically for his underwear at the side of the bed.

Throwing off one corner of the quilt, he listened for further indication of his sister's approach, ready to go into action when necessary.

'Takamori.' Tomoe's voice on the staircase was unusually soft this morning. 'Takamori,' she called again.

'I'm up. But I'm enjoying a quiet morning meditation. I don't want to break the spell.'

'Come down. I want you to take a look at the morning paper.'

He heard her come up the stairs. In a moment she was in the room. She had the newspaper in her hands.

'What do you want? I've been meditating on the meaning of life and death. I don't want you and the world breaking in on my meditation.' He spoke from under the covers, so that he sounded as if he had cotton wool in his mouth.

'Stop that nonsense.'

'As Goethe says . . .'

'There's something in this morning's paper about a man that might be Gaston.'

'What's that?'

Takamori had been led by Gaston's dog to the diviner who had given Gaston food and a night's lodging, and he had arranged with the old man to get in touch with him when Gaston turned up again.

'Where?' he asked, as he took the newspaper from her hands.

'Here.' Tomoe pointed to an article right at the foot of an inside page. It was a daily column reporting unusual happenings about the city.

'On Monday night a foreigner in a car that was stopped by the Meguro police in a routine road check handed the policeman a man's loincloth.' This first sentence of the article caught Takamori's eye immediately.

Tomoe looked at her brother as he lay on his stomach scanning the article. 'Couldn't that be Gaston?'

'Monday night, eh?'

'The day before yesterday.'

The article stated that the foreigner was riding in a Ford with two Japanese men.

'Loincloth, it says. Remember how he embarrassed us at the *sushi* place in Yokohama? It must be Gaston.'

'I wonder if he's in danger? He may have wanted to get a message to us through that loincloth.'

Takamori jumped out of bed. 'I'll leave at once.'

'Where are you going?'

'I'll go and see the old diviner. Remember, I told you about him the day before yesterday. Come along, if you like.'

Takamori, who was usually so unexcitable, was suddenly full of energy at the thought of Gaston. Tomoe looked at her brother as if she were seeing him for the first time.

Takamori usually passed the time on the bus ogling the young girls about him, but today in the bus for Shibuya his eyebrows were knit in thought and his knees moved back and forth nervously.

'Takamori, you've really grown to like him, haven't you?'

Takamori nodded. 'What about you? Don't you like him too?'

'I . . .' She raised her eyebrows and smiled scornfully. 'Don't be ridiculous. That foreigner's a fool, a complete idiot. I hate him.'

'A fool, eh? You still don't have the sense to recognize a real man when you see one,' answered Takamori in a low voice, obviously disappointed in his sister's attitude. He looked out the window and saw that summer was very near.

In Shibuya the sun was shining brightly. The streets around Shibuya station were thronged with people, as if for a festival. Among them were family groups on a Sunday shopping expedition to the department stores, and young men and women meeting in front of the station.

'Where is it? . . . that diviner's place?'

'Wait a second. I'll have to look at the map he drew me.'

They began to walk, according to the directions of the map. The street was lined with bars, and at each bar women were performing their morning tasks – sweeping the street in front with brooms that had been worn to a stump, emptying waste food into garbage pails, and so on.

'If you're looking for the *sensei*, you'll find him still asleep on the second floor of that building over there,' answered the woman of whom they had made inquiry, without taking her toothbrush out of her mouth. She pointed to a bar five or six buildings down.

But when they reached the place that had been pointed out to them, they ran into the old man himself. He was returning from the communal toilet, still buttoning up his trousers.

'Oh, it's you.' Chotei blinked his eyes and looked at Takamori and Tomoe. The morning sun was too strong for his eyes.

'This is my sister,' said Takamori, introducing Tomoe. 'We've come to see about Gaston.'

'In fact, I was just going to phone you.' He began to

tell them what he had learned. A woman he knew in Shibuya had brought unexpected news. She had seen Gaston brought to an inn in Sanya, an unsavoury section of Tokyo bordering on Asakusa. She had herself spent the night at the same Iwate Inn.

'The man who was with Gaston was Endo, a member of the Hoshino gang. He's a well-known killer. Quite by chance, he happens to be a former student of mine. The woman who gave me this information was pretty roughly treated by him.'

'A killer? . . . Endo?' Takamori was taken aback. He had heard the name of Endo before. Two months earlier when the Hoshino gang had intimidated a certain business man and then actually roughed him up, Endo's picture had appeared in the newspapers and weekly magazines. His face had a dark look of despair that had fixed itself in Takamori's memory.

One hour later Takamori, in the company of a Sanya policeman, was inquiring about Gaston at the Iwate Inn.

'We get all kinds of guests here,' the proprietor answered with a Kansai accent from behind the sliding panels of his room. He sounded annoyed.

'Foreigner? There was a very tall foreigner who left this morning with another man. I don't know where they were headed for.'

He seemed to be telling the truth. Takamori stood alone on the narrow street of Sanya and looked about him. A black cat crossed the street, which was struck by the hot sun. Where could the man have taken Gaston? The neighbourhood was wrapped in an eerie silence.

Just a few hours before Takamori arrived at the Sanya inn, Gaston had taken his departure with Endo. The rain, which had continued steadily for two days, had finally stopped. The sky was still clouded and the ground was black and muddy. A milk-coloured mist curled around the low roofs of the inns. Elsewhere in the city the houses still wore the silence of night, even though the milkman on his bicycle was already announcing the beginning of a new day.

'Morning comes early here in Sanya,' explained Endo. Gaston could see this for himself. For some time he had been marvelling at the unusual early morning activity of the place. From the inns on the right and left men dressed in working clothes with towels wound around their necks came out and walked off in twos and threes.

'What are those people doing?'

'They're going off to get work for the day. At Namida Bridge near here there's an employment office that assigns jobs for the day,' Endo explained, between coughs. Namida Bridge – literally, 'Bridge of Tears' – was so named because in olden days criminals condemned to death would walk as far as the bridge accompanied by their families, then go on from there alone to their execution. It is a place with a sad history.

'If I had lived at that time, sooner or later I would also have had to say my goodbyes at that bridge,' said Endo, smiling. 'I wish all the "respectable" people in Tokyo could see what goes on there in early morning. The workmen come together like ants and wait in front of the office. Pedlars circulate among them selling rice patties for twenty yen. Even at that price, there are some who cannot afford to eat breakfast. But at least they're still alive.'

In the alley between two inns a man dressed in an undershirt and covered with dirt lay as if dead.

'Is he ill?' asked Gaston.

'No. He probably couldn't get work because of the rain and, not having the forty yen for a bed in an inn, settled for a shot of dope.' Endo cleared his throat and spat in the road. In the viscuous yellow liquid were threads of red blood.

'Why don't you go to a doctor?'

'Doctor?' Endo smiled sarcastically. 'I'll take care of myself. Foreigner, you'd better worry about your own problems. But you're a strange one, aren't you? Yesterday all day you had plenty of chance to get away from me if you had wanted to. Why didn't you?'

Gaston shrugged his shoulders. His mouth opened wide in a good-natured smile.

'But don't get me wrong. I'm going to keep my eye on you all the same. I hate sentimentality. I think you can imagine what I want you for. What's your name?'

'Gas.'

'Gas?' Then Endo's voice became hard and cold again. 'The fact is, Gas, I'm going to bump off a man. That man . . .' Endo's eyes suddenly filled with hatred. They glared long at Gaston, almost as if Gaston himself were the object of his hate.

'Have you ever been to war?'

Gaston shook his head.

'Well, I have! My brother was killed in the war.'

Endo kept on talking, closing his eyes every so often, as if the memory were too painful to bear. It began to drizzle again, but he did not even bother to put up the collar of his raincoat. Workers on their way to find work for the day passed them one after the other. They did not seem particularly surprised at the sight of Gaston. They were too concerned about their prospects for that day's employment to be curious about how a foreigner had found his way to Sanya.

'My brother . . . was executed for war crimes.'

'War crimes?'

'How do you say it in your language? *Guerre criminel?*'

'Yes. Yes.'

As Endo continued his explanation, mixing in an occasional French expression, Gaston listened with eyes turned down. Once in a while he stole a glance at his companion and wondered: Why did a man who has even studied a foreign language ever fall into such a miserable profession? He could not understand.

'It happened twelve years ago, at the end of the war.'

Endo, having finished middle school, had become a trainee at Kasumi-ga-ura. When he returned to Tokyo, he found that his home in Aoyama had been burnt down in an air raid at the beginning of May. His parents and younger sister had tried to escape to Jingu Park, but they had never been seen again. Their bodies were never recovered.

The only living member of his immediate family was his elder brother, who had been conscripted into service and sent with other students to a tiny island in the South Seas. Fortunately, young Endo was taken in by relatives and lived with them while he attended high school. He planned to work on the side and go on to a university.

After the war had ended, ships loaded with soldiers returning from China and the South Sea islands came into port one after the other. But Endo was unable to get any word of his brother. Busy as he was with his exhausting job and beset by loneliness in the absence of any near relative, he pinned all his hopes on the return of his brother. But search as he would, he never managed to spot the face of his brother among the soldiers on the returning ships.

'Two years later when I entered the university I finally learned what had happened to him.'

Endo spat again, then wiped his mouth slowly with his white handkerchief.

'On the charge of having committed a war crime, he was taken into custody and sent to prison. He was said to have killed some of the natives of the island.'

'Did he kill them?'

'No.' For the first time since their meeting, Endo's voice had a tearful tone. 'No. It was a false charge. He kept protesting his innocence in his letters to me. He kept asking that I at least believe in his innocence.'

Endo, who was still only a student, had not been able to find a way of helping his brother. The latter had written him that the charge was false, but for some reason he would never reveal the details. If the courts are on the side of justice, then they would hardly convict an innocent man. Endo, who was still young, wanted to believe this. Still . . .

As the days passed, between the lines of his brother's letters Endo saw the shadow of despair gradually grow darker and darker. 'I will no longer try to vindicate myself or explain. Someone brought me a Bible and I have been reading it. I no longer want to live in this world, so full of lies and falsehoods. But I want to think that you at least believe in my innocence.'

Endo had replied at once. If there was anything at all that he could do, he asked his brother to let him know at once. But no answer came to his letter. He didn't even know if it had ever been delivered. One hot evening in August, he later learned, his brother had been executed.

In place of a will his brother's effects were sent to Endo. Among them was the Bible that he had read with such pleasure in prison. Fighting against fear of death, his brother had read it over and over again. Its worn cover testified to that. My brother was innocent, thought Endo. Who then was responsible for his death?

From that day, Endo's life underwent a complete change. He visited the demobilization offices and looked up the names of the soldiers who had returned from the island on which his brother had been stationed. He walked about, interrogating one after another of the men in his brother's unit.

The rain had started up again. Endo continued talking, but more to himself than to Gaston. His face was completely wet with sweat and rain.

'It took me half a year, but I finally discovered the facts. What I'm telling you is the truth. There are people still living who ought to be executed. They've made an easy return to Japan and live with lips sealed about their past. My brother's superior officers! They laid all their crimes on my brother's shoulders. They denied having given the

orders. The circumstances of the time were so complicated
that it was easy enough for them to do so. But when they
got back to Japan, they even took the precaution of
changing their names. They must have been afraid that the
truth would out. For that reason it has taken me all this
time to ferret them out. But now I have their addresses.'

'Their addresses?'

'There are three of them. One of them is in Tokyo, the
other two in other parts of Japan. But, Gas, no matter
where they go, they won't be able to get away from me . . .
Tokyo, this very Tokyo where we're standing! But they
won't escape.'

Endo put his hand in his raincoat pocket and came to
a halt. He was smiling. Gaston knew that he had his hand
curled around the Colt in his pocket.

There were cheap restaurants all over Sanya for the
people lodged in the inns. They sold bean-paste soup for
ten yen, pickled vegetables for five. Cigarettes could still
be bought individually, as few or as many as one liked.

Gaston was not finicky about his food. He found whatever he was given tasty. *O-den*, sardines, whatever it was –
since arriving in Japan he had found nothing he disliked.
Now too, when he was taken by Endo to a cheap eating
place in Sanya, he sipped his bean-paste soup, and plopped
chunks of pickled radish into his huge mouth, under the
astonished stares of the waitresses and workers.

His face didn't show it, but in his heart Gaston had
come little by little to feel a deep compassion for Endo.
The fear and trepidation he had initially felt towards this
man had all but disappeared. Two nights spent together in
the shabby cubbyhole of a room were hardly grounds for
postulating a bond carried over from a previous existence,
but he had begun to feel an indescribable intimacy with
this killer – an intimacy that could not quite be designated
'friendship' or 'affection' but was more like the feeling he
had had for the stray dog.

The pain in Endo's eyes as he told Gaston about his

brother was more than sufficient proof of the truth of his words. His eyes overflowed with human feeling.

Gaston, of course, was still unable to make out what kind of man Endo really was. The previous morning when he had whipped the woman from Shibuya with his belt, the expression in his face had been that of a cold, bloodless man who did not know compassion. Seeing him then, Gaston could well believe that he was able to kill a man in cold blood and feel nothing. But that very cruel man had, just a few minutes ago when speaking of his brother, given expression – for the first time – to human sorrow. Since then he had not opened his mouth. He had eaten only a little and then had stuck a crumpled cigarette between his lips and was now lost in his thoughts.

Endo *san*, you mustn't do it. You mustn't go through with your plan. An act so full of hatred . . . doesn't it frighten you? Gaston sought for the right words to dissuade Endo from his plan of revenge and to dissipate the hatred in his heart. But with his limited vocabulary there was finally nothing he could say.

In his present mood Endo was not likely to accept any advice that Gaston might give him in his poor Japanese. There was nothing for him to do then but to follow along mutely. Perhaps somewhere along the way he might find the means of bringing peace to this man's troubled spirit.

'Endo *san*, don't you eat? If you don't eat, bad for your body, very bad.' But Endo merely threw a quick glance at Gaston. The sad, human expression of a few minutes before had vanished completely and had left in its place the cold, serpent-like mask of the killer.

When Takamori and Tomoe left the dark corridors of the police station and stepped out into the street, their eyes were dazzled by the bright midday sun. It had been drizzling in the morning, but suddenly the sky had cleared. This day too a stream of cars flowed along the street going from the Sakurada Gate of the Imperial Palace, where it

was still wet, to Yurakucho. When the stream came to a
stop as the pedestrians' light turned green, a restless, vortex-
like tangle of people rushed across.

'I wonder if the police will be able to find him,' said
Tomoe. She had her hand to her forehead to shield her
eyes from the sun. It was a hot day signalling the beginning
of summer. When Takamori did not answer her, she added,
'It'll be all right, won't it?'

The two had just been to the police station to ask the
police to look for Gaston. 'He should be easy to find. He's
tall with a very long face. He reminds you somehow of the
Sumo-wrestler, Ouchiyama,' Takamori had explained, and
the policeman had smiled. But when he went on to say
that Gaston had been taken away by Endo of the Hoshino
gang, their faces, at the mention of Endo, had stopped
smiling and become very sober.

There was at present no warrant out for Endo's arrest,
the police explained. But since he was a very dangerous
man, his activity was under surveillance.

'This is the man,' said the detective, pointing to one of
the posters above his desk. 'He's famous as a gangster of
some intelligence. He has a university degree.' The pictures
on the poster had been taken both from the front and
from the side.

'Let me take down your information. You say he was
in Sanya until yesterday?'

On the way to Yurakucho Takamori walked along with
bent head, trying to remember something.

'What are you thinking about, Takamori?'

'It seems to me I've seen that face somewhere.'

'What face?'

'Endo's.'

He had once seen Endo's face in a weekly magazine, at
the time when the Hoshino gang was putting pressure on a
certain big businessman. It had made no particular impression on him at the time, but now that he had had a closer
look at the man's face and expression in the police station,

it seemed that there was something about the man he
should recall.

'Endo's face?'

'I've got it!' exclaimed Takamori in such a loud voice
that he startled his sister.

'Don't scare me like that.'

'I wonder if it's possible!'

'What's the matter?'

'The detective said that he was a smart gangster who'd
graduated from college, didn't he? That university may
be . . . He certainly resembles him. . . .'

'What are you talking about?'

'When I was at school, there was a student there who
looked a lot like Endo in that picture. Yes, it's got to be.
It's the same face.'

Tomoe's nose went up a degree in her familiar gesture
of scorn, and she smiled sarcastically.

'What's the matter, Tomoe?'

'You've been seeing too many third-rate films. The
criminal always turns out to be a childhood pal of the
detective chasing him. You're letting your imagination run
away with you.'

'Do you think so?' Takamori said in a low voice; she
made him feel ridiculous.

When they reached the Hibiya intersection, they prepared to part. He had to return to his bank in Otemachi
and she was to meet Osako at the Nikkatsu Building. She
raised her hand slightly in a farewell gesture and called,
as a parting shot, 'Don't be carried away by your romantic
fancy, Takamori.'

'What do you call romantic fancy?'

'I'm sure I don't have to explain,' she said in a low voice
close to his ear. 'I know that you'd like nothing better than
to play the hero and go chasing after Gaston and Endo
by yourself.'

Takamori did not answer.

'This isn't a detective novel, brother. You're foolish if

you think that Gaston'll be able to get the killer to mend his ways.'

Thus attacked by his sister, Takamori wet his lips with his tongue. He wore a sheepish expression.

'In place of such heroics, you'd better get the police to find Gaston at once.'

'What do you think we should do about him?'

'I have little use for that fool. I'm fed up with him. For a guest to be such a bother. . . .'

Back straight and head high, Tomoe entered into the stream of people, clicking her high heels as she walked. Watching her until she was out of sight, Takamori reflected, 'How practical she is! Gaston has become something of an ideal for me, but to her he's nothing but a fool.'

When they had finished breakfast, Endo and Gaston left the restaurant. The sky was still clouded and a light rain was falling. Endo looked at his watch. It was seven o'clock.

'Our inn is over there.' After two days in Sanya, Gaston more or less knew his way around. Proudly he began to walk in the direction of Iwate Inn, where they had been staying.

'We're not going back to the inn,' Endo told him in a sharp voice. Sometimes he would suddenly become very gentle with Gaston, and at other times his face wore the cold look of the killer.

'Where are we going?'

Endo did not answer. He was staring into the distance as if looking for something on the street, which was shrouded in mist. A black car was approaching slowly from the direction of the streetcar tracks. Gaston recognized it at once. When it got close enough, Gaston also recognized the driver. It was the same man who had brought them here.

The driver greeted Endo and flicked away his cigarette. It fell on the wet street but did not go out at once. For several seconds smoke kept rising from it.

'Gas, get in.'

'The foreigner's name is Gas, is it? What a stinky name.'

'Did you look up what I asked you to?' asked Endo in a tired voice as he got into the car.

'There's nothing to be afraid of.' The driver handed Endo a sheet of paper. The latter ran his eyes over it quickly, then put his hand into an inside pocket of his raincoat and pulled out a thick pad of tags and handed it to the driver, who received it with one hand silently as he steered the car with the other.

'Endo, why didn't you decide to do the job at night?'

'A killer doesn't do his work by night.'

'Why not?'

'Even a man who's on his guard will relax while it's light. He will be cautious at night, but in the daytime all you have to do is to call him and he'll turn around. He leaves himself wide open.'

'So that's it.'

'Besides,' continued Endo smiling, 'there's something nice about the sound of the words "murder at noon".'

The driver said nothing more. The car passed through Asakusa and headed in the direction of the Ginza.

' "Murder at noon" – do you understand what that means, Mr Gas?'

'Noon?'

'Yes. The time of the day when the sun is highest in the sky.'

'Murder?'

'Making red blood flow.'

Gaston began to tremble. Looking at Endo, he shook his head vigorously and covered Endo's hand with his big paw. That was all that it was in his power to do. Silently he laid his huge palm over Endo's hand, and his horseface was convulsed with feeling as he tried to find words to express his thoughts : No, Endo *san*, no. You mustn't. I know how hard it is to be ill. I know how you feel about your brother's execution. But even so, you mustn't. To hate men . . . to hate . . . nothing but a dead end.

What in his poor Japanese he could not say, he tried to get across somehow with his eyes. 'No . . . you mustn't.'

Endo looked intently at Gaston. Certainly something of what Gaston was trying so desperately to say did get across to the sensitive core of his heart. But finally he wrenched his eyes away and pulled his hand away from Gaston's.

'I hate sentimentality.' He sounded as if he were talking to himself. 'Get a move on!'

'The streets are slippery. This is the worst kind of rain for driving.'

'Never mind. Step on it. This fellow's liable to jump out and get away. . . . I can read his mind.'

Turning to Gaston, he asked, 'You'd like to get away, wouldn't you?'

Gaston shook his head. Even if the car were to stop and the door to fly open with Endo facing the other way, he would have no thought of escaping now.

'Dog *san*!'

'What?'

'You.' Gaston's big mouth fell open in a grin. 'You are like Napoleon *san*.'

Gaston had not forgotten the old dog, Napoleon, who always seemed to be making a pathetic appeal to him, as if wishing to be consoled for all the teasings and beatings he had taken. Now, looking at Endo's profile, Gaston somehow felt the presence of that very same appeal in the killer's face.

'Endo *san*, you like dogs, don't you?'

Endo was taken aback by the question. 'Why?'

'I like dogs. Endo *san*, do you like children?'

'Shut up!'

'Do you like? Do you hate?'

'Shut up! I don't know.'

The driver looked back and remarked, 'The man's crazy. You sure know how to pick 'em.'

Endo did not answer. He sat with his eyes turned down.
'We've reached the Ginza.'

The rain had gradually lifted. The grey skies were giving
way to blue, and the sun had become so strong that it was
hard on the eyes.

After parting from her brother, Tomoe crossed the Hibiya
road junction and headed in the direction of the Nikkatsu
Building. Though it had been raining that morning, the
skies were now perfectly clear and the wet pavements
reflected the brilliant rays of the sun. The windows of the
buildings too were sparkling. Foreigners and Japanese with
briefcases poured out of the doors, intent on their business.
A taxi pulled up and discharged its passenger, only to pick
up another. Another busy day had begun.

Tomoe was supposed to meet Osako at the coffee shop in
the basement of the Nikkatsu Building. An influential
patron of the Disanto Trading Company at which they
worked was due to arrive at Haneda from abroad today
and Tomoe and Osako had to select a welcoming gift for
him.

They had arranged to meet at ten o'clock, but Osako
had not yet made his appearance when she arrived. As she
ordered a glass of lemonade, she reflected on how rude it
was to keep a lady waiting.

As a result of the Shinjuku incident, Tomoe had come
to look down on Osako. Ordinarily so well groomed, he
had cut a ridiculous figure as he ran away screaming in a
shrill voice. It had been very funny. More than funny, it
had been disgraceful. When he had shown up at the office
the following morning, he had looked sheepish and had
gone to great lengths to defend his actions of the previous
day. 'The reason I ran off, Tomoe, was to call the police.'
Tomoe had raised her nose, smiled, and turned away.

'I'd like to meet a man I can really depend on,' thought
Tomoe as she raised her glass to her lips and sighed. On
reflection she realized that of all the men she knew there

was not a single one that was really dependable. Osako, Takamori, Gaston . . . not one.

'For the time being I'll have to forget about marriage . . . if all men are like Osako and my brother.' Suddenly there came to mind the words that Takamori had so often thrown at her recently : 'You don't recognize a real man when you see one.' How insulting! How dare he make fun of her! Let him fall hook, line and sinker for that fool Gaston! That's his business. But what right does he have to say I don't recognize a real man just because I have no use for Gaston?

She recalled the first time she had seen his face in the fourth-class cabin when they had gone in search of him on the *Vietnam*. It had been all she could do to keep from saying 'horse' or breaking into a laugh. Men liked by other men, and men liked by women, are they really so different? However she looked at him, Gaston was for her nothing but a simpleton – yes, to be exact, a fool.

'Excuse me for being late, Tomoe,' said Osako in his usual effeminate voice, when he finally made his appearance. He was elegantly dressed in a dark jacket above which projected an immaculately white collar. His necktie was in the best of taste and tied in a Windsor knot. He was so elegantly attired that the waitresses could not take their eyes off him.

'I'm afraid I've kept you waiting a long time,' he said, snapping his fingers.

'Not at all,' answered Tomoe, not without sarcasm. 'Only ten minutes.'

He bent his head to look down into her uplifted face and apologized again. Tomoe was not appeased. Quite the contrary. The more affected he became, the more ridiculous he appeared in her eyes.

'Tomoe,' he said in a voice that sounded pained, 'ever since that business in Shinjuku, I'm afraid you've had the wrong opinion of me.'

'I have no wrong opinion of you.' A malicious smile

came over her face as she proceeded to take him down a peg. 'I haven't thought enough about you to have any opinion.'

Osako gave her a hurt look and began to play with his coffee spoon.

'I don't believe you've ever been serious about a man.'

'Why do you say that? I'm a girl, after all. If the man is someone I like . . .'

'Is there such a person?'

'There might be.'

She experienced a peculiar pleasure in deflating him like this. Observing the dejected look that came into his face, she felt all the more inclined to prick the vanity of this conceited grandson of a peer.

'Who is he?' he asked in a hoarse voice. 'It's not that Frenchman by any chance, is it?'

'That Frenchman?'

'Yes, the one who calls himself Monsieur Gaston.'

Tomoe laughed so loudly that the waitress turned around startled. Even Osako, in spite of himself, had to smile.

'Of course not. How could you possibly fall in love with that soft-brained idiot of a foreigner who looks as if he'd just come off the farm? I must say, he did give me a start. Is he really a Frenchman? He has no intelligence and hardly any education. He must be about the lowest specimen of a Frenchman. Those clothes and that face!'

There was probably a certain amount of jealousy in Osako's condemnation of Gaston. For some reason, the more he abused Gaston, the angrier Tomoe became. Even though just a minute before she herself had made fun of him to her brother, now that someone like Osako did the same, she rose to his defence.

'You have no right to talk about him in that way. I think much more of him than I do of you.' She herself was surprised at what she had said.

'This is the place.'

There were few people on the Ginza pavements, although the rain had lifted. With a prolonged screech the metal shutters of a camera shop in front of them were being rolled up. At the coffee shop next to it a waiter in his white jacket was energetically cleaning the window.

Gaston wondered where Endo was going, and what he planned to do. An overhead railway carriage filled with passengers passed near them. Even after it had passed, they could still hear the pounding of its wheels on the tracks. About thirty yards away was a fence enclosing a construction area and sounds could be heard coming from there too.

When Gaston put his eye to one of the cracks in the fence, he could see the fierce white flame of an acetylene torch cutting into steel. The workers, with towels wound around their necks just like the men he had seen in Sanya, had already begun working.

The driver stopped the car and opened the door for Endo.

'Fine.' Endo pulled out the piece of paper the driver had given him earlier and looked at it again.

'I'll be waiting for you.'

'OK Gas, get out.'

Once again Endo studied the piece of paper. 'Hey, Gas.' He looked about to make sure no one saw them and then motioned to Gaston to enter through a small opening in the fence. The wall of the building under construction was still nothing more than a framework of steel bars. The air smelled of cement. Pushing Gaston ahead of him, Endo made his way between the fence of the enclosure and the steel framework.

They came to a staircase on which had been deposited a number of wooden boards, and Gaston asked, 'Where are we going, Endo *san*?'

'Don't ask any questions. Just come along. Be careful not to raise your voice.'

Of course, even had Gaston raised his voice, it would

not have been heard above the noise of the construction, especially that of drilling into steel.

Occasionally a drop of water fell onto Gaston's head. The cement was probably still damp. The roar of the overhead railway seemed to come from close at hand. Endo stood still and listened to the sound. Then he said, 'Let's go back.'

Dull-witted Gaston had not the slightest idea why Endo had come here. But, at any rate, nothing had happened.

'We've finished, haven't we? What do we do now?' he asked, with a sigh of relief.

Endo gave him a big smile, showing his teeth. 'You're really a simple fellow, aren't you?'

'Why?'

'You still don't know why I came here?'

Gaston shook his head.

'Just listen to that noise. When I fire my pistol, no one's going to hear. A fine place for a killing, isn't it, Gas?'

When they got back to the car, the driver was waiting for them. He was chewing gum.

'All right. Let's get ready.'

'OK.'

Opening the car boot, the driver pulled out a brown suitcase. Endo got into the car and took off his raincoat, jacket and tie. Inside the suitcase the driver brought him was a brand new shirt, a light blue jacket, and cream-coloured shoes.

'Gas, here, hold these.' Endo handed him the suit he had been wearing, which was badly crumpled after their two days in Sanya, and the raincoat, and he slowly began to put on the fresh clothes. When he was dressed, he took out an electric razor, battery-run, and began to shave his blackening chin. Gaston was amazed at the transformation. He was now a handsome young gentleman.

'Oh, Endo *san*!' exclaimed Gaston. '*Beau garçon, n'est-ce pas.*'

'Of course. . . . Oh, hand me my pistol.'

Endo put on a shoulder holster over his shirt and took the pistol from the pocket of the raincoat Gaston was holding.

'Gas, wait for me here.' Then in his gentleman's attire Endo opened the door of the car, stepped onto the pavement, where the stream of people had begun to swell, and vanished into the crowd. The sun was now hard on his eyes. It was ten o'clock, the hour when city life begins to pulse at high pitch.

Where was he going? Anxiety like a black cloud began to spread across Gaston's spirit. The notion of murder, which until this moment had totally eluded him, suddenly took on a concrete reality. That it had taken so long for this to happen was due to the fact that, although Endo had occasionally been cruel to him during the two days at Sanya and later, Gaston had not been able to find in his heart any hatred for the man. With the same kind of feeling as when on a rainy day one looks across to a far-off hill which alone is bathed in sunshine, Gaston had looked upon the action which Endo was preparing to perform.

'Have some gum, foreigner?' The driver extended a pack of chewing gum to him. 'But don't try anything funny.'

'Endo *san*. . . . Where did he go?'

'He went to get a man.'

'To get a man?'

'The man he's planning to bump off.'

Gaston pressed his long face against the window. A policeman wearing a white helmet had stopped his motorcycle at the intersection and was looking vacantly in their direction. The white helmet glittered in the sun. Gaston could easily have opened the window and shouted to him. But the pitiful image of Endo convulsed in a coughing spell flitted through his mind. 'Poor Endo,' he thought. 'I can't abandon him.' The policeman stepped on his accelerator and disappeared.

Endo finally reappeared, blinking his eyes in the strong sun.

'How did it go?'

'I disguised my voice over the phone and he fell for it. He'll come to that coffee shop there at eleven. All I have to do is lead him to the construction site and pull the trigger.'

Ten forty-five. Endo sat with his elbows against the window of the car watching the stream of people passing by. The driver, still chewing gum, was absorbed in the morning paper, which was spread out on his knees.

'Anything important in the paper?' asked Endo, coughing dryly.

'The Giants lost a double header to the Swallows.'

'I mean in the news.'

'In politics? Same old stuff, I guess. . . . That's a bit out of our line.' Without looking up, he handed Endo the part of the paper he wasn't reading. Endo ran his eyes over the front page.

'Gas, your country's having its problems too, isn't it? What's going to happen in Algeria?' he asked, smiling.

'Algeria?'

'Aren't the French and the natives fighting each other bitterly? They hate each other.'

Hate each other . . . fighting. . . . Gaston looked at Endo and shook his head sadly. But it wasn't only Algeria. It wasn't only France. Here at this very moment. . .

There seemed to be nothing but hatred and enmity in the world. One country hating another, one man distrusting another. Love and trust had fled far away. Dulles was suspicious of Khrushchev, Khrushchev of Dulles. The French hated the Algerians, and the Algerians the French. And that was not all. Here before his very eyes, here under the dazzling sun of the Ginza, one man was preparing to murder another. Eyes flashing with hatred, he awaited his prey.

'Just like you . . .' said Gaston, in a low voice. But Endo was no longer paying attention to him. He was staring out of the window.

Ten fifty-five. The driver turned on the radio. A young lady's voice was intoning a commercial. 'Good nails mean lasting buildings. Buy your nails at Yamato.' The sweet feminine voice gave place to that of the male announcer.

'The police are searching for Gaston Bonaparte. Gaston, if you hear this, get in touch with the police immediately.'

The announcer said nothing more. The three men in the car were silent. Then the driver laughed and turned to Gaston. 'That's you! . . . Endo, this is getting risky.'

'What are you talking about? No one knows Gas is with me.'

A couple of young lovers, starting to cross the street, looked into the car.

Eleven o'clock. Endo suddenly sprang back from the window. 'He's come. Right on the dot.' There flashed across his cheeks, made hollow by his illness, a satisfied grin. 'Don't stare at him,' he ordered in a low voice. 'Umezaki, don't turn the radio off.'

Umezaki did as he was told. With the radio still playing, he pretended to be absorbed in his newspaper. Endo sat with one elbow against the window, yawning and feigning boredom.

A mass of people were moving along in both directions on the Ginza. There was no way for Gaston to know which of all these people was Endo's target.

'He's come to a stop.'

Gaston caught sight of a half-bald Japanese pushing open the door of the coffee shop in front of them. He was a short, pudgy man. His balding head and short, squat body made an unpleasant impression even on Gaston.

'Gas, get out.'

'I . . .'

'I said get out.'

'I . . . I . . . What are you going to do?' Gaston shook his head vigorously and held tight to the car door. Fear had a firm hold upon the cowardly heart in his massive body.

'Didn't you hear me? I said "Get out".' Endo began

to kick Gaston roughly on the thigh, again and again.

'You won't get out?'

Just then the car door flew open with the weight of Gaston's body leaning against it. Endo grabbed him as he was about to fall out.

'You want me to kill you too?'

Gaston looked as if he were about to cry. Holding his face between his hands, he lowered his legs to the space between the car and the pavement.

'I . . . You don't need me. . . . That man . . . I don't know him.'

'You won't have to talk. . . . Just sit in front of him and let me do the talking.' Endo manoeuvred Gaston along the pavement in the direction of the coffee shop. None of the passers-by paid any attention to them. The Ginza crowd was too blasé to be interested even in so unusual a species of foreigner as Gaston.

Endo pushed open the door of the shop. At a cosy table near the entrance, the pudgy man was sitting comfortably, smoking a cigarette. Beads of perspiration stood out on his hairless forehead.

'Are you Mr Kanai?' asked Endo, bowing politely. 'I am a member of the Cultural Exchange Society. As I told you over the phone, in determining what kind of Caucasian girl would suit you, I thought it best to bring along the man in charge.' Turning to Gaston, he continued. 'I would like you to meet Mr Sade.'

The pudgy man wiped the perspiration off his brow and smiled obscenely. 'Are you really serious about this?'

'What do you mean "serious"?'

Endo had a sarcastic smile on his face, but the man did not notice.

'How far can I believe what you say? In the first place, I've never heard of any group of white prostitutes operating in Tokyo.'

'Of course you haven't. We're set up as a private club. This Mr Sade here. . . .'

Endo and the pudgy man, sitting across the table from each other, began talking in a low voice so that the waitresses would not overhear the conversation. In the meantime Gaston was shaking his head furiously and blinking his eyes and doing everything in his power to alert the man to the danger he was in. But the man hardly even noticed him.

'White women? What kind've you got?'

Endo spun his water glass, still half-full of water, on the palm of his hand, and continued to speak in hushed tones.

After the red-light districts in Tokyo were closed by the law against prostitution, prostitution went underground and continued to be practised in private clubs, referred to as 'white-light'. But completely unconnected with this, there had existed from long before groups of white call girls at the disposal of executive class Japanese businessmen and their foreign guests. White strippers employed at cabarets and foreign jazz singers entering the country on tours by way of Hong-Kong would establish contact with these groups in order to earn a little extra money.

The longer Endo continued his hushed explanation, the more the pudgy man, who had at first been sceptical, manifested interest in his leering face.

'Is it safe? They'll act responsibly if the police find out?' asked Kanai, wiping his brow.

'Mr Sade here is taking care of that right now.'

Only then did the man notice Gaston's shaking head and blinking eyes. 'Is something wrong with him?' he asked.

'Ah. Mr Sade has a nervous affliction. He can't control his facial muscles. . . . But how about it? In fact, I brought two of those girls along for you to look at.'

'What? You certainly came well prepared. But I can't use them now. I can't find an interested customer until tonight. I'll give you a call when the party breaks up.'

'I'm afraid that won't be satisfactory. You see, these

foreign women are pretty fussy. If there's not a contract drawn up before hand . . .'

Kanai took the bait. 'So that's the way it is. Well, then I suppose I might as well have a look at them. Of course, I can't speak any other language except Japanese.' And he rose from the table.

Endo quickly grabbed the bill and called the waitress. Then in a low voice, but sharp, he whispered in Gaston's ear, '*Tais-toi, sacré Gas.* . . . Don't try anything funny.'

Endo placed himself between Kanai and Gaston and began to walk in the direction of the construction site. He wished to prevent Gaston from talking to Kanai. They could hear close at hand the ear-splitting noise of steel being pounded and of the acetylene torch at work.

8   Trust and Suspicion

'Where are we going?' Kanai asked Endo suspiciously, coming to a halt.

'Just over there,' answered Endo, with an air of innocence. 'These women aren't Japanese, so they don't like to be seen in public. I told them to wait over there.'

The noise of construction beyond the fence was now quite loud. The three men, Gaston towering between the other two, turned a corner and entered an alley.

Gaston should have walked more slowly. If he had been inspired to detain Endo and Kanai in the coffee shop for another five minutes, he might have seen Tomoe and Osako pass by. Tomoe was just then walking with Osako along the street from the Nikkatsu Building to Owaricho. She stopped often to look into shops at objects that caught her eye or to inspect window displays. 'It's always noisy around here, isn't it?' she remarked as they passed near the construction area into which Gaston had disappeared.

'It certainly is. In recent months it's been one new building after another here on the Ginza. Tokyo's dirty, isn't it? There's no regard here for urban beauty as there is in Paris.' Osako, as usual, had nothing good to say about his own country.

When the three men came to the entrance leading to the basement of the new construction, Endo looked about him. Near the entrance was a pile of gravel, and beside it were large boxes full of sand and sacks of cement. The sun was beating down on the cement sacks.

'The women are waiting in such a place? Is this a joke?' asked Kanai, uneasily. He seemed at last to suspect something.

'Why would I joke with you?' Endo spoke in Kanai's Osaka dialect. 'The women are right here in front of you.'

'What's all this about?'

'Take a good look at me. You don't remember? Don't I look like someone you once knew? Of course, the man is now dead . . . A lieutenant you killed. I'm his younger brother.'

All at once a look of consternation and fear spread over Kanai's face. Taking two or three steps backwards, he stumbled against the cement sacks and fell to the ground. Endo had not yet drawn his gun but Kanai, without trying to rise, brought his right hand up to protect his face, and let out a shout.

'I've been looking for you a long time, Kanai.'

'It wasn't me. It wasn't me.'

'You've still got the nerve to deny it?'

'It wasn't me. Kobayashi was responsible.'

'Now you can join my brother.'

'Let me tell you my side of the story, at least.'

Endo looked down silently at the pudgy man stretched out over the cement sacks at his feet. Beads of perspiration stood out on the man's bald forehead. A chilling smile was on Endo's face. The noise of the pounding and melting of steel was loud in their ears. Endo now had the Colt in his hand. He spun it around on his fingertips, and at each spin the cold black metal glittered in the sun. Kanai clung to the cement sacks, looking into the mouth of the pistol.

'Don't do anything foolish,' shouted Kanai.

'Stand up,' ordered Endo in a low voice. 'Now get into that basement.' He pointed to a dark hole which smelled of wet cement.

'Endo, I tell you. It wasn't me. It wasn't me. It was Major Kobayashi who pinned the blame on your brother. At least give me a chance to explain.'

'I'll get around to Kobayashi in good time. But before that, I'll take care of you. Now get into that cellar.'

'No, no. Forgive me! No, forgive me!'

'My brother, Kanai . . . My brother was thrown into a prison cell that was colder and blacker than this.'

The killer's hoarse voice suddenly stopped as a fit of coughing took possession of him. Without loosening his hold on the gun in his right hand, he covered his mouth with his left. For a few moments his shoulders shook with the violence of his coughing. When it finally stopped, he spat on the cement sacks. This time too there was a red thread of blood in his spittle.

'Kanai, my brother . . . for a crime he never committed . . .'

Kanai let out a loud shout, but it was absorbed into the noise of the construction.

'Try that again and I'll shoot you on the spot!' He lifted his foot and brought it down mercilessly on Kanai's hands, which were still holding on to the cement sacks. The skin on all five fingers was abraded and blood began to trickle.

'Oh, *non, non.*' Now for the first time Gaston found his voice. Until this moment he had been too dumb with fear to speak and had just stood there gaping at the two Japanese.

'Gas, you get in there too. If anyone comes along, pretend that we're having a look around.'

'Endo *san*,' Gaston cried desperately, 'Dog *san*, you like! You like children. You like dogs. . . . You like children. I know. You like children.'

Taking his cue from Gaston's words, Kanai brought his bleeding hands together in the gesture of petition. 'I've got a wife . . . and children . . . two children!'

Endo's hands began to tremble slightly. There was no doubt that his heart had been touched by Gaston's plea. But he steeled himself against it, took a new grip on his pistol, put its mouth against the temple of Kanai, who was still sprawled over the cement sacks, and pulled the trigger.

A train was passing somewhere nearby. The noise of the construction seemed louder than ever. It was close to high noon.

Kanai's bleeding fingers, still clinging to the cement sacks, began to move across them like an inchworm. Endo just stood there staring at his pistol. He still did not grasp what had happened. He pulled the trigger a second time and then a third. But his faithful pistol gave off only empty sound. Whenever fire jumped out of its barrel, Endo felt a pleasurable shock that went from the palm of his hand to his arms and then through his entire body. But now there was only the dull click of the spring being released. The pistol had no bullets!

'No bullets! No bullets! No bullets!' He seemed to hear someone, not himself, shout in his ear in derision. Then he turned and fixed his eyes on Gaston.

Gaston had both hands up to his face, supporting his cheeks. Like a child that has been scolded by its mother, he was looking at Endo with a face that seemed about to collapse in tears.

'You . . . You . . .' Endo's lips quivered with anger and hatred. 'Did you take out the bullets?'

Endo's attention being thus diverted elsewhere, Kanai chose this opportunity to raise himself from the cement sacks, and without any regard for appearances ran away screaming at the top of his voice. Unexpectedly, his short squat body seemed to have greater velocity than a bullet. Before Endo could put out a hand to stop him, he had run the length of the wall and practically fallen out of the construction-site entrance, and then vanished onto the street.

Gaston and Endo stood in silent confrontation for a moment.

'You . . .'

'Yes.'

On the horseface of the big man was a pitiful smile that bespoke both fear and repentance for what he had done. 'Excuse me. Excuse me.'

Suddenly Endo's right hand came crashing down on Gaston. It was a blow aimed at no particular part of the body, but at everything it could reach. At the same time he kicked him again and again in the knees.

'You . . .'

'You're hurting me!'

'You don't know how I've worked and suffered for this day.'

'It hurts!'

Endo kept on hitting and kicking. Tears were flowing from his eyes. 'The pain of waiting for this day!' Finally his strength gave out and he leaned against the wall, his shoulders shaking violently.

'When did you take out the bullets?'

Gaston didn't answer, and Endo repeated the question.

'A while ago.'

'When a while ago?'

'In the car . . . while you were changing into your suit,' answered Gaston, sobbing, as he wiped away the blood that was trickling from his nose, the result of one of Endo's blows. At the slightest movement of Endo's body, as he leaned there against the wall trying to catch his breath, Gaston flinched in fright.

'You plan to get away?'

'*Non. Non.*'

Endo looked at this ungainly monster of a man as if he were seeing him for the first time. Though more of a coward than even a stray dog, all you had to do was be a little nice to him and a friendly smile came over his big horseface. Just when you had him down as an idiot, he manages to remove the bullets from your gun. Not enough self respect to keep him from crying out when hit. But it had been a mistake to relax his guard with him.

'Was it when you held my raincoat?' Endo remembered having handed his raincoat with the pistol in the pocket to Gaston as he changed clothes. How had he dared try to remove the bullets in this short time? Where had this dull-witted foreigner acquired such skill?

With the sun shining directly into his long, foolish-look-

ing face, Gaston kept wiping away the blood from his
nose. Watching him, Endo felt there was something uncanny about him.

'What are you, anyway?'

'What am I?'

'Where did you come from?'

'France.'

His answers were about as satisfying as candy floss.

'Why . . . why did you come to Japan?'

'By ship.' Gaston had mistaken the word 'why' for
'how', the same word in Japanese.

'Bastard! I'm asking for what reason you came.' Gaston
smiled as if troubled for an answer and kept quiet.

'You're not an actor by any chance, are you?' Yes, that
was it. This man was just pretending to be a fool. In
reality, he was a very clever man, aware of everything
going on around him. Endo decided that this must be the
answer.

Endo looked fixedly at him with newly-awakened suspicion. He spat and started walking toward the entrance.

The noise of construction was as loud as ever. Endo
looked back and saw that Gaston was following hesitantly
behind.

'Why are you following me?'

Gaston did not answer.

'I asked why you were following me. Don't you want
to get away?'

'I won't go away, Endo *san*.' The amiable smile, now so
familiar, came to his blood-stained lips and he shook his
head. 'You and I . . . friends.'

'Friends? You're kidding! I don't need you any more.
Get the hell out of here. Leave me alone.'

In the original plan Gaston was to have helped in the
get-away. There are many Japanese who are soft on
foreigners. The police earlier had hesitated to stop the car
when they had seen a foreigner inside. Kanai too would
not have believed his story so readily if Gaston had not

been along. Just by being a foreigner, he could be put to profitable use.

But now! The circumstances had changed. It wasn't very likely, but Kanai might run and call the police, in which case Gaston would be a great handicap. If Endo were seen in the company of a giant foreigner like Gaston, he would soon be picked out by the police, who would be lying in wait at each station.

'What are you waiting for? Get out!' Endo opened the small door out of the construction enclosure and pointed to the street. 'You're lucky to be alive. . . . I probably would have killed you too afterwards.'

The killer said this half in threat, but he was not joking. Several times since leaving Sanya Endo had thought of killing Gaston if he should betray him. After all, he was like a stray dog, a tramp without a place to stay.

'I said, get going!'

'You. . . . Where do you go?' asked Gaston sadly.

'Where? That's my own damn business.'

'Where do you go?'

'You're a real pest, aren't you?'

'I go with you.'

'With me?' Endo raised his face in surprise. Tell him to leave and he says he wants to come along. He even seems to think it the natural thing to do.

'So you want to know where I'm going, eh? Well, I'll tell you. I'm going to get the other guy that framed my brother. You want to come along and louse that one up too?'

'If you go, I go with you.'

'Why?'

'Because I like you. I want to help you.'

'Help? You want to help me bump off that other man?'

'No, not that.' Gaston's face was screwed up in frustration at not being able to find the Japanese words to communicate his feeling.

'Endo . . . all alone . . . All alone, so you need friend.'

Endo's eyes lit up with raw hatred and he stared at Gaston. 'You son of a bitch. Get the hell away from here. If there's anything I hate it's mush.' He raised his hand as if to strike Gaston another blow, and the latter backed away a few steps.

Having put a safe distance between himself and the killer, he announced once again, 'I go with you,' this time in a whisper, as if talking to himself.

'The hell you will. You want the life beaten out of you?'

'No. I don't want to be beaten.'

'Then get lost.'

'I go with you.'

Endo's patience was exhausted. He grasped his pistol and advanced to hit Gaston with the butt.

Gaston's eyes filled with fear. 'Oh, *non, non.*' He raised his hands to his face and prepared to ward off Endo's blow.

'Then move!'

'Oh, *non, non.*'

'Why don't you go, if you don't want to get hurt?'

Gaston did not answer.

'Did you hear me? I asked you a question.'

'I made a resolution.' Gaston's low voice filtered through the fingers covering his face. He looked at Endo with knit eyebrows like a child being scolded by its parents.

'Resolution? What the hell kind of resolution?'

'Not to leave you . . . to go with you.'

His voice was as low as the singing of a mosquito, but Endo had no trouble catching his words. 'Not leave you . . . go with you.' To this killer, who had steeled himself against all human affection and feeling, no words could have been more offensive. He grabbed Gaston by the collar.

'Look here. . . . There's only one thing I trust. That's hate!'

'You lie.'

'Lie? Why?' Endo put pressure on Gaston's neck until he had to struggle for his breath. 'Does it hurt, Gas? Are you in pain?'

'It hurts!'

'If it hurts, then listen. You're the kind of bastard I dislike most. Not dislike, *hate*.'

'You're hurting me.'

'You can stop the clowning. You don't fool me. I know how much good will there is in the world! "Love", "trust" — words that everyone uses for their own convenience. . . . I'm smarter now. I won't be fooled again.'

'You're hurting me.'

'If you take even one step after me, I swear to God I'll kill you. Just try it!'

With that Endo let go of him and began to walk away. But when he turned and saw Gaston pulling himself along the wall behind him, he rushed back to him and brought the butt of his pistol down full strength against Gaston's temple. It made a sound like that of an iron bar falling to the ground. Gaston spun around like a top and fell like a huge log.

Although spring had given way to summer, the evening air was humid. The two wind bells Tomoe had just bought in the Ginza tinkled occasionally when a slight breeze stirred them, and then were still.

Takamori, who had come home unusually early, sat cross-legged on the veranda, greedily devouring a sweet rice-cake, dessert after the evening meal. This too Tomoe had brought back from the Ginza as a present.

'Look, you've got bean jam on your kimono!' Tomoe began to lecture him from her chair.

'I'm sorry.'

'You should be. That's a fresh kimono.'

'So it is. I said I was sorry.'

But his attention was elsewhere and he was soon rubbing his sticky fingers on his kimono again.

'Takamori.'

'Yes.'

'I feel sorry for your wife.'

'You needn't,' he answered, wiping his fingers on a piece of newspaper.

'From where I sit, you look just like an overgrown child.'

'Oh? It seems to me that it's the man you marry that will need the pity. . . . You can't keep from nagging even while you're eating.'

Takamori pulled out his packet of cigarettes. 'Match, please!'

'They're right next to you. . . . And be sure to put your ash in the ashtray. Mother was complaining about that again this morning. "Takamori seems to think that everything in the house is an ashtray." '

Like most men Takamori was careless about his cigarette ash. Anything convenient served as an ashtray – a flower vase, Tomoe's cream jars.

'Takamori.'

'What now?'

'I've already had an offer of marriage.'

'Oh? He must have a screw loose.'

'Osako in my office . . .'

'That fellow with a face that looks like the bottom of my foot.' As he spoke, Takamori rose and stretched, then stepped into the dark garden. Looking up at the night sky, he saw a falling star streak across it. He turned his eyes away as if it were a bad omen.

The telephone was ringing. Tomoe went to answer it. There was a strange tone in her voice. 'The Ginza? . . . all right. . . .' She put down the receiver and called her brother.

'Takamori! Gaston's been hurt. He's at the police station. The Marunouchi station just phoned.'

All Japanese police stations seem to have been built according to the same blueprint. Like the station Takamori and Tomoe had visited earlier, this one had its entrance at a higher level than a normal building, not the kind of place one finds easy to enter. The position of the entrance and the stone steps leading up to it at right and left gave the entire building a stiff official feeling. They ought to lower the entrance and get rid of these useless steps, thought Takamori. That way the police could get closer to the people. This was the thought that came to mind as he entered the Marunouchi police station. Someone of Takamori's age – who had been a boy at the time of the war – could not get rid of a certain feeling of dread whenever he entered a police station. But once inside the feeling left him. Even the young policeman sitting at the reception desk was very courteous in telling them where to go. 'If you're looking for that foreigner, he's resting in the infirmary. Please go down to the basement floor and wait in the corridor there.'

The narrow basement corridor was lit only by one dim light. On the corridor were a room for interrogation and the detectives' office. The door of the interrogation room was ajar and they could see two detectives sitting cross-legged on the mat eating noodles.

'You've come for the foreigner?' asked a detective who hurried out of the office, putting on his coat as he spoke. He was thick-shouldered and had the look of a man who has been trained in judo.

'We got your call.'

'It was Police Headquarters that called. . . . Let's see, what did he call himself? . . . Gaston Bonaparte. We heard that you were his guarantor.'

He seemed to have just finished his evening meal. He picked at his teeth with a toothpick as he talked.

'We were told that he was hurt.'

'Nothing to worry about. Only a few bruises where he was hit. He's a Frenchman, so we were more concerned about the possible repercussions. But, fortunately, there doesn't seem to be any crime involved.'

Hearing that there was no crime involved, Takamori and Tomoe both breathed a sigh of relief.

The detective proceeded to explain to them what had happened. Just a little after twelve o'clock noon, Gaston had been found unconscious on the Ginza by a group of workers. Since blood was trickling from a gash on his forehead, there was some excitement for a time. The Marunouchi police had investigated and learned from Gaston that one of the steel bars being used for construction had fallen and hit him on the head. They had treated his injury in the police station infirmary, where he was still resting.

'The foreigner doesn't let anything bother him, does he? He ate everything we gave him for supper and when I looked in on him a minute ago he was comfortably tucked in under the covers, sleeping soundly.'

Takamori could not help laughing. That was Gaston, all right. But what was he doing at the construction site in the first place? When and how had he escaped from Endo?

'Then Gaston wasn't with Endo?' Tomoe had the same question. The detective, seeing her puzzled look, spat out his tooth-pick, and explained. 'You don't have to worry about Endo. The foreigner says that they parted company in the morning on the Ginza.'

'But why did Endo take him away in the first place?'

'We can't make much out of Gaston's explanation. But at any rate, Police Headquarters informs us that Endo is not at present wanted by the police. They told us to go ahead and release the foreigner.'

Takamori and Tomoe were relieved to hear this.

'Come along. I'll take you to him.'

The detective buttoned up his suitcoat and began to walk down the dimly lit corridor. Takamori and Tomoe followed timidly behind him.

'Let me have the key, please.' The detective received the key from a young, uniformed policeman, unlocked a door that opened into what looked like a prison compartment, and disappeared within.

'By "infirmary" did he mean "prison cell?" ' Tomoe, knowing nothing about places like this, asked her brother fearfully.

'No. The infirmary is the place where they take care of drunks for the night. The prisoners in the cells have to give up their belts, neckties and anything else they might injure themselves with. But not those in the infirmary.'

'You seem to have a pretty detailed knowledge of such places.'

'Of course.'

'It wouldn't be from first-hand experience, would it? . . . after a night of drinking?'

Through the half-opened door they could see a row of cells with straw sandals lined up before the cage-like door of each cell. From the number of sandals they judged that one cell contained three or four prisoners.

A woman with a limp was returning from the toilet accompanied by a police guard. As she entered her cell, she flashed a mysterious smile at them.

The detective returned and led them to the infirmary. There was Gaston. It seemed ages since they had seen him. Still wearing the same suit that was much too small for him, he was sitting hunched on his bed. It was also the same old horseface, but now with a large bandage on the forehead. Still, the wound didn't seem to be much.

'Gas.'

Recognizing Takamori, Gaston lunged forward. He shot out his huge hand and grasped Takamori's in a firm handshake.

'You really had us worried, Gas.'

'Nothing to worry about.'

'How's your head?'

'It's all right. Hurt all gone.'

On the bus between Hibiya and Kyodo, Takamori and Tomoe made Gaston sit between them and treated him as if he were someone special. The night sky was illumined with a rainbow of neon lights. Standing in front of them hanging on the straps were two girls, apparently high school students, who, judging from their conversation, were returning from a concert at Hibiya Hall. With faces that seemed still under the spell of the music, they were having an enthusiastic discussion about the pianist.

Gaston seemed to be embarrassed. He sat stiffly with both hands primly resting on his knees.

Takamori was recalling the night Gaston had left their house in Kyodo. It was a night such as this, with a multitude of silvery stars twinkling in the cloudless sky. Takamori could see vividly the figure of Gaston walking off into the night, turning back again and again to wave them goodbye.

Even now Takamori did not really understand his motive in leaving them. But in his simpleton's face there had been clear sign of a definite purpose, as, blinking his eyes, he looked sadly at them and tried to explain in his halting Japanese.

'I am going.' When he said this, his face had had such a beautiful expression that Takamori could not help being moved. Since that day, what had Gaston seen? What adventures had he had?

Takamori asked him again if he were not in pain. Reassured that he was not, he asked, 'You were hit by a steel bar?'

'Yes.' Gaston shook his head, but avoided meeting Takamori's eyes.

'What were you doing at that construction site?'

Gaston was obviously at a loss for an answer.

'You were with a professional killer by the name of Endo, weren't you, Gas?'

'Yes.'

'We were really worried about you. You were lucky to be able to get away from him.'

'Yes.'

'Did you know what kind of man Endo was, Gas?'

'He not a bad man, Takamori.'

Takamori saw that Gaston was holding something back, that there was something he did not want to tell them.

'Gaston, we've reached Shibuya,' announced Tomoe. 'You remember Shibuya, don't you?'

'Oh, Shibuya!' He pressed his bandaged forehead to the window and looked out intently at the brilliantly lighted streets, as if he were searching for something. Here too the night sky was aflame with neon lights.

'*Sensei*!' Gaston muttered to himself.

'*Sensei*? You mean Chotei *san*?'

'Yes. Is dog *san* with him, I wonder.'

'Dog *san*? Oh, you mean that stray mongrel.'

'I want to see dog *san*.' He looked at Takamori with eyes filled with longing.

9 Shine, All You Stars

Takamori knew Shibuya well, as well as he knew Shinjuku. That is to say, he was familiar with all the rat holes here too. And Gaston had his own lively memories of the place.

The three got off the bus and started down the street, which even at this late hour was crowded with people. Gaston stopped frequently to look about him, as if he remembered having been here before. When they reached a certain cinema, he came to a halt and stood there for a long time without saying anything.

'What's the matter, Gas?'

'Takamori *san*, I was here that night.'

Gaston had said hardly a word since leaving the Marunouchi police station and had even seemed to be embarrassed in the company of Takamori and his sister. But now finally he looked more at ease, and he began to tell them about the events of that night. For the first time they learned of what had taken place at the Hilltop Hotel, the *shoben* incident, and of how he had been befriended by the women of the street and treated to hot *o-den*, and of how he had spent the night at Chotei's.

'That's an interesting story, Gas. Say, Tomoe, I'll bet you didn't know that the word *shoben* had that other meaning.'

Tomoe was all too familiar with the way her brother's eyes lit up whenever the conversation turned vulgar, and so she remained silent, pretending not to have heard him.

'Tomoe, even the other word, *unchi*, has taken on another meaning recently,' he informed her with gleeful face. 'Gaston, it's good for you to know this too. *Unchi* in

Japanese means "shit" but in recent slang it also has the meaning of . . .'

'Stop that foul talk, Takamori.'

'No, no. Listen, Gaston. As Confucius says, search out the way today, tomorrow you may be dead. Tomoe simply doesn't have a thirst for truth. Here's what it means, Gaston. A fellow who's tone deaf is called an *onchi*. But a fellow who keeps failing his driving test is an *unchi*. *Un* is the word for "driving" and *chi* means "idiot".'

Even after Takamori's explanation, Gaston still had not grasped the point.

'There's this famous writer of historical novels, Gomi Kōsuke, who's always flunking his driving test. So his friends call him Gomi Unchi. Do you get it? *Gomi* means "dirt". "Dirt Shit" – sounds as if he had some connection with the Public Health Department, doesn't it?'

Takamori kept up this kind of talk until they reached their destination, much to Tomoe's disgust.

When they approached the railway underpass, they could see the candle flickering in the stall of the old diviner, Chotei, and they knew he was open for business again tonight.

'Gas, shall we give the old man a surprise?'

At Takamori's suggestion, Gaston slipped away from the other two and concealed himself in the shadow of a telephone pole.

Chotei was sitting with both hands in his lap, looking meditatively into the candle flame. 'Oh, it's you,' he exclaimed when he recognized them. He seemed happy to see them.

'*Sensei*, today we've come to have our fortunes read.'

'I'm afraid you can't put much faith in my readings. . . . Is it an affair of the heart?' Then seeing something in their faces, he guessed the truth. 'You've found Gaston! But I have bad news for him. Today a dog catcher caught his dog. I'm afraid I've let him down.' Chotei spoke as if he himself were responsible for the incident.

From the night Gaston disappeared, the dog had made his home with the old man. During the day he lay in the street in front of the bars, and the waitresses fed him left-over rice and fish tails. At night when Chotei departed for work, the dog would limp along behind him.

'Old man, is that your dog?' customers at the bars would call out to him when they saw Napoleon. 'He's all skin and bones.'

'No, he's not my dog,' Chotei answered. 'A foreigner left him with me to take care of for a while.'

'A foreigner's dog? What a mongrel! He looks as if he's on his last legs.'

Then this very evening the dog catcher had got hold of him. It happened while Chotei was in his room putting on his *hakama* and *haori* before going to work. From a crack in his broken window he heard the bar waitresses making a fuss in the street. He looked out and saw the dog catcher pulling Napoleon along by a rope tied round his neck. Napoleon resisted and tried to get away, but to no avail. He was thrown into the cage with the other barking dogs.

'What a shame! Let him out! This fellow's not human.' The waitresses hurled imprecations and insults at the dog catcher but the man, not even bothering to answer them, merely snapped the lock on the cage. Chotei rushed down and with trembling voice tried to talk to the man.

'Old man, it's against the law to let mongrels like this run around loose. Look, he doesn't even have a dog tag.' The dog catcher quickly disposed of the old man's objections.

Takamori and Tomoe, who had intended to give Chotei a pleasant surprise, listened crestfallen to his account. Gaston, who had heard everything from his place of concealment, presented himself. He looked as if he were about to cry. The others could not bear to look at him.

'Napoleon *san*, dog *san*,' exclaimed Gaston mournfully. 'Poor Napoleon.'

'It's too early to give up hope, Gas. They keep the dogs at least three days. We may still be able to save him.'

'Where? Where?'

When Chotei told him where the dogs were probably caged, Gaston announced, 'I go there. Now.' He looked at them pleadingly, like a coaxing child.

They were finally able to persuade him to wait until the following day, but Gaston's face was as drained of life as a Morning Glory at high noon. Takamori would never have imagined that a dog could mean so much to him.

'We'll come with you,' said Tomoe. Even she seemed eager to console him.

It was about eleven o'clock when Takamori and Tomoe finally brought Gaston back to their home. From the enthusiastic way he was received by Shizu and Matchan, one would have thought he were a son home for summer vacation. They prepared a bath for him and treated him to another light meal. On the second floor, fresh sheets and soft quilts had been laid. It seemed a long time since he had slept in such a warm bed. The night he had left Takamori's and found a night's lodging in Chotei's room, and then later at the inn in Sanya, he had just stretched himself out on the mat without even taking off his clothes.

Watching him force himself to smile as Shizu and Matchan ministered to him, Takamori and Tomoe realized that he was trying to conceal from them his sadness at the loss of Napoleon.

That night Takamori laid his bed next to Gaston's. When he chanced to wake up in the middle of the night, he saw that Gaston was standing by the window in his night clothes, looking out at the sky.

'Gas *san*.'

'Yes.'

Takamori also got up and lit a cigarette. The lighted tip glowed in the dark. Everything was still. Takamori knew that Gaston was thinking about Napoleon, so he carefully avoided bringing up the subject.

'The stars are very beautiful, aren't they, Gas?'

'Yes.'

'You really enjoy looking at them, don't you?'

'Yes.'

Clouds of stars shone brightly in the black night sky. Takamori had never before met anyone as simple and pure as Gaston. Just as the stars strove bravely to illumine the night sky with their tiny lamps, so this foreigner did his utmost to give strength to men with the purity of his heart. Looking at Gaston, who had his eyes fixed on the brightly shining stars of the Milky Way, Takamori was suddenly reminded of *The Tale of the Bamboo Cutter*.

Princess Kaguya was said to have come down to the earth from the moon. Hadn't Gaston, perhaps, come from the stars? Wouldn't he be returning there one day? To Takamori in his present mood it all seemed very possible.

'Let's get back to bed. I promise you that we'll find Napoleon tomorrow.'

The following day Takamori had to report to the bank for work at the usual time, but Tomoe got permission from Mr Disanto to come in later.

Gaston was in somewhat better spirits than the night before. It was as if he were anticipating the joy of having Napoleon back again. From early morning his horseface was all smiles.

Tomoe and Gaston boarded a bus for the part of town where Chotei surmised the dog catcher had taken Napoleon. It was a very hot day, reminiscent of mid-summer. Getting off the bus, they found before them a dirty black stream, on either side of which were rows of houses that looked like matchboxes and whose roofs seemed ready to fall in.

They stopped at a police box to ask the way to the dog pound. A policeman came out of an inner room, wiping

his head with a towel. On his forehead, beaded with perspiration, was a red line where the band of his cap had
rested.

'Do you see that chimney over there? The dog pound
is directly beneath it.'

Tomoe could not imagine why a dog pound should need
so high a chimney, but she and Gaston crossed the muddy
stream and headed in the direction pointed out to them.
There were fluffy white clouds in the sky. This section of
town seemed to have many factories. Except for the ice-
cream man that passed by ringing his bell, the streets were
empty of people. They turned a corner and suddenly found
the air filled with a strange stench. It was like having a
handkerchief doused in cheap perfume thrust into one's
face.

'Could that be the smell of the dogs?'

It was really more like the smell of some chemical
compound. It was not unlike the unpleasant odour of the
pupae that Takamori sometimes used as bait when he went
fishing.

Just then a small truck passed them. On the back of the
truck was a large cage from which stuck out the heads of
four or five dogs, all barking plaintively.

'Oh! Dog *san*!' Gaston forgot Tomoe and began to run
after the truck, moving his long legs in an awkward manner. He was caught up in the cloud of yellow dust raised
by the truck as it passed. As Tomoe watched, he disappeared at the end of the long wall that enclosed the dog
pound.

Gaston's desperate chase after the dog catcher struck
Tomoe, who had no great love for animals, as ridiculous.
Just like a child, she thought. Is he really that fond of
dogs?

The wall enclosing the dog pound was longer than she
thought. On the other side of the wall she could see the
chimney they had spotted before, towering into the sky.
When she finally reached the stone gate that led into the

enclosure, she found Gaston arguing about something with a young man who wore a white laboratory coat.

'It's no use,' said Gaston to Tomoe when he saw her. 'Napoleon *san* has no ticket.' There was a note of sad appeal in his voice.

'Ticket?'

'A certificate issued by the district office,' explained the young man. 'You need the certificate to show that you're the dog's owner.'

'Isn't there any way of getting around it?' Tomoe's voice too was pleading.

'You put me in a difficult position.' The young man blinked his eyes as he spoke. 'Do you remember his licence number?'

'Licence number?' How could a stray mongrel like Napoleon have a licence number? Or be registered at the ward office? Tomoe was at a loss for an answer. 'He doesn't have a licence, but since this foreigner has been taking very special care of him . . .'

'I'm sorry. If he doesn't have a licence, there's nothing I can do.'

'Can't you find some way?'

The man in the laboratory coat may have been moved to pity at the sight of Gaston's face, which was as crestfallen as a wilting flower on a hot summer's day. He finally succumbed to their entreaties.

'Then, just this once. . . . Come inside. I must warn you, though, that the dog you're looking for has probably been disposed of already. Stray dogs are not treated the same as those that have owners. We generally kill them on the day they come in.'

Passing through the gate, they found a small office at their right. Sitting at desks inside the office were several young men, also wearing white laboratory coats.

The man led them across a courtyard. The dog catchers who had just driven in with their load of dogs were squatting beside a water tap, stripped to their undershirts,

washing their arms and legs. They stared suspiciously
at Tomoe and Gaston as they passed. The pungent smell
they had noticed earlier filled the courtyard.

'What in the world is that smell?' asked Tomoe.

'You get used to it. That's the smell of the chemicals
used in the hide factories in this neighbourhood. There are
two or three such factories that skin and tan the hides of
the dogs we kill.' He pointed to the tall chimney which
they had first seen from the police box.

They were now close enough to hear an ear-splitting
chorus of barking dogs. Plaintive barks, angry barks, pleading barks – if they could have spoken, their words would
have expressed every kind of grief and resentment.

There were white dogs, black dogs, spotted dogs, big
dogs, sleeping dogs. When their guide opened the door into
the dog compound, close on a hundred dogs, startled by the
light that entered their dark cages, began to bark.

Following their guide inside, Gaston and Tomoe were
overwhelmed by appeals for help from the caged dogs.
Jumping at the wire mesh of their cages, wagging their
tails furiously, they all seemed to be saying, 'I'm the one.
I'm the one. Please help me!'

Dogs have an instinct for recognizing those who are
fond of them. As Gaston approached each cage, the dogs
inside struggled to get near him, joy written all over their
faces. They wagged their tails so vigorously that they
seemed in danger of losing them.

'He must really like dogs,' remarked the young man to
Tomoe, in admiration.

Gaston put his fingers through the wire mesh and greeted
each dog in turn, speaking soft words to them and gently
stroking their heads. But when he came to the corner of
the room, he stopped abruptly and stared ahead of him.
On a straw matting lay two dogs, their bodies stiff in
death. One of the dogs was Napoleon.

The afternoon sun filtered in through the cracks in the
wall boards. Some rays fell almost directly upon the heads

of the two dogs that lay there unmoving. They had probably been dead for several hours. Napoleon's skinny body was lying on its side with his front legs turned in as if he were swimming. Traces of foam-like spittle remained on his lower chin, suggesting that he may have been in pain when he died.

Gaston squatted down. He covered his face with his hands and did not move. Tomoe stood behind him looking down at his shoulders, completely helpless. There was nothing she could do. A couple of flies were buzzing about Napoleon's grey fur.

'We were too late,' said the young man, heaving a sigh. 'If you'd just come a few hours earlier, we might have been in time.'

'But he doesn't seem to have suffered.' Tomoe did not expect that her words would be of any consolation to Gaston, but she had to say them, if only for her own sake.

'That's because we give them injections. It's not like the old days,' the young man explained weakly.

'So the dogs don't suffer. . . .'

The dogs in the cages seemed to sense something was wrong. They no longer barked as before, but turned misty eyes toward the three.

Gaston remained squatting there for a long time. A fly left Napoleon and settled near Gaston's ear, but he made no attempt to brush it away.

'We'd better be going,' said Tomoe finally, putting her hand on Gaston's shoulder. At this he stood up, but he looked as if he had been drained of life.

The afternoon sun had begun to decline when Gaston and Tomoe left the dog pound. They both found the stretch of road from the entrance of the dog compound to the main street extremely long. The ice-cream man who had passed them earlier passed them once again, perhaps on his return route. He inspected them carefully as he drove by.

'Gaston, shall we find you another dog to take the place

of Napoleon?' asked Tomoe in a soft voice. But Gaston
only shook his head weakly.

'You mustn't take it so hard, Gaston. Tonight let's invite
Takamori along and go out and have a party.'

'Tomoe *san*, I . . .' Gaston stopped, rested one hand on
the wall, and continued in a low voice. 'Tonight I leave
Tokyo.'

'Leave Tokyo? Where will you go?'

'North.' His long face looked as if it were about to break
down. His nose and mouth were screwed up in such a
way as to hold back the tears that were welling up behind
his eyelids.'

'North? I don't understand.'

'Endo's place.'

'Endo?' Tomoe exclaimed in amazement. 'You don't
mean *the* Endo?'

Gaston was silent.

'Not *that* Endo, is it, Gaston? It couldn't be !'

'I'm going,' repeated Gaston in a low voice. 'Tonight.'

Dusk was already falling as they walked along the tree-
lined path that connects Ichigaya and Yotsuya. An evening
haze made the dark green leaves of the trees darker still.
Except for two boys playing catch in a corner of the park,
no one else was around.

Tomoe was still stunned by Gaston's sudden decision to
leave Tokyo, especially for such a destination. With all the
authority of an older sister trying to talk sense into her
younger brother, she sought to dissuade him from his
purpose. She had even given up going to work for the day,
though she had promised to report in at noon. For over
three hours she had been trying to win him over to her
point of view. As she argued with him, the train reached
Yotsuya and they had got off, intending to catch the
underground for the Ginza at Yotsuya Station. But since
Gaston had still not given in, they had begun walking along
the moat in the direction of Ichigaya.

'Then there's nothing I can say to make you change your mind?'

'No. I'm going, Tomoe *san*.'

What Tomoe did not know was that when Gaston had first caught sight of the dead carcass of Napoleon lying there on the mat, the face of Endo had flashed into his mind.

He himself did not understand why the image of the dead dog should have been overlaid with the face of the killer. Was it because the carcass of the dog somehow associated itself in his imagination with the man Endo was planning to kill? Or was it because Napoleon's eyes, unmoving and emptied of life, reminded him of that pitiful young man convulsed in a coughing fit on the rain-soaked street of Sanya?

The plaintive barking of the dogs in the compound may have suggested to him that Endo was doomed to walk the same path as these dogs, to eventual slaughter. Before long Endo might also be, like Napoleon, just a stiff corpse, exposed in the same way to the eyes of men. Gaston had tried to express all this to Tomoe, but his Japanese was simply not up to it.

'Then you're definitely set on going?'

'Yes. Endo *san* is my friend . . . just like Napoleon.'

'Do you know about that man, Gaston?'

'Yes.'

'You can't possibly. Don't you realize what he may do to you? Aren't you afraid?'

'Yes, I'm afraid.'

Tomoe threw up her hands in despair, and looked once again into the huge man's face. He was even denser than she had thought. Unless he were a complete idiot, he should be able to follow the logic of her argument. Even a three-year-old child would understand.

'Hey, will you throw us the ball, please?' shouted one of the boys playing catch some distance from where they were standing. Gaston spotted the ball near his feet, picked it up, and threw it to the boys with a happy face.

'The children are enjoying themselves.'

'We're not talking about the children. I asked you if you weren't afraid.'

'Afraid?' replied Gaston. 'Yes, I'm afraid.'

'If you're afraid, then why do you go, Gaston?'

Then it was that Tomoe, without reflection, finally put into words the impression she had had of him from the beginning. 'You're a real fool, aren't you?'

Fool! From the moment she had set eyes on him in the smelly hold of the *Vietnam* she had had many occasions to wonder if he were not a fool, an idiot. His face, his clumsy movements, his dress, everything could not but invite Tomoe's pity and contempt.

She admitted that her brother was right in saying that he had a good heart, a heart such as one seldom found these days. He might even be called a saint, or, if that sounded exaggerated, at least an extraordinarily good-natured man.

But to be a saint or a man of too good a nature in today's pragmatic world, with everyone out to get the other fellow, was equivalent to being a fool, wasn't it? At least, to a young girl like Tomoe, Gaston was lacking in all modern appeal. He was just a huge, inert, useless tree. Yes, a big useless tree. The tree stood before her now, staring vacantly at the children playing catch. At the furthest corner of the sky floated two or three clouds tinged with the rose of sunset. Directly below where they stood, trains filled with people on their way home from work slowly picked up speed after leaving Yotsuya Station.

This fellow has absolutely no common sense, thought Tomoe. Can he possibly realize what a desperate character Endo is? The police may not have anything on him just at the moment, but they are having him watched, as a dangerous person. Does Gaston know what he may be getting himself into by going off so nonchalantly in search of this killer? If he did, then he would be too apprehensive to stand here like this, watching children play ball with that foolish smile on his long horseface.

'Now, look here, Gaston . . .'

'Yes.'

One more time Tomoe had to repeat the question she had already asked so often. Her tone was that of a mother talking to a slow-witted child.

'You really intend to go through with this?'

'Yes.'

'In the first place, do you know where you can find Endo?'

Gaston nodded. He pulled a slip of paper from his pocket, and pointed with his long index finger to an address written in pencil : Mr Kobayashi, Yamagata City, Yamagata Prefecture.

'Where did you get this?'

Gaston stared at the ground, at a loss for an answer. The fact was that the slip of paper had been in the pocket of Endo's raincoat together with the pistol whose bullets Gaston had removed. It was the same paper that the driver, Umezaki, had handed to Endo on the way from Sanya to the Ginza.

'Then Endo is staying with this Kobayashi in Yamagata?'

Gaston shrugged his shoulders. But he couldn't tell Tomoe about what had taken place at the construction site.

'I'm going to tell the police!'

'*Non. Non.* You mustn't.' Desperately Gaston snatched the slip of paper from Tomoe's hand. 'Endo won't do anything bad.'

Tomoe had no reply to this. After all, even the Marunouchi police, who had taken care of Gaston, had indicated that there was at present no reason for detaining Endo.

'Tomoe *san*. Where can I catch a train for Yamagata?'

'At Ueno,' replied Tomoe, but she immediately added, 'This is no joke, Gaston. . . . I'll call Takamori and ask him to talk some sense into you.'

Keeping an eye on Gaston, who stood just outside the telephone booth, Tomoe got Takamori's bank on the line and in as soft a voice as she could muster, said, 'This is Takamori Higaki's sister. . . .'

Before she could say more, the girl at the switchboard, in no less soft a voice, answered, 'Just a moment. I'll call him.' Soon she was back on the line to say that unfortunately Mr Higaki had left the bank ten minutes earlier. Not knowing what to do next, Tomoe called home, but of course her brother had not arrived back yet.

'What shall I do? He's already left work.'

Gaston, with a dejected look on his face, was kicking at the ground with his old shoes. 'I'm sorry I won't see Takamori before I go.'

'Then why don't you come back home with me, tonight at least? How about it?' Tomoe tried desperately to win his assent. 'You can have a good talk with him, and then if you're still set on going to Yamagata, you can go after a good night's rest.'

'No, that's no good.'

'Why is it no good?'

'Because I've got to get there quickly.'

Gaston was afraid that if he delayed even one day Endo might get to Kobayashi before he arrived. Even a simpleton like Gaston could make that much of a calculation.

Now it was evening. The children playing in the park tied their equipment onto their bicycles and drove off. The rose-coloured clouds had turned a greyish-blue.

'At least, let's get something to eat.'

As they walked along the moat beyond Yotsuya Station, Tomoe reflected that there was nothing more she could say that could possibly make him change his mind. If he's going to be so pig-headed, she thought, then let him do as he pleases. I've had my fill of him. I can't waste all my time on this stubborn fool. Fool – that's what he is! An absolute idiot! I'll bet he doesn't even know that one and one make two.

They sat across from each other in silence in a restaurant in Yotsuya. Tomoe was too tired and depressed to speak, as she mechanically moved her fork up and down. Gaston, with his usual table manners, shovelled the food into his hippopotamus mouth.

'Look here, Gaston . . .'

'Yes.' But Gaston's mouth was full of macaroni, and the sound of his 'yes' was more like the moan of a cow.

'I've been meaning to ask you this for a long time. . . . Why did you come to Japan?'

He was still moving his jaws up and down so that his one-word answer was indecipherable.

'I know it's rude of me to ask.'

'No, not rude.'

'Then won't you tell me? I've wondered about this ever since you arrived, Gaston.'

For what possible reason had he come to Japan? From the beginning this had been a deep mystery to both sister and brother. Business? Trade? Impossible! Looking more like a tramp than anything, he had neither the presence nor the wit to deal with buyers.

Had he come as a tourist? Tourism was fast becoming a major industry in Japan. But Gaston had no interest in seeing Nikko or Kyoto or Nara, and he never spoke of Fujiyama, *geisha*, or other such things that seemed to be on every foreigner's tongue.

Had he come to do a report on Japan? But in his sleepy face could be found not an iota of the uncanny discernment that ought to sparkle in a journalist's eyes.

'Why, Gaston?' she pressed her question boldly. 'Why did you come to Japan?'

Gaston merely spluttered. His eyes were blinking like a

cow's and his jaws kept up their movement. But not a word in answer to Tomoe's question.

He's hiding something, decided Tomoe. She was suddenly filled with suspicion. Why does he always try to get off this subject whenever it comes up? She stopped eating and just stared at him for a while. She was possessed by a feeling that was neither quite suspicion nor yet mere curiosity. What in the world was this fellow? Did he have normal masculine feelings? Had he ever been in love, for example? Had he ever felt passion for anyone?

'Gaston, have you got a girl friend?'

'Girl friend?'

'Yes, a girl that you're in love with.'

Gaston lifted his face from his plate and exclaimed, 'I'm in love with you, Tomoe.'

Tomoe made a wry face and closed her eyes. Of course, she realized immediately that Gaston did not know the precise meaning of the Japanese word for 'love' that she had used. Still, she could not keep from blushing at his answer.

'That's not what I mean, Gaston.'

'But I do love you.'

'Thank you, Gaston. But you and I are not exactly lovers.' She became even more serious. 'We're not lovers,' she repeated. Then realizing that she had said this in too loud a voice, she became the more flustered. All the same it was at that very moment that Gaston, whom she had never before been able to think of as a member of the opposite sex, first appeared to her as a man.

It was not clear whether Gaston was aware of Tomoe's consternation as he stared at her, smiling.

Her nose went up a notch and she averted her face. What an insult! This man and I lovers!

At the end of the meal Gaston rose and took up the bill. 'I'll take care of it,' said Tomoe, hastily. 'This is on me.'

'No, Tomoe *san*. I'll pay for it.'

Tomoe knew how little money Gaston had had on him when he passed through Yokohama customs, so naturally, when she had invited Gaston to dinner she had had no intention of letting him pay the bill.

'You're a traveller, Gaston. You've got to take good care of your money,' she said, trying to sound casual.

'I have no need for money,' answered Gaston softly, smiling. He was silent for a moment and then announced decisively, 'I want to treat you to dinner.'

Tomoe had learned from their foregoing conversation how unyielding he could be once his mind was made up. So she did not argue with him further.

When they left the restaurant, the yellow street lights of Yotsuya were already on. There were fluorescent lights still shining in the windows of Sophia University, which loomed above them like a huge ship. The bells of St Ignatius Church struck the hour of eight. The dark of night enfolded the neighbourhood.

'Goodbye,' said Gaston, stopping in front of the restaurant and extending his hand to Tomoe. 'Goodbye, Tomoe *san.*'

'Goodbye? Where are you going? You can't be serious.'

'Yes, I'm going.'

'Gaston!'

But Gaston only shook his head sadly.

'Don't go through with it, Gaston!'

People on the street turned and looked strangely at them as they passed. But Tomoe no longer cared what people thought. She forgot all about herself as she took hold of Gaston's coat and tried to detain him, saying, 'Don't go, Gaston. You don't know. You really don't know.'

'I know,' he answered softly. 'I know.'

'What do you know?'

'I know that life is very difficult. Tomoe, I'm a weakling. So I've got to be careful all my life. It's a problem.'

One, two, several silvery tears flowed down from the

sleepy-looking eyes in his huge face. It was like seeing a horse cry.

'Goodbye, Tomoe *san*. I really love you.' And he turned around and began to walk off. The lights at the crossroads turned green and he crossed the street. Soon his large hulk had melted into the crowd.

'Tomoe, you can't recognize a real man.' Takamori's words suddenly came back to her, and they reverberated within her head with more resonance than the bells of St Ignatius.

The busy station of Ueno. A long line of people waiting to buy their tickets. A melancholy voice announcing train departures over the loudspeaker: 'The train for Takasaki will depart at 8.26 from Platform 14. The Takasaki-bound train from Platform 14.'

In a telephone booth Tomoe was frantically trying to discover her brother's whereabouts. Where in the world could he be loitering? He still hadn't returned. She had called the homes of his friends and acquaintances, but to no avail. She stepped out of the booth.

'It's no use. I can't find him.' She sounded completely disheartened.

'I'm sorry I can't meet Takamori *san*,' said Gaston. He too sounded disheartened.

'Then you're still determined to go?' Though she knew it was useless to ask, she could not help doing so. Beyond the gate the train was getting ready to depart for the Tohoku region. People were already forming lines at the gate and others were hurriedly converging there from the waiting room and from behind pillars of the station, suitcases and knapsacks in their hands.

'You really have to go, Gaston?'

Gaston smiled and placed his large hand on her shoulder in a gesture of consolation. She felt the warmth of his palm through her clothes.

'Please don't go!'

'It's all right. There's nothing to worry about.' Gaston was smiling as if it were not he who was the cause of her worry.

'I just don't understand.'

'What don't you understand?'

'I just don't understand you.' There was a note of vexation in her voice. Gaston who until now had been nothing more than an object of her ridicule and pity, seemed suddenly transformed into a man of extraordinary power. Since she had always held men in secret contempt, this was a new sensation for her.

'I'm a fool . . . a weakling!' He pointed at his own head, poking fun at himself to make her laugh. But since that was exactly the opinion she herself had had of him until now, the words stabbed her with their unconscious irony. Her face turned red and she lowered her eyes.

The train blew its melancholy whistle. 'The 8.35 train for Aomori via Fukushima, Yonezawa, Yamagata, and Akita is now ready for boarding. Go to Platform number 12.'

'This is it, then, Gaston,' said Tomoe in a voice so low as to be barely audible.

'Goodbye.' He grasped her hand a second time in a warm handshake.

'Goodbye, Tomoe *san*. I really love you.'

He turned around and walked off into the crowd of people moving towards the gate. Tomoe stood there unable to take her eyes off his receding figure. The suit too small for him, his awkward way of walking as he bumped into Japanese carrying suitcases.

'You don't know a real man when you see one. . . .' Again her brother's words echoed through her head. A feeling compounded of loneliness and regret, and something else too, attacked her, causing pain.

'Wait!' She ran after him through the crowd. 'Wait, Gaston, wait!'

People bumped into her with their suitcases, but she

paid no attention. It didn't even matter that they turned and looked at her with strange expressions on their faces.

'Gaston!' But when she finally reached him and saw his amazement to see her running after him like this, she did not know what to say. When she finally recovered her wits, she managed to stammer out, 'We'll be waiting for you when you come back. I had forgotten to tell you that.'

'Thank you.' Gaston acknowledged her words with a deep nod of the head and walked on.

Tomoe took a stand at the gate and kept her eyes on the platform. She could have gone all the way with him and waited at his window for the train to pull out. But she didn't want to do that. The train began to move away, hands waved. The special melancholy of platform farewells was distasteful to her now. Instead she preferred to stand here, unknown to him, and watch the train pull away from a distance.

He's not a fool. He's not a fool. Or, if he is, he's a wonderful fool.

For the first time in her life Tomoe came to the realization that there are fools and fools. A man who loves others with an open-hearted simplicity, who trusts others, no matter who they are, even if he is deceived or even betrayed – such a man in the present-day world is bound to be written off as a fool. And so he is. But not just an ordinary fool. He is a wonderful fool. He is a wonderful fool who will never allow the little light which he sheds along man's way to go out. It was the first time this thought had occurred to her.

Gaston could no longer be seen. Dim lights were shining in all the windows of the train waiting to depart from Platform 12. The bell announcing departure rang. Under which of those lights was he sitting?

'Wonderful fool!' Tomoe placed her hands to her mouth and spoke the words to herself. 'Wonderful fool, hurry back.'

Finally the bell stopped ringing. The train blew its whistle into the black sky and began to shuffle off slowly, carrying the wonderful fool to the north.

For some time after leaving Ueno Station the passengers in the third-class coach of the northbound train ate their box lunches and engaged each other in loud conversation, but after Akabane, Omiya, and Koyama had been left behind, they seemed to have nothing more to talk about and one by one dropped off to sleep.

Gaston sat close to the window, gazing at the lights of Koyama, which fast receded into the distance. He also saw the lights of the rickety shops along the railway tracks, and occasionally caught a glimpse of families gathered around the dinner table within.

His thoughts turned to the Higaki home in Kyodo. The train was already two hours out of Ueno, so Tomoe would certainly be home by now. She was probably in the parlour telling Takamori and the rest of the family what had happened.

The everyday life of people . . . the joy of parents and children gathered together in an intimate circle. The happiness of not being alone. In contrast, Gaston was resigned to being by himself. He had come all the way to Japan, and now he was on a rocking train plunging northward through the dark night.

Yamagata. What a lonely place that would be for him. He was travelling by himself to a strange town he had never seen before. What destiny awaited him there? He could not guess.

Occasionally a passenger stumbled down the aisle of the swaying car to the toilet. The toilet door opened with a grating sound and he vanished inside. A passenger awakened at the sound and turned to ask the man next to him where they were, then closed his eyes again.

The space between the seats was so narrow that Gaston's long legs, crammed so long in one position, began to ache. The middle-aged man sitting across from him in his under-wear occasionally threw him a curious look from behind his newspaper. But he too finally folded the newspaper and went off to sleep. The little, old, hunch-backed lady who sat next to him opened her lunch box and began to nibble at the large riceballs like a little mouse. She turned to Gaston and, half-smiling, asked him, 'You're an American?'

'No . . .' Gaston flustered, shook his head.

'Won't you have a riceball?'

'No, thanks. I've already eaten.'

'Where are you going?'

She herself was on her way to Akita to visit her son and his wife and her three grandchildren.

As he listened to her, Gaston reviewed again his reasons for going in search of Endo. As Tomoe had pointed out, he had absolutely no idea what kind of reception he would get. He knew only too well what a rash, imprudent venture this was.

Still, earlier that day at the dog pound when he had seen the already decomposing carcass of Napoleon lying there on the matting under the cruel rays of the afternoon sun, he had smelled the stench of death. It was not just the smell of the dog, but a smell more universal – a smell that in the present-day world surrounded men everywhere.

After each turn of the carriage, Tomoe's white fingertips moved over the keys of her typewriter with the speed of a machine-gun. The sound had a pleasant rhythm to it. Tomoe's face, so self-possessed as she pounded the black letters onto the white paper, was overflowing with that sprightly charm that characterizes the modern girl.

'Miss Higaki, would you please take care of this?' She

was handed another document to type from Mr Disanto's office.

'Fine. Just leave it here.' She gave a smile of acknowledgement but her fingers did not lose a beat. In this way the documents stacked on her desk were disposed of one by one.

Every half hour she took a five-minute break. Taking a bottle of eye medicine from her drawer, she put several drops in her eyes, then rested them by looking out of the window. This served to relieve the eye fatigue resulting from prolonged staring with taut nerves at small letters. In this way she sought to protect herself against near-sightedness, the arch-enemy of a young girl concerned about her appearance. Besides, if she were to work on with tired eyes, she would make many spelling mistakes. This five-minute break, therefore, was anything but a waste of time.

Today as she massaged her fingertips and looked out at the sky, she had something on her mind. It was already close to noon, 11.30 to be exact. Since it took the ordinary train about nine hours to reach Yamagata from Tokyo, Gaston would have arrived there this morning while it was still dark.

Tomoe had never been to Yamagata, but she could imagine Gaston arriving at the station before the break of day. The lights would still be on in the waiting room, which would be chilly at that time of morning. Several local men and women would be sitting on the benches, their luggage piled beside them, waiting sleepily for the train to pull in. A station employee would be sweeping the floor. . . .

Finally the train from Tokyo slipped quietly into the station. Following behind the Japanese passengers, Gaston made his way to the gate, a slightly anxious look on his face. His huge body and strange appearance drew the eyes of the people sitting in the waiting room.

The square in front of the station was still asleep. The

milk-white haze of dawn had already begun to lift the curtain of night. Buses were not yet running, the shops were all closed. The desolate scene was illumined by an occasional street lamp. Gaston leaned against the front wall of the station and looked up at the morning stars.

'Wonderful fool!' Tomoe had exclaimed the night before as his train started off into the dark. She repeated the words to herself now. She wondered if she had been wrong in her critical estimation of men. Tomoe's feeling towards Gaston was not, of course, that of a girl towards her lover. That this simpleton, whom she had secretly despised and made fun of, should have become such a mystery to her now – this was certainly quite a shock to a girl as self-assured as Tomoe. It was not just that he was a mystery, but also that she had, yes, lost out to him, fool though he was. This feeling of having been beaten was to Tomoe, who prided herself on being a very knowledgeable young lady, particularly disagreeable.

For all her spirit of independence, she suddenly felt the need to talk with her brother. She was, after all, only a young girl. Since she had no one she could really call a boy friend, Takamori was the only person with whom she could discuss the subject of men. She dialled his number. His voice at the other end of the line sounded unusually businesslike. However easy-going he might be about the house, she realized, at the bank he was attentive to his duties.

'Oh, it's you.' When he discovered it was only his sister, his manner of speaking changed abruptly. 'What do you mean calling me up like this? I'll get in trouble with the boss. We're not supposed to take personal calls during business hours.'

Tomoe surmised that his immediate boss, whom he stood in fear of, was within earshot.

'I'm sorry.' Her tone of voice was unusually apologetic. 'I just wanted to ask if we could meet somewhere on the way home from work.'

'Well . . .' He sounded apprehensive, not knowing what she wanted of him. He knew she wanted something, since such an invitation was almost without precedent.

'You can't make it?'

'I suppose I could. . . .' His voice suddenly became very low. 'Will you treat me to dinner? I'm broke.'

'What did you say?'

'I said I might consider it if you agree to take me to dinner.'

At five o'clock Tomoe put the cover over her typewriter and went to the ladies' room to freshen her make-up. When she came out, Osako was in the corridor, standing straight as a matchstick.

'Tomoe, I wonder if you would like to go to a film with me? I have two tickets for *The Tempest*.'

'Thank you, but today I already have a date,' she answered politely. 'Perhaps another time.'

She brushed him off gently and rushed to keep her appointment with Takamori at a coffee shop in Yurakucho. He was on time for a change. When she arrived, he was sitting against the wall, smoking a cigarette and staring at a fish-bowl filled with tropical fish.

'What did you want to see me about?'

'Well . . .'

'Something to do with Gaston, I'll bet.'

'How did you guess?'

'Because he's been on my mind all day too.'

'I wonder what he's doing in Yamagata just about now.'

'Tomoe, I . . .' Takamori ground out his cigarette firmly in the ashtray. 'I'm thinking of asking for a week's leave. Last year I didn't take a single day, so I'm due for it. I'd like to go to Yamagata. I somehow feel that to abandon Gaston now would be like throwing away the best part of myself. That's the way I feel.'

After this open declaration of his feelings, he began to scratch his head in embarrassment. 'I'm going to Yamagata,' he announced with decision.

'I wonder if I might come along too.' Tomoe put her spoon in her coffee cup and closed her eyes.

'But there's no need for you to go as well! You needn't put yourself out any further for Gaston. Aren't you the one who was always complaining about him?' Takamori's words were intentionally needling.

'Then why are you going?'

'I told you. I have my own view of Gaston. You've always made fun of him. I haven't.'

It was unusual for Takamori to take advantage of his sister's vulnerability like this. For once she had no comeback, other than a pathetic look of appeal. It was painful for her to admit the truth to her brother.

'I wasn't necessarily looking down on him. Even I could see that he was a good man – too good, in fact. Still, I don't find anything attractive in that kind of man.'

'Attractive?'

'Yes, attractive. He's lacking in all the manly virtues.' Finally Tomoe found the words to ward off her brother's attack. 'That face, those clothes . . . But that's not the worst. What about his weakness, his cowardice? Doesn't he break down and cry like a girl? I don't think you could exactly call him a man to appeal to women.'

'Is that so? Yes, I suppose it is.' He lit his second cigarette.

'Don't you think I had reason then for getting the wrong impression of him?' Tomoe was beginning to taste a little the pride of victory.

'But look here, Tomoe. Not all men are handsome and strong. There are some who are cowards from birth. There are some who are weak by nature. There are even some who cry easily. But for such a man, a man both weak and cowardly, to bear the burden of his weakness and struggle valiantly to live a beautiful life – that's what I call great. The reason I'm so fond of Gaston is not because he has a strong will or a good head. Rather it's because, weakling and coward that he is, he keeps on fighting in his own way.

I feel much more drawn to Gaston than I would to a splendid saint or hero.'

The two were silent for a time. Tomoe had never heard Takamori speak so seriously about anything before. He was usually too embarrassed to air his deepest thoughts like this. Whenever a conversation became the least bit serious, he usually interjected a frivolous note or diverted it to other channels. This was the Takamori who was now defending Gaston so earnestly.

'Why do you suppose he ever came to Japan?' Tomoe asked her brother the same question she had asked Gaston in the restaurant in Yotsuya.

'I haven't the slightest idea. He's a mysterious one, that Gaston.'

It was a beautifully clear day. The express train, Aoba, had left Ueno Station at nine that morning and was now beyond Koyama and Utsunomiya. The volcanic range of Nasu could be seen far to the left.

'Don't you ever stop eating?' Tomoe lifted her face from her magazine and gave her brother a look of disgust.

A grunt was his only answer. Still moving his jaws, he turned his face to the window. Neither he nor Tomoe had ever been to the Tohoku region. As children they had once or twice been all the way south to Kagoshima, where their grandparents had lived, but this was the first time they had travelled north.

In the blue sky were a couple of woolly clouds. A gentle wind was blowing through the green groves of trees. The backs of the leaves, turned upward by the wind, had a silvery sheen. Even the far-off mountains of Nasu seemed to sparkle in the sun.

'Tomoe, this is where the Tohoku region begins,' pointed out Takamori. 'From here on out we're in north country.'

'Be careful not to drop ice cream on your trousers.'

'It's good to be away from Tokyo. It's been a long time

since I've seen open country like this. Tokyo shrinks people's hearts. They become irritable like you. That's not for me.'

'If you eat any more, you're sure to upset your stomach.'

Takamori pressed his face to the window. He could see a river flowing along, raising a cold spray. A girl of the village was riding a bicycle across a bridge.

Gas must have passed here too, thought Takamori. He must have looked out over this very scene. But no, Gaston was on the night train. It would have been pitch dark when he passed here. Everyone else would have been fast asleep.

Takamori imagined Gaston as he sat in the night coach, his long legs awkwardly contracted to fit into the narrow space between the seats. He would be the only one still awake. What would he be looking at? Had he kept his eyes fixed on the stars in the black sky, as he had that other night when the two had looked at them together? The wind threatened to blow them out, but they would submit to no threat and kept on guarding their flames all through the night.

From Fukushima the train gradually began to climb into the steep mountains. It was hemmed in on both sides by mountains covered with pine and cryptomeria. It passed through tunnel after tunnel and finally reached the famous Itaya Peak.

'The snow must really pile up here in winter.' Takamori thought he would enjoy coming here again with Gaston when there was snow.

After reaching Itaya Peak the number of passengers using the Tohoku dialect seemed suddenly to increase.

The sky was now somewhat clouded. Fruit orchards were to be seen everywhere. On the terraced mountain sides were trellised grape vines the height of a man. In autumn the grapes probably reflected the light of the setting sun. Chestnut trees covered with white flowers stood out strikingly from the other trees in the groves. There were also apple and peach trees, their fruit covered with paper bags for protection; and cherry trees, loaded down with bright red cherries. As the train plunged deeper into Tohoku country, the trees became more and more numerous.

'Do you know what they call that kind of cherry? They call it "Napoleon".'

Tomoe and Takamori were startled to overhear this fragment of conversation from a neighbouring seat. It was an uncanny coincidence that here in this region, which both they and Gaston were visiting for the first time, they should hear the name Napoleon.

The cherry trees, their silvery leaves fluttering in a slight breeze, proudly displayed cluster after cluster of ruby-coloured cherries. There were also cherries that had not yet turned red. Why had they named this cherry 'Napoleon'? Was it because it was the most imperial of the cherries? But as they looked out of the window at the cherry trees, Takamori and Tomoe had a different Bonaparte on their minds.

Four o'clock. After seven hours the train finally reached Yamagata. The sky which had been so clear when they left Tokyo was now quite clouded over. They had not noticed it so much in the train, but when they got out onto the station platform they found that it was a very sultry day. Walking outside the building, they noticed in the far sky heavy grey clouds that seemed to be drawing nearer. They were in for a thunder shower.

'Where will we stay?' asked Tomoe, suitcase in hand. She was afraid that it was going to start to rain.

'There seems to be one famous hotel here.' Takamori unfolded a map of the town which he had just bought in the station. 'Let's see. Araki Mataimon . . . Araki Mataimon.'

'What's that?'

'That's the name of the inn. It's not on the map. I don't suppose it's so famous after all.'

But when he gave the name of the inn to the driver of

one of the taxis lined up in front of the station, the driver knew where it was. They got into the taxi and the driver spoke to them, not in the native Tohoku dialect, but in standard Tokyo Japanese, which he seemed to be very proud of knowing.

'You must be from Tokyo. I used to live in Tokyo. Can you understand the Tohoku dialect? I had a hard time with it when I first moved here. But I've been here five years now and I get along all right in it.'

It began to rain. This old castle city, surrounded by the mountains, had not been bombed during the war, so there were still ancient camphor trees and the remains of old stone walls, covered with moss, and old houses reminiscent of the samurai houses of former ages.

The inn was near the centre of the town. 'That's the best inn in Yamagata,' the driver assured them.

It was indeed a splendid inn. From their second floor room Takamori and Tomoe looked down upon a beautiful Japanese garden with an artful arrangement of trees and stones, and even a fountain. There seemed to be hardly any other guests. When the elderly maid had shown them to their room, they had walked along winding corridors and had passed well-appointed rooms that seemed to be un-occupied.

'You must be tired from your long journey. Are you from Tokyo?' the maid asked in her Tohoku dialect as she folded Takamori's suit neatly.

'Tomoe, why don't you run along to the bath? I'll go a little later.'

Tomoe did as he suggested. Takamori asked the maid to teach him a few expressions in the Tohoku dialect. After she left the room, his ears were caught by the sound of the falling rain.

Raindrops fell steadily in the garden below. Occasion-ally a carp rose to the surface of the water in the fountain and then submerged again. Beyond the garden wall, which was concealed by trees, lay, apparently, a busy street.

Takamori could just faintly make out the sound of footsteps and of passing cars. As he lit a cigarette, he thought
how strange it was to be here in Yamagata like this.

Where is Gaston at this moment, he wondered. He must
be somewhere in the town, listening to the gently falling
rain. Or, knowing him, he's very likely somewhere out in
the rain by himself, looking like a stray dog.

Gaston was in fact walking through the rain along a back
street of the town. Occasionally the strains of a popular
song, from the radio of one of the houses he passed, reached
his ears, but otherwise everything was still.

Very few of the houses had tiled roofs. Instead, the roofs
were made of zinc sheeting, or else stones had been fitted
together in the ancient style. Here you could see the dark
poverty of the Tohoku area. But even these little houses, so
primitively built, had, unlike the houses of Tokyo, each its
little garden. The green leaves of the trees were wet with
rain and reflected whatever light still reached them. Large
pink flowers, whose name he did not know, were in bloom
in the hedges that enclosed the houses.

With one hand Gaston wiped the rain from his forehead, as with the other he munched on a chunk of bread.
He turned onto the main street and stopped, looking around
him for some sign of an inn. Finding one, he went to the
entrance and called out, 'Excuse me.'

When the maid came hurrying to the door, he asked in
a low voice, 'Is there a Mr Endo staying here?'

The maid looked at him with frightened eyes. Even
under ordinary circumstances Gaston's appearance was
startling, but now he was completely drenched and had
the look of an abandoned dog.

'Endo?' The maid turned to the clerk at the desk and
asked if anyone by that name was registered at the inn.
This man also gave Gaston a suspicious look and answered,
'Endo? No one by that name here.' When Gaston had
shuffled out of the door, the two exchanged glances and

the clerk spoke what was in both of their minds. 'He looks like a tramp.'

At the next place too Gaston got the same answer. Since the previous day, he had walked all over the city and inquired at countless inns. The response was always the same. The maids and the clerks gave him strange looks and told him there was no one by the name of Endo staying with them.

It had never occurred to him that Endo might have registered under an assumed name. So he had kept going from one inn to another, standing at the entrance of each and inquiring after a man by the name of Endo.

The rain had soaked through his clothes and was damp to the skin. He was tired and hungry. All he had had in his mouth since morning was the rain and a bit of bread he had bought at a bakery along the way.

It was already evening. He crossed the main street slowly and came to a stand in front of the inn where Takamori and Tomoe had just arrived. At this very moment Takamori was sitting in the rattan chair in his room looking out at the rain. Tomoe, up to her neck in clear, hot water, was luxuriating in her bath, her white fawn-like legs stretched out full length in complete relaxation.

At this inn too Gaston received the usual disappointing answer. Not dreaming, of course, that Takamori and Tomoe were there, Gaston, dragging along his tired legs, disappeared once more into the streets.

'Kobayashi? There are at least a hundred Kobayashis in Yamagata,' said the elderly policeman, looking up at Gaston. 'But don't stand out there in the rain. Come in and sit down.'

Gaston's appearance must have moved him to pity. The good-natured policeman was sipping lukewarm tea from a cracked teacup. He opened a drawer and drew from it an aluminium lunch box which he put before Gaston. 'Foreigner, won't you have something to eat?' As if to encourage him, he himself took a riceball into his hand and began to eat it.

'You're looking for someone named Kobayashi. Right?'

'Yes.'

'As I told you, there are at least a hundred Kobayashis in this town. Can you give me a further description of him?'

Gaston knew nothing at all about Kobayashi except what Endo had told him – that he had once been a soldier and had been stationed on a South Sea island.

'A soldier, you say? In the South Seas?' The old policeman thought a while and then said, 'You probably mean Ihei Kobayashi.'

Fortunately, Yamagata, unlike Tokyo, is only a town, and the inhabitants are simple and have a lively curiosity. In the long winter evenings they have nothing better to do than to sit around the fire and exchange news and gossip. The old policeman was acquainted with a Kobayashi that had been a soldier in the South Seas.

'If that's the one, he lives near Kosho-*machi*.'

'Kosho-*machi*?'

'It used to be the red light district,' the old man said smiling. 'But I don't expect you know the meaning of "red light", do you?'

Ten minutes later the policeman put on his raincoat and, pushing his bicycle, led Gaston to Kosho-*machi*.

'I'll leave you here. You'll find Kobayashi's house just around that corner.'

The rain had lessened considerably. This part of the town had once been the pleasure quarters of Yamagata. There were still a number of two- and three-storey buildings built in the old Edo style. But since the passing of the anti-prostitution law the place had lost all its gay activity and was now very sombre, even melancholy.

Gaston turned the corner as he had been told. The street was very narrow. On the left side was a pharmacy with the name of Takahashi, and next to it a shop that sold *sake.* Two houses beyond that Gaston saw hanging on the dirty glass door of a small house a sign that read 'Kobayashi – Land Surveyor'. He came up to it and looked in through the window. Imagine his surprise when he saw standing there near the door the very man he had been searching for!

Endo seemed to be waiting there for someone. His coat was flung over one arm, and a cigarette dangled from his lips. He was turned in such a way that he could not see Gaston looking in at him through the dirty glass of the door. When he had smoked the cigarette down almost to his lips, he flipped the butt to the floor and stamped it out with his cream-coloured summer shoes.

Gaston stood there staring, taking in the cocky angle of his shoulders, the slender nape of his neck, his white face, and his perfectly straight nose. Endo wiped his mouth with his handkerchief, as he had done so often during those two days in Sanya.

Suddenly another man was with him. From the dark interior of the house emerged a thin, feeble-looking man of over fifty. He had the face of a rat, especially round the eyes, which had a mean and shifty look.

'That must be Kobayashi!' Gaston decided. Knowing that Kobayashi had once been a soldier in the South Seas, he had expected to see a man much larger and better built, but he had been wrong. The man squatted in the doorway leading to the inner part of the house. The collar of his kimono was not pulled together at the neck, so that Gaston could see even his ribs. He scratched his legs, then unfolded a piece of paper for Endo to inspect and pointed repeatedly to one section of it. Endo was bent down, studying the paper. Kobayashi was explaining something to him with an obsequious smile on his rat-like face.

The situation struck Gaston as strange. He knew what Kobayashi meant to Endo. He had seen Endo's eyes fill with hatred and anger when at the construction site he had revealed his reason for going to Yamagata. How then explain the fact that the two men were now bent over that one piece of paper, laughing and talking as amicably as if they were old friends?

Rain began to pour down again. Large drops trickled off the eaves down Gaston's neck. Three children with running noses were staring curiously at him from the grocery store across the way.

Endo waved his hand, then made a sign with three fingers. Kobayashi nodded. Gaston heaved a heavy sigh. He suddenly felt very tired. In place of the fearful scene he had imagined, here were the two men conversing amiably together. While he was relieved to see it, he also felt a little as if he had been deceived.

Their conversation seemed to be at an end. Endo began to put on his coat. Kobayashi handed him an old umbrella. Endo slid open the glass door, which did not fit well on its runners, and, looking out at the grey skies, said goodbye to Kobayashi. 'I'll see you tomorrow, then.' Kobayashi saw him out of the door with the same obsequious smile as before.

Gaston let Endo walk about ten yards down the puddle-filled, muddy street before running after him and tapping him on the shoulder.

'Endo *san*!'

Endo's eyes opened wide in surprise, and he stood there wordlessly staring at Gaston, the old umbrella gripped in his right hand. The expression on his face was one of absolute astonishment. It was obvious that Gaston was the last person in the world he had expected to find standing there in front of him.

'Endo *san*!' With an amiable smile on his face, Gaston tapped him again on the shoulder, greatly delighted to have given him such a shock by his sudden appearance.

'You!'. Endo finally found his voice. 'You.' He added nothing more but turned his face aside quickly. He spat once on the ground and began to walk off rapidly, using the umbrella to conceal his face.

'Endo *san*, wait for me!'

But the man with TB did not even look back. When he heard Gaston's footsteps behind him on the puddle-strewn street, he walked all the faster. The street curved to the right and then to the left.

Not another soul was to be seen on this backstreet of Yamagata. Everything was enveloped in a mist of rain. Above a stone wall that had half-collapsed was a huge camphor tree whose wet leaves filled the air with a pleasant fragrance. Along this street were many temples. It seemed as if the white walls of the temple enclosures went on forever. Meizen-ji, Shinen-ji, Enryo-ji, Taiho-in. Where the wall of one temple came to an end, that of the next one began. From behind the walls could be heard the chanting of sutras and the hollow beating of a drum. The sound served but to deepen the stillness of the street.

Endo came to a halt and listened for the footsteps of the odd foreigner, but they were no longer to be heard. He felt oppressed. 'What's he trying to do to me? Following me all the way here to Yamagata . . .'

There was something eerie about this fool of a foreigner. Endo had not the slightest idea why Gaston should have followed him to Yamagata and searched him out like this.

The chanting of the sutras was in time with the beat of the drum. Endo was now in front of Sensho-ji, which was spread over a larger area than the other temples. Beyond the gate to this temple stood a towering gingko tree that must have been two or three hundred years old.

Suddenly from the foot of the gingko tree someone called his name. It was the idiot voice of Gaston, whom he thought he had left far behind. He might just as well have been a ghost come swimming through the rain. How had he ever managed to find a short cut on his own and to ambush him here like this? The man was uncanny.

'Endo *san*, I want to talk to you.'

Strange to say, Endo just stood there vacantly and allowed Gaston to draw near him. Then suddenly he felt a pain in his chest, probably brought on by the over-exertion. A lump of something came welling up in his throat. He spat it out. It hit a stone of the temple gate, and bright red blood formed a pattern in the rainwater collected there.

The rain had stopped. By nightfall it was sweltering. Yamagata, surrounded as it is on all sides by mountains, becomes far hotter than is usual for that latitude. The record for the highest temperature ever reached in Japan was set in Yamagata.

This evening too it was very hot and there was no breeze. The blinds clung motionless to the dirty windows, and even the mats were sticky with the oppressive heat.

In olden days the house had been a brothel, but with the suppression of prostitution it had been converted into an inn. The smell of the men and women who had spent their lustful nights here still seemed to exude from the walls and the sliding doors, still decorated with flowers and birds. No one had bothered to brush off the remains of swatted mosquitoes.

Endo lay moistening his dry lips with his tongue and staring at the ceiling. The shade of the ceiling lamp cast a shadow that resembled a bat.

Gaston was sitting in his shirtsleeves at his side. Occasionally he wrung out a wet cloth from a basin beside him and wiped Endo's face.

After the incident at the entrance to Sensho Temple, the killer had managed with Gaston's help to return to his inn. Discovering that he had a high temperature, he had gone to bed. The heat, the rain and the long journey had worn him out completely.

A moth flew in through the window blinds and began to circle round and round the lamp. Gaston got up, caught it and let it fly out of the window but, attracted by the light, it only flew back in again, dropping from its wings a powdery substance.

'Kill it! Why don't you kill it?' barked Endo impatiently. When he saw that Gaston had caught the moth by its wings but was hesitating to kill it, he was instantly filled with an overpowering hatred for this man.

'You hypocrite!' Endo snatched the moth from him and crushed it mercilessly with his pillow. 'How long do you plan to hang around this room? You intend to keep on dogging me, do you?'

'Endo *san* . . . ill. I'll leave when you get well.'

Now that Gaston had seen that Endo had no intention of harming Kobayashi, his only remaining function, he thought, was to nurse the sick man.

'I'm not going to lie here in Yamagata forever, let me tell you.' He began to cough again. 'I'm getting up to-morrow.'

'Tomorrow? No, no! . . . You're ill.'

'Tomorrow I have to get up.' Looking up at the shadow cast by the lamp-shade, Endo thought of what he had to do the following day. On the morrow he was planning to climb Mt Takamori and Mt Shirataka, two of the mountains encircling Yamagata, with Kobayashi. To understand the reason for this expedition, it is necessary to go back three days.

Endo, upon arriving in Yamagata and taking up lodging at this inn in Kosho-*machi*, quickly discovered Kobayashi's house and began to keep a close watch over his comings and goings. He carefully planned the place and opportunity for confrontation.

Kobayashi, who had a sign that read 'Land Surveyor' over his door, was scurrying about Yamagata like a rat. He was, it seemed, providing people with many services. He looked into the registration of land, compared the recorded dimensions with the actual ones and prepared valuations for the buyer. He also gave information to the land speculators who roamed the mountains of the Tohoku region, prepared to buy up entire mountains, if only it were profitable.

The figure of Kobayashi in his drab, worn-out kimono, making the rounds of local government offices, the land-registry office and surveyors, did indeed remind Endo of a rat scurrying about for food. The people in the neighbourhood regarded him with pity and contempt.

'So the grand Major of the Japanese Army has come down to this!' thought Endo, watching him.

After following him around for two days, even Endo, to whom this man was the enemy, could not help being moved to something akin to pity.

When Endo looked into Kobayashi's small, flimsily-built home, he always saw Kobayashi's wife, worn down by her household duties, sitting at the kitchen door, legs outstretched, scrubbing clothes that were no better than rags. A little boy with a swollen stomach always played beside her. Every time he looked in upon this scene, Endo, hard as he was, had to steel himself against a feeling of compassion. He kept watch at a window of his inn from which he could see everything that took place at Kobayashi's. One day, two days he watched, waiting for the chance he needed.

On the afternoon of the third day he saw Kobayashi, who had been indoors all morning, emerge busily from his hole. As usual his emaciated chest could be seen between the folds of his loosely worn, dirty kimono. Endo hastily put on his coat and prepared to follow him.

Although the day had started out clear, from about noon the Yamagata skies had begun to cloud over. The rays of the sun reached the earth through the filter of grey clouds.

Kobayashi began to walk down the street. Endo followed him to Seventh-day-*machi*, the liveliest section of town and known as the 'Yamagata Ginza'. Occasionally Kobayashi passed someone he knew, and a shifty rat-like smile came over his face as he bowed obsequiously.

'Where're you headed for?' a man on a bicycle called out to him.

'I have some business over in Umamigasaki,' answered Kobayashi.

When he heard 'Umamigasaki', Endo saw his opportunity. The day he had arrived in Yamagata he had made the rounds of the town, map in hand. For his meeting with Kobayashi he had to find a place that would be deserted. The field of Umamigasaki was perfect. It was close to town, but even in the middle of the day almost no one was to be seen there.

Kobayashi had not noticed that he was being followed. He walked along with short, quick steps in his old, worn-down wooden clogs. When he came to the local government offices, he entered the office of the Notary Public and stood there talking for a time with the man who seemed to be in charge.

Five minutes later he emerged and began walking in the direction of Miyata-*machi*. From Miyata-*machi* it is only a short distance to the river.

Except on rainy days there is almost no water in the river at Umamigasaki. All that can be seen in the white river bed are massive stones scattered here and there. At night it is an ideal rendezvous for lovers.

When they reached the river bank, Endo quickened his pace to draw near to the man. He caught up to him and whispered his own name in his ear. Kobayashi's emaciated face turned as pale as wax.

'Will you walk with me down to the river bed?'

Fortunately, there was no one to be seen either on the road or in the fields. The only sign of another human presence was a truck that crossed a bridge in the distance and quickly vanished from sight.

'A . . . A . . . A . . . Ah' Kobayashi moved his lips, but could only stutter.

'What's the matter?'

Somewhere over to their left was the dump where all the

town's refuse was hauled and burned. The offensive stink of rot and decay was in the air.

'What's the matter, Mr Kobayashi?' Endo asked with exaggerated politeness.

That day at the construction site on the Ginza, the more politely Endo had addressed this man's accomplice, Kanai, the more that man had lost his self-possession and manifested surprise and fear. So it was now with Kobayashi. He shrank away from Endo, his lean chest still visible through the opening of his kimono. He could only stutter a response.

'What's that you say, Mr Kobayashi?'

As if pushing him with his body, Endo inched the rodent-like man in the direction of the white river bed where large stones lay scattered. Crickets, which until then had been singing between the stones, suddenly fell still, perhaps in token of approaching rain. There was a town-owned plant for crushing stones not very far away, and a small shack for the workers who came to collect the stones stood on the river bank.

'Let's go in here. . . . Here.'

'I'll re . . . re . . . re . . . turn it,' Kobayashi stuttered.

'Return?' When they reached the entrance to the shack, Endo put his hand into his coat. His fingers touched the hard steel of his pistol. 'Return? What will you return?'

Then looking into the other's face, Endo set a trap.

'So you were hiding it after all!'

Of course Endo had not the slightest notion of what it was Kobayashi was hiding. For that very reason he led him on.

Intuitively he realized that it had something to do with his brother, who had been killed for a crime he had not committed.

'Mr Kobayashi, let's hear the whole story inside. . . . Besides, it's started to rain.' From the clouded skies raindrops had begun to fall, staining the stones of the white river bed.

It was dark inside the shack. Against the wall, which had been made of lumber scraps, rested a shovel and a basket for carrying earth.

'Then suppose you bring out what you've been hiding.'

'Not . . . not . . . not . . . here . . . Swamp.'

'Swamp?'

Endo heard the full story now for the first time. Fourteen years earlier Kanai and Kobayashi, of the same battalion as his brother, had plotted together and succeeded in hiding away a portion of the bars of silver that had been confiscated from the local bank. So that no one would be able to reveal their secret, Kanai had ordered all the natives who had helped in burying the silver to be killed, and he and Kobayashi had laid the blame on Endo's brother. Now at last Endo had an inkling of why his brother had never written him the full details.

'What swamp?' Endo's manner of speech changed abruptly. 'You bastard! You hid the bars in a swamp?'

'It wasn't me. Kanai made me do it.'

'All right, all right. Which swamp?'

'A place called "Big Swamp".'

In a trembling voice Kobayashi stammered out his confession.

In July of 1944, a year before the end of the war, Kobayashi and Kanai returned to Japan from the South Sea island where they had been stationed. Kanai had seen clearly that the war was not going well and had wangled a change of assignment for them from central command. Kobayashi had become an instructor to a regiment at Headquarters and Kanai had found a supply job with the Eastern Army. Neither of them ever intended to return to the front. Kanai took charge of two-thirds of the silver they had secretly carried off the island and Kobayashi of the remaining third.

When the war ended, Kanai sold his silver bars to a Korean and with the profits started a trading company. But Kobayashi, not as bold as Kanai and afflicted with both pangs of conscience and fears of discovery, could not bring himself to touch the silver. He was even afraid that his family would come to know of it, and so he decided to hide the bars.

They could hear the rain beating down on the roof of the shack. Their eyes had gradually grown accustomed to the dark.

'Are you telling me the truth, Kobayashi?' asked Endo, smiling sarcastically. He lit his cigarette lighter and surveyed the other man's face. In the feeble light ugly black shadows lay over his face, which had the look of dried tangerine peel.

'Where is this "Big Swamp"?'

Hoping to be able to appease Endo, Kobayashi earnestly began to explain the position of the swamp. Crossing over the nearest mountains one came to a series of swamp ponds, the result, perhaps, of an ancient volcano. The largest of these was Big Swamp.

An ancient legend was associated with it. The dragon god of this swamp was wont to invade a neighbouring swamp to carry off the lady who was its mistress. One day a samurai by the name of Fujigoro was sound asleep at the edge of the swamp when a maiden appeared to him in a vivid dream and begged him to save her. She asked him to rescue her from the master of Big Swamp. When he awoke, waves were stirring in the deep, dark waters. He put an arrow to his bow and shot into the waves, and the swamp became still again.

Endo imagined the gloomy swamp in the heart of the mountains. He could not really give full credence to Kobayashi's tale of having hidden the silver bars there. The man might just possibly be setting a trap for him. If the story were true, he would have clear proof of his brother's innocence. In either case, he had to go. He had nothing to lose by it.

'All right, then. Take me there.'

Kobayashi pointed out that they would need tools. He

begged Endo to accompany him home, at least to have a look at the map. This was reasonable enough.

It was decided that the following morning Kobayashi would lead Endo to the mountains. But in his present physical condition, how would he ever make it?

Endo looked vacantly at Gaston, who was wiping his forehead with a wet cloth. Suddenly he thought of a way of making use of this foreigner.

The most depressing thing about country inns is generally the food. Guests from Tokyo would like nothing better than to taste the food that is the speciality of the region in which they are travelling. But in most second-class inns only the most ordinary kinds of food, such as one can find anywhere at any time, are served.

But the meal that was served that evening at the Araki Mataimon did not disappoint even such discerning gourmets as Takamori and Tomoe. They were treated to well-cooked fish and vegetables native to Yamagata. The last dish to be served was a cut-glass sauce dish heaped up with yellow cherries.

'I wonder if these are Napoleons?' Tomoe put a cherry into her mouth to see how it tasted. It was sweeter than the cherries she had eaten in Tokyo.

'I'm afraid they're not very tasty,' the maid apologized. 'It's still a little early. The season's late this year.'

'Oh, no. These are delicious.'

As brother and sister ate the cherries, they were silent, their thoughts on Gaston. They felt somehow apologetic to Gaston to be sitting here like this after a good meal eating this delicious dessert.

The rain finally stopped, and they were visited by a hot, windless, sultry night.

While Tomoe explained to the maid that they were searching in Yamagata for a foreigner friend of theirs, Takamori lay stretched out on the mat before a map of Yamagata.

The names of the various sections of Yamagata were very interesting. Many of the sections seemed to be named after the objects made by the craftsmen who lived there : Lacquer-*machi*, Silver-*machi*, Candle-*machi*, Bucket-*machi*. Then there were Seventh-day-*machi*, Eighth-day-*machi*, Tenth-day-*machi* – all named according to the day of market in that section. There were also Farmer-*machi*, Inn-*machi*, and Carpenter-*machi*.

'How did you make out?' Takamori asked Tomoe in a low voice when she ended her conversation with the maid in the corridor and returned to the room.

'She says the town's not very large. A foreigner is so conspicuous here that he should be easy to find. She's promised to telephone all the inns in town this evening.' Tomoe sat down beside her brother.

'That's kind of her.'

'I wonder if we oughtn't to get in touch with the police.'

'Let's do that last. After we've tried everything else. We don't want to have Gaston treated like a criminal.'

This sounded reasonable also to Tomoe.

'What are you looking at?'

'A map. There are many places here with interesting names. Here, for example, "Fox-Crossing Road". See how many ponds and swamps there are in the vicinity of Yamagata. Mountain ponds are rather romantic, don't you think, Tomoe? If we find Gaston, how about going there on a hike, the three of us?'

They could hear the sound of the television downstairs. Someone was watching a night baseball game.

When the maid came to put down their bedding, she told them she had called the seven or eight major inns in Yamagata but that there was no foreigner by the name of Gaston Bonaparte staying at any of them.

'But I'll also phone up to the spa hotel on the mountain.' She added that this was a spa similar to those in Atami.

'Then maybe it's time we called the police,' Takamori

and Tomoe decided as they lay down and prepared to get
some rest.

In this condition, spitting up blood as he was, he would
have a hard time climbing the mountains tomorrow. Checking his map, he saw that Big Swamp was between Mt
Higashi-Kuromori, which was 2,300 feet high, and Mt
Takamori, 2,400 feet high. Of course, in contrast to the
old days, there was now a bus going there. But Endo
thought it best to leave early, before dawn, so as to avoid
meeting anyone on the way.

According to Kobayashi, even at these mountain swamps
one occasionally ran into woodcutters or fishermen with
poles, come to fish for carp. For that reason he too urged
that they leave while it was still dark, so that no one
would see them pull out the silver.

There was no need for Endo to explain to Gaston why
he was climbing the mountain. Even without explanation,
Gaston would be sure to follow him to the swamp. If he
were not able to struggle up a particularly steep slope, he
could get this huge man to carry him on his back. Gaston
would also be of help in pulling the heavy silver bars out
of the pond.

Endo lay on his back staring vacantly at the shadows
cast on the ceiling by the gently swaying light. The
time for revenge on Kobayashi has finally come, he
thought.

It would be after they had found the silver bars. But if
Gaston should try the same kind of stunt he had the last
time, then what? Will I kill him? Endo wondered.

He stole a look at Gaston, who was sitting up against
the wall with his long legs drawn up to his chest and
encircled in his arms. He had fallen off to sleep. It seemed
as if the fatigue of that long day's activity had finally taken
its toll.

What a stupid-looking face! His mouth was slightly
open, and there were drops of saliva drooling down his

chin. From that long face came the sound of a gentle snoring.

'If it should come to that, would I really kill him?'

He didn't want to. But supposing that tomorrow circumstances seemed to require his death, he might very well pump a bullet into this big face with the drooling mouth. For some reason, even imagining this possibility gave Endo a feeling of cruel, dark regret.

'Hey!' He called to Gaston in a low voice. 'Hey, Gas!'

Gaston opened his eyes and looked about him, still in a daze. He had probably been dreaming. Blinking his eyes, he looked at Endo and then about the room. He mumbled something in French, and then, 'Oh, Endo *san*, I'll change the towel at once.' In consternation he reached for the water basin.

'Do you know what I was just thinking?' asked Endo, wetting his feverish lips with his tongue. 'Someday I may kill you. . . . Sometimes you give me such a pain that I can't stand you. You fake! Pretending to be a good man! Who do you think you're fooling? Hypocrite! I'd like to pull that skin off your face, pull off that mask.' And he laughed.

It was four-thirty in the morning. Gaston opened his eyes to find Endo shaking his shoulders. The blinds drawn down over the open windows of the room were just the least bit light, but the sky was still very dark. Not a sound could be heard in the inn, which was still steeped in sleep.

'Time to get up.'

Endo already had his shirt and trousers on. The hotel kimono he had worn for sleeping was rolled up in a ball at the foot of his bed. As he put on his coat, he coughed up some phlegm. Gaston caught a glimpse of the Colt pistol in its holster under his suitcoat.

'Where are we going, Endo *san*? You shouldn't move.'

Without answering him, Endo opened the door into the corridor, and motioned Gaston to go out.

The front hall was still dark when they came down, but someone, evidently alerted by their footsteps, turned on a light. A clerk appeared. He looked as if he had just left his bed.

'I'm not sure we'll be coming back here,' explained Endo as he put on his shoes. 'So I'll pay the bill now.' He pulled several notes from his pocket and handed them to the clerk, whose thick lips broke into a wide smile that revealed the gold in his teeth.

The street too was still dark. An occasional fluorescent street-lamp broke the darkness. The squeaking wheels of a small truck – a milk truck, perhaps, or else the truck of a farmer bringing his vegetables to market – could be heard on the otherwise silent, empty street.

When they reached the corner in front of Yamagata Bank, Endo stopped. Across the street, metal shutters were pulled down over the entrances to a cinema and a bank.

'Where are we going, Endo *san*?'

'It doesn't matter. If you don't want to come along, you can go back.' The killer had his left hand over his heart. It seemed to be painful for him to breathe. 'I never told you to follow me.' When Gaston didn't answer, he urged, 'That's true, isn't it?'

Gaston blinked his eyes and looked up at Endo with an expression of appeal that was now quite familiar.

'Endo *san*, do you hate me?'

' "Hate" is not the word. From the bottom of my heart I detest you.' He had a wry smile on his face. 'That long stupid face of yours makes me want to puke.'

Neither spoke for a while. Endo looked at his watch and saw that it was five o'clock.

The bank and cinema across the way were already more visible than before. The day had begun to break. A newspaper boy drove by on his bicycle. Now they could hear footsteps in the distance. The steps stopped for a moment and then came on again. Kobayashi came into sight. He was wearing an old raincoat and had on high boots.

Endo whistled to him. He saw them and came in their direction. Catching his first glimpse of Gaston, the rat-faced man looked up at him suspiciously. Endo walked up to him and began to explain something, turning occasionally to look back at Gaston.

12   The Dark Swamp

When Endo had finished his conversation with Kobayashi, he called Gaston over and gave him the thick rope and large shovel the man had brought with him.

Gaston had not the slightest idea what the rope and shovel were for, nor even where they were going. It was enough for him that Endo was speaking amicably with Kobayashi and seemed to have forgotten the hostility and hatred he had once borne him. He did not know how the two had come to make their peace with each other, but, however it had come about, it was certainly preferable to senseless and bloody murder.

'You've made up?' Gaston said smiling, looking at the faces of the two men. He was so pleased to make up a third in their party that he began to whistle.

'Knock off that racket!' Endo shouted at Gaston, who stopped in mid-note, his lips still puckered.

The three began to walk in silence. Kobayashi and Endo walked in front and Gaston followed behind with the shovel and the rope. The street of Fifth-day-*machi* was still wrapped in sleep.

'Are you sure you can trust that foreigner?' asked Kobayashi in a voice loud enough for Gaston to hear. 'I don't distrust him but . . .'

'I'm giving the orders around here,' answered Endo sharply in a low voice. 'Just do as you're told.'

Kobayashi laughed obsequiously and said nothing more.

Day gradually began to break. Dark purple clouds still covered the sky, but there was a rim of light over the mountains.

'Is it far from here?' asked Endo. He had to stop from time to time to spit.

Yamagata had seemed to be hemmed in by mountains, but emerging now onto a broad plain, they found that the road they were following seemed to go on for ever and the mountains to be a great distance off.

'Endo *san*, are you all right?' asked Gaston, worried to see Endo stop so often to spit. In reply Endo merely glared at him fiercely.

'Are you ill?' asked Kobayashi. He seemed surprised. Even in the dim light of early morning Endo did not fail to note that Kobayashi, until now so obsequious, wore a strange smile.

'Why do you smile, Kobayashi *san*? It's true I'm not well. There's a hole in my lung. But try anything funny and you'll have a hole to match mine.'

There now came into view the low, narrow roofs of the first village along the way. How far had they gone?

They came to the end of the plain and started up the slope of Mt Toyoshima. Though only a small mountain, no more than about 1,200 feet high, the ascent was quite steep. From the plain it had seemed that the skies over the mountains were clear, but after they had climbed for a time they ran into the same misty rain they had encountered the day before.

To their right were fields that seemed to bear few crops. In narrow strips of cultivated land surrounded by mulberry trees grew onions and scraggy clusters of wheat and corn. Nothing else.

The path had many turns, so that it seemed as if they would never reach the top. Beyond this mountain they still had to pass through the valley that lay between Mt Matsumori and Mt Takamori.

Endo was finding it hard to breathe. Gaston, walking behind him with the shovel and rope, could see the rapid pump-like movement of his shoulders as he struggled for air. When Endo looked back at him, as he did at regular intervals, Gaston could see that he was in pain. Beads of perspiration stood out on his forehead and his hair was plastered to his head in sweat.

'We'll take a short rest,' announced Endo, as he plopped himself down on a boulder at the side of the road. He seemed unable to make it even one step further. Breathing heavily, he held his head in his hands.

A wind-driven mist came blowing down from the mountain to the grove of cryptomeria* where they rested. A fine rain, rather than mist, it made its way through their clothes all the way to the skin.

Kobayashi was protected from the weather by his raincoat and hood. Moreover, he had once been an army officer and was still unexpectedly robust for his age. Looking at Endo stretched out on the boulder as if he had not the energy to go another step, the strange smile returned to his hollow cheeks. He seemed to be amused at the sight of this killer who had so little physical stamina. It was apparent that he had something in mind, perhaps a plan of escape, as he looked in the direction of the cryptomeria grove, which was now hidden in the misty rain.

Endo got up and began to climb again in silence. Ordinarily Gaston would have found this an easy climb, but he had not had a single decent meal since reaching Yamagata and only two or three hours of sleep the night before. Besides, he was carrying the equipment on his back.

'Are we almost there?'

'No,' Kobayashi answered coldly. 'We haven't gone one-third of the way yet.'

Endo coughed up more phlegm. He sounded as if he were scraping it out of his throat. Bright red threads of blood were again to be seen in the phlegm as he spat it out.

'You've got a pretty bad dose of TB, haven't you?' said Kobayashi, taken aback at the sight of the blood. Then

---

* A Japanese cedar, *cryptomeria japonica.*

he smiled the same strange smile and added, 'You'll never make it to Big Swamp.'

'Just don't try to get away from me, I warn you,' Endo snapped back at him.

'All right. I get you.'

Suddenly Endo had the Colt in his hand. Gaston took one surprised look at it and shouted, 'Endo *san*, you promised.'

'I'm not going to shoot him, Gas . . . unless he tries to run away.'

The higher they climbed, the denser grew the fog. Trees and rocks only a few yards ahead of them were enshrouded in the milk-like mist and revealed only their outlines.

Endo lagged a little behind the other two, so that at times he was hidden in the fog. By his painful coughing, however, they knew he was still with them. The plain from which they had begun their ascent was no longer to be seen, and there were no more houses or fields along the road. Everything was one all-enclosing sheet of fog. Walking in that fog was like travelling through another world, like being inside a grey dream. It felt as if one were being sucked to the bottom of a milk-coloured swamp where neither time nor space existed.

Gaston didn't know where he was walking. He had lost even the awareness that he was in Japan. In his native Savoy, which bordered on the Swiss Alps, there were many mountains over 6,000 feet high.

'Where am I walking? Am I climbing one of the mountains of Savoy? Am I on my way to gather firewood with my friends?'

The illusion was broken by the dry coughing of Endo behind him. And ahead of him he saw the rubber boots and worn-out old raincoat of Kobayashi.

Yes, certainly, this was Japan. And he was on a mountain near a town called Yamagata which he had never even dreamed of before.

Why had he come to Japan? Yes, he had finally come,

but so far he had only given people trouble. He had only wandered about like a stray dog. He had only won the hatred of this man, Endo, whom he had wanted to help.

He was of no use to anyone. If he should die now here on this mountain, he realized sorrowfully, there would be no one to mourn for him. Takamori and Tomoe might be surprised, it was true, but in a month they would have forgotten him.

'All I've ever done is tag along behind people.' It was the same now with Endo. He had been unable to induce in him a change of heart or even to calm his troubled spirit. All he was able to do was follow along behind.

Endo wiped the sweat off his forehead with his hand and dragged his tired feet along, telling himself 'only another hundred yards, only another hundred yards'. When those hundred yards had been covered, he concentrated on getting over the next hundred. In this fog it was hard to know what Kobayashi might try. He recalled the well-used Bible his brother had sent him just after he had been conscripted into the army. He recalled also the night he had first coughed up blood.

'In this physical condition I'd be dead now, had it not been for my hatred of this man. Hatred can also give strength to live.'

At last way off in the distance the blue-black surface of a pond appeared through the rents opened in the fog by a slight wind. On the bank of the pond was a shack. They had arrived at Big Swamp. They could not tell how far it was from one side of the pond to the other, since a heavy mist clung to the cold-looking, black surface of the water. A portion of the opposite bank, covered by a small copse, floated up out of the mist like an island. Since the fog moved wave-like across the pond, it seemed as if even this island were slowly moving.

On the rain-soaked bank of the pond was the chassis of an old bus that had been abandoned here. Beyond the chassis was the shack they had spotted earlier. It had probably been built to give shelter and refreshment to hikers who made their way here in summer, but today there was no one in sight. Still, Endo took the precaution of making certain.

'Gas, go over and take a look,' Endo told Gaston. 'See if you can find something to drink . . . water at least.'

'It's dangerous to send the foreigner. He's bound to arouse suspicion. I'll get the water.' Kobayashi intercepted Gaston, afraid of what the reaction to Gaston's strange appearance might be.

Endo and Gaston concealed themselves in the abandoned bus, while Kobayashi, walking through the puddles of water in his high boots, approached the shack. When he knocked, a man dressed like a farmer came to the door. Kobayashi spoke to him, and he disappeared again inside.

Resting against the wall of the dilapidated bus as drops of rain fell down on them through the leaking roof, Endo started to polish his pistol. Sweat was running down his forehead. His sunken cheeks, far more hollow now than they had been in Tokyo, and the dark shadows below his eyes, indicative of illness, gave evidence of all that he had been through these past three days.

'Endo *san*, let's go home,' Gaston urged in a low voice.

Endo did not answer him, but his hands continued their activity. He pulled the cartridge out of his pistol, examined the bullets, put the cartridge back in again, engaged the safety catch, then put the pistol back into his pocket.

Kobayashi returned, his boots squishing in the puddles. He brought with him three bottles of orange soda.

'This is all there was.'

'The man didn't get suspicious, did he?'

'No, it's all right. He's here to fish.'

'You didn't telephone to Yamagata from there, by any chance?'

'Talk sense! How would that help me?'

All the same Endo continued to eye Kobayashi with suspicion, even as he drank his soda. He finished only half of

the bottle and then threw it out of window of the bus into
the swamp below. Making almost no sound, the bottle
disappeared into the fog.

'All right. Lead me to the place.'

'Don't be in such a hurry. I'm still drinking.' Kobayashi's
attitude had changed. In contrast to his previous air of
servility, there was now a tone of arrogance in his voice.

'What did you say?' Endo barked out.

'It's only a hundred yards ahead of us. What we're looking for won't disappear before we get there.'

If Gaston wasn't staying at an inn in town, he might be at
the mountain spa hotel, the maid and the clerk of their
inn suggested to Takamori and Tomoe. So they telephoned
to the spa hotel and discovered that there was no foreigner
of Gaston's description staying there, but that four or five
days earlier a guest at the hotel had reported seeing a
foreigner walking along the street with a Japanese.

'How about going there and inquiring direct?' suggested the fat proprietor of the inn. Takamori and Tomoe
had learned from the maid upon their arrival that this
man was an influential member of the Mountain Climbers'
Association.

'It's a very small village. If he's still there, you should be
able to find him at once.'

It would take only half an hour by car. Until about a
year ago, according to the proprietor's explanation, it had
been a highly prospering spa. But after the anti-prostitution
bill had become law, it had quickly deteriorated to its
present unflourishing state.

After lunch Takamori and Tomoe called a taxi and
started for the top of the mountain. They left the town
and climbed along a smooth asphalt road. In the hedges
of farmhouses along the way and at the gate of a school
large-petalled magnolias were in bloom.

The village at the top was like all spa villages in Japan.
Lined up along both sides of the street were shops selling

wooden *kokeshi* dolls* and cake boxes, pachinko parlours, shooting galleries and the like and beyond these were a number of hotels and inns.

Seeing that they were here, Tomoe decided to pick out gifts for the family. She bought a small Nambu iron kettle for her mother and a doll modelled after a Yamagata farm girl for Matchan.

When Takamori asked the girl attending the shop if she had seen a foreigner of Gaston's description, she answered, blushing a deep red, 'I wonder if it could be the foreigner that came to the common bath.'

The 'common bath' was a bath where the people of the village, irrespective of sex, came to bathe at any time of the day for only two yen. Takamori could well picture Gaston entering one of these.

'Where do you suppose he was staying?'

'I heard he was at Hoshioka Hotel.'

The village was so small that a foreigner as conspicuous as Gaston would soon be the subject of village gossip.

But when the brother and sister paid a visit to Hoshioka Hotel, they were disappointed. It was true that a foreigner was staying there, but he was a teacher of a university in Sendai.

It was already evening when they returned to Yamagata, worn out from their fruitless search.

The pot-bellied proprietor of their inn was standing at the entrance when they drew up. 'I gather you didn't find him.' He knew the results of their search even before Takamori had had a chance to explain. 'I've just heard that a huge foreigner stayed at an inn in Kosho-*machi* last night.'

They began to walk the last hundred yards. Kobayashi left the road and began to descend the slope to the swampy pond. After him Endo and then Gaston ploughed through

* Limbless, wooden dolls.

the wet grass. Their trouser legs were wet and muddy. Beyond the grass banks was a reddish-black stretch of ground, lapped by the black waves of the pond.

'This is the place,' said Kobayashi in a low voice, craftily observing Endo's expression. 'See over there . . . that tree sticking out of the water. It's at the foot of that.'

Kobayashi pointed to a dead tree rising out of the fog-covered water. It was probably a remnant from the time when this had been a cryptomeria forest, before the swamp had come into existence. Now it was stripped of bark and stood out above the water, a whitened trunk that looked like a man's rib.

'I'll stand guard here,' said Endo, turning to Kobayashi, who stood a little behind him. 'Go out there and get it.'

'You're asking me to get it?' asked Kobayashi, as if surprised. 'An old man like me? I've got a weak heart. I can't go into cold water like this.'

'You'll have something worse than a weak heart if you don't do as I say.' With a pinched smile on his face, Endo put his hand into his pocket. When he drew it out again, it was gripping the black weapon.

'I see.' Kobayashi blinked his rat-like eyes and looked up at the killer in appeal. 'Forgive me, forgive me. Endo *san*, I really have got a bad heart.'

At this point Gaston, who had not taken his eyes off the other two, sat down on the ground and began to untie the laces of his old shoes.

'What are you doing, Gas?' Endo asked suspiciously.

'Kobayashi *san*'s an old man. I'll go into the water,' explained Gaston smiling, as he lowered his big feet into the swamp. 'Oh, this water is ice-cold. . . . Endo *san*, what are we looking for?'

'At the foot of that tree over there is a box,' said Kobayashi, relieved. 'Tie this rope to it and pull it out.'

The wind began to blow harder and the fog became still thicker. Even the withered tree trunk was now covered by the fog. Gaston went deeper into the swamp water, sinking first to his knees and then to his hips. The two on shore saw the outline of his body gradually disappear into the fog.

Just then Kobayashi's small rodent eyes were drawn to the shovel which Gaston had left on the bank. Endo, who was still gripping the pistol, had turned toward Gaston as he made his way through the water, and so he had momentarily taken his eyes off his enemy.

Despite his huge physique Gaston did not know how to swim. Since he had been born and raised in a mountain country, the only water he was familiar with was that of the mountain streams, deep enough only for wading. Thus there had been no opportunity to learn to swim.

Moreover, he had not noticed the peculiar nature of the swamp. It was only when the water was up to his waist that he noticed that the ground at his feet was soft and was sucking down his legs. But it was too late. When he lifted one leg out of the mud, the other only sank deeper into it.

'My feet!' he cried out, stunned. 'Endo *san*, my feet!'

But the fog had cut off all sight of Endo on shore. Gaston could not even guess his direction. When he stopped struggling and stood still, he seemed to sink still deeper into the mud. And the more he struggled, the harder it was to free himself.

Endo heard Gaston's cry. Unfortunately, from where he stood he could not catch sight of Gaston's ungainly figure. He put the hand that held the Colt to his mouth and started to shout to him. But just then out of the corner of his eye he saw Kobayashi quickly pick up the shovel that lay on the bank.

Endo had been distracted by Gaston for only a moment, but it was enough to put him completely off his guard. Kobayashi took advantage of this to come at Endo full strength with his shovel. Though he was an old man, he had the strength born of desperation. Endo, trying to sidestep his attack, slipped on the wet ground and fell, still clutching the pistol.

Kobayashi directed blow after blow at the hand holding the pistol until it fell from the killer's hand, which was now covered with blood, but not before a dull gun report had echoed across the swamp.

'Die, you bastard! Die! Die!' shouted Kobayashi as he rained blow after blow upon Endo. The latter, trying to dodge the blows, attempted to rise to his feet, but he could get no firm foothold. He felt a burning pain in his left shoulder and saw Kobayashi's inflamed face immediately before his eyes. He grabbed Kobayashi's legs and would not let go even when the shovel hit him several times on the hips and on the arms.

When Endo finally succeeded in rising to his feet, his suit was ripped to shreds, as if it had been cut off him by a sharp knife. From the rents in the material bright red blood was flowing, staining his arms and chest.

Both adversaries were breathing hard. They stood for a time merely glaring at each other, trying to catch their breath. Endo, who could not use his left shoulder, had his back to the swamp. He started to move backwards step by step, while Kobayashi, shovel still in hand and breathing so heavily that his shoulders moved rapidly up and down, pressed in on him.

'Endo *san*!' called Gaston at the top of his voice when he heard the gun discharge. His legs remained stuck in the swamp mud.

The wind was still blowing over the surface of the water. Just then a blast of wind opened a pocket in the fog, revealing enough of the shore for Gaston to catch sight of Kobayashi coming with the shovel at Endo, who was standing in the swamp.

At this sight Gaston instinctively lurched forward in an attempt to run to shore where he saw a life and death struggle taking place, but his legs, still clutched by the swamp, would not move at his command. Losing his balance, he fell into the water with a heavy plop such as a telegraph pole might make.

The water in the swamp was not very deep, but Gaston, who could not swim, swallowed a good deal of the muddy water. When he raised his head out of the water again, it looked like the face of a pop-eyed goldfish floating up to the surface for air.

He began to move his arms and legs desperately, like a mongrel that has been thrown into a pond. He inched forward slowly, but when he raised his head and tried to call out to Endo, he lost his balance again and sank once more into the water.

Meanwhile on the shore Endo and Kobayashi, their shoulders heaving, were still glaring at each other. When Endo made a quick move to retrieve the pistol that had fallen to the ground, Kobayashi rushed forward with the shovel raised above his head to keep Endo from reaching it.

Kobayashi aimed blow after blow at his enemy. Endo succeeded in dodging the blows, and the shovel bit into the ground each time with a ringing sound. Kobayashi always brought the shovel down full strength so that it had the cutting edge of a sharp instrument.

Little by little Endo was moving further into the water. Blood was gushing from his knees, where his trousers were torn, and mixing with the water like black ink seeping into clear liquid.

Endo's strategy was obvious. The ground on the bank was hard. So Kobayashi had no trouble pulling up his shovel after each blow. But in the swamp the pressure of the water would count against him. Then the two would have to fight it out hand to hand.

But if Endo went too far out into the water, it would make it hard for him to sidestep Kobayashi's blows. So he took a stand about two yards from the bank. Kobashayi, staring at him with bloodshot eyes, moved along the bank to the right. There was a crafty smile on his face. He had not been a soldier for nothing. He had quickly divined the strategy of his enemy.

'Die, you bastard! Die!' Swinging the shovel around his head with no particular aim, Kobayashi approached little by little the place where the pistol had fallen. Determined that Kobayashi should not get to it, Endo kept clear of the swinging blade and watched for a chance to rush him.

Gaston had by now managed to swim up almost to the shore, if that strange crawling motion could be called swimming. Taking up a position between the two men, he stretched out his long arms and called out in a loud, drawling voice, 'No! No! No! You mustn't do that!'

Kobayashi's shovel came down heavily on his head. Unlike Endo, he had not the agility to dodge it. Surprisingly he did not fall under the weight of the blow, but just stood there, feet apart, like a colossus, with both arms dangling at his sides. He closed his eyes, as if the better to bear the pain. Both Kobayashi and Endo were frozen for a moment, their eyes glued on Gaston.

A red liquid began to gush from the wound in Gaston's head, and flowed slowly down the side of his face. Still he did not move; he did not even wipe away the blood. Kobayashi was driven to a new frenzy by the sight of blood. He raised his shovel and brought it down once again with all his strength on the motionless giant.

This time Gaston began to stagger. Kobayashi was all the more infuriated and came at him with another blow and then still another. For some reason he could not fathom, there was something unbearably eerie about this man standing before him. Under the impact of the blows Gaston fell prone into the swamp like a heavy log and sank down into the water.

In the meantime Endo had regained his wits. He scampered up the bank like a rabbit in flight and quickly retrieved the Colt pistol that lay on the wet ground. It was firmly in his hand by the time Kobayashi, breathing heavily, had lowered his shovel after the last blow.

'Kobayashi!' Pointing the black barrel at his enemy, Endo shouted, 'Now I'll be revenged for my brother's death. Throw away the shovel. . . . Get into the water. . . . Or wait, maybe I'd better have you dig your grave first. I'm sure you don't want anyone to catch sight of your ugly corpse.'

The shovel fell from Kobayashi's hand. His rodent eyes became as large as saucers and a look of anguish and fear distorted his face. He thrust both hands out in front of him and emitted a loud cry. Like the moan of an animal, it refused to form itself into words.

'*Non.*'

'What did you say?'

'*Non. Non. Non.*'

The sound had not come from Kobashayi. Gaston had raised his head from the water. Covered with blood, it looked more than ever like the head of a hippopotamus. He shouted again, '*Non, non,* Endo *san.*' He shook his head violently and with all the strength remaining in him made a gesture of appeal for clemency. 'I . . . ask you.' Then the hippopotamus head was once more submerged in the water.

The milk-white fog drifted in again and began to enfold both Gaston in the water and Endo and Kobayashi on shore.

Without shame or worry about appearances, Kobayashi got down on his knees and prostrated himself before Endo, who stood, pistol in hand, summoning up the remains of his energy for the final job he had to do.

The fact was that Kobayashi's figure was reflected but dimly in his eyes. Not only Kobayashi, but also the bank covered with fog and the field and the dead tree. It was as though he were viewing the scene through a badly-focused lens. On the point of losing consciousness, he realized that all he had to do was pull back the finger on the trigger. But it would not move, as if it were glued to its present position.

'Pull! All you have to do is pull!' a far-off voice some-where in his head ordered.

'Pull! Now! Just pull!' Kobayashi's distorted face, eyes closed, was pointed up at him. He made one last effort to concentrate his remaining strength into that trigger finger.

'*Non. Non. Non.*' The voice of Gaston, now very feeble, came up at him again from the water. 'I ask you.' Endo had the illusion that he had heard this voice before in the long distant past. It resembled the voice of his sister who with his parents had burned to death in the shrine gardens the day of the big Tokyo air raid.

'Pull! Pull!'

'*Non, non, non.* I ask you.'

The two voices began to merge in his head. He lost consciousness and fell into the water next to Gaston.

At the sound of the fall Kobayashi opened his eyes. This was an unexpected turn of fortune. He picked up the shovel and lifted it over his head. He walked into the water with the intention of splitting Endo's head open like a watermelon. He didn't have to be afraid of killing him. After all, the man had come at him with a gun. He would have no trouble proving that he had done it in self-defence.

But just as he was getting ready to bring down the shovel, Gaston's battered head plunged up once again out of the water.

'Stop!' The voice was loud enough to reach across the swamp. And this strange monster of a man stretched his huge hands over the fallen body of his friend in a protect-ing gesture.

Shovel upraised, Kobayashi stared at Gaston in astonish-ment. This time chills of fright ran up and down his spine. He dropped the shovel and scurried with rat-like speed toward the road.

Then everything was still. The swamp was enshrouded in silence, as if it had already forgotten the desperate battle that had taken place. At a blast of wind the deep fog scattered and at another blast came together again. There was no sound but that of the branches of the trees trying to shake off the raindrops that had settled on them.

13 The Egret

According to the proprietor of Araki Mataimon Inn, a man had seen a foreigner and a Japanese enter a cheap hotel in Kosho-*machi* the previous evening.

'This fellow who saw them works at a *sake* shop in the neighbourhood. He says the Japanese had a very pale face and seemed to be ill. The foreigner was exactly as you described him. Tall, built like a Sumo-wrestler, with a long, flat face.'

'That must have been Gaston.'

'Why don't you go and have a look?'

Kosho-*machi* was not far from the inn at which they were staying. It was a walk of less than ten minutes. Takamori and Tomoe followed the proprietor's instructions and turned right at Seventh-day-*machi*. As he walked, Takamori was full of joyful expectation at the prospect of seeing Gaston again.

'Don't walk so fast!'

'I can't help it. My feet won't go any slower.'

Takamori's eagerness brought out the perverse streak in his sister. Purposely she stopped from time to time to point out Yamagata landmarks to him.

'Takamori, have you ever seen so many temples? This is really a temple town, isn't it?' Among the houses built in the style of the ancient samurai manors were many quiet temple compounds. 'I'd love to live here. Maybe I ought to find myself a husband in Yamagata.'

'We can discuss that after we've seen Gas.'

'What's all the rush? He's not going to disappear.'

But when they reached the inn where Gaston was supposed to be staying, Tomoe's words were given the lie.

'He left early this morning.' The clerk at the inn, a man with so many gold teeth that his face looked like the tiger mask used in the local festival dances, examined Tomoe carefully from head to foot and continued. 'He got up while it was still dark. Let me see, what time was it?'

The clerk did not know where he had gone. He had paid his bill, and since he had no luggage there was no reason for him to return to the inn.

It was already dusk. The last rays of the sun struck the roofs of the old houses of Kosho-*machi*. A young girl with her little brother strapped to her back was leaning against the wall of a temple and singing him a lullaby. There was something in her song that made Takamori feel sad. Or more than sad, it made him wonder about men. What was this strange creature man, anyway?

'After coming all the way to Yamagata . . .' There was disappointment and a touch of melancholy in Tomoe's voice.

'I have a premonition something's happened to him.'

'Don't be silly.'

Just then someone came riding up from behind on a bicycle and called to them. When they turned round, they saw that it was the proprietor of their inn. The fat man got off his bicycle, all out of breath.

'Something terrible's happened! Endo's just been found over at Big Swamp. The police called to let you know.'

Today for the first time since they had arrived in Yamagata the sky was blue all over. Their homeward-bound train was passing through a plain of rice fields that looked like a lake of bluish-green water. The train occasionally blew its whistle loudly and gradually picked up speed. A refreshing breeze was blowing in through the window. Boys and girls at the farms they passed waved their hands at the train.

Takamori and Tomoe, sitting close to the window with their elbows on the ledge, looked up at the fluffy clouds of pure white that floated above the mountain peaks. The peak in the middle that rose above all the others was named Mt Shirataka or Mt White Falcon. Immediately below it was Big Swamp. Neither brother nor sister could take their eyes away from this mountain, which shone now with a golden splendour. The same thought was in both their minds.

The three days that had followed the discovery of Endo had been full of activity. That very evening the proprietor of their inn had taken them to the Yamagata Police Station, immediately behind the Yamagata District Building, where the man in charge had explained to them that about ten o'clock that morning a young man had been found lying in the shallow water of the swamp, a pistol gripped in his hand. The first to discover him had been the old man of the nearby rest house who had gone to the swamp to fish. As he drew near the water, he had seen about a hundred yards from the bank a long, dark brown object lapped over by the slight waves of the pond. The police and detectives had come immediately from Yamagata to investigate. Four hours later they knew from the letters and the small notebook they found in the man's pocket that he was Endo of the Hoshino gang in Tokyo. The man had been taken immediately to a hospital in Yamagata.

About the swamp were to be seen the traces of a desperate struggle. Endo was lucky enough to be still alive, but he had been severely injured.

'According to the man who found him, a man in a raincoat had stopped by at his place that morning and bought three bottles of soft drink. We're investigating that now,' the detective at the desk explained, as he wiped the sweat from his neck.

Takamori asked about Gaston and the detective replied, 'A foreigner, you say? As of now, we've heard nothing about a foreigner being involved in the case.'

Strange that Endo should have been the only one found at the swamp. Takamori explained everything he knew about the case as the detective scribbled notes in his pad.

'So you say that Endo and your foreign friend left the inn together this morning?'

'Yes.' Takamori was not accustomed to this kind of investigation, and he answered the detective's questions as apprehensively as if he himself were under suspicion. 'But it's inconceivable that the foreigner should have tried to kill Endo. I'll lay my life on that.'

'In any case, we'll know what happened when Endo comes to. It's the police's job to investigate every possible lead.' Then he added, 'I'm sorry, but I'm afraid I'll have to ask you to stay in Yamagata for another two or three days.'

The next day men in boats dragged the pond carefully, but they found nothing – neither Gaston's body nor anything belonging to any of the three men.

'I suppose he might have run off with the man who bought the soft drinks.'

'Ridiculous!' replied Takamori. It was the following day and he had again dropped by at the police station. 'Gas – that foreigner – isn't involved in the crime. Of course he might have been forced to go along with them.'

The third day when Endo, who was still in the hospital in a very weak condition, told his story to the detectives, the mystery only deepened. Endo confessed that he had led both Kobayashi and Gaston to Big Swamp. He had not explained to the foreigner the purpose of the trip. He told how Gaston had taken Kobayashi's blows on himself in order to save him, and how finally, seriously injured, he had collapsed in the shallows of the swamp.

'Then what happened to him?'

Endo shook his bandaged head so vigorously that it must have given him pain. Then he remembered that some time after he had lost consciousness he had felt the drifting fog wet on his cheeks and had opened his eyes slightly. One corner of the sky was a cloudless blue and he saw a lone egret, flapping snow-white wings, heading in that direction. But he had seen it only dimly.

That was all he remembered. And even this he could not be quite sure of.

He thought he had really seen the blue sky and the egret with the pure white wings, but he admitted that it could just as well have been an illusion or a dream. After that he had lost consciousness again and had lain there until discovered, his head half under water.

Where had Gaston disappeared to?

There was no indication that he had died in the swamp. The only trace of him found there was an old jacket, which someone pulled out of a shallow part of the swamp a day or so later. Endo confirmed the fact that the coat was indeed Gaston's.

That was the end of it. The detectives were reluctant to put any further questions to Endo, who was still in a critical condition.

Had Gaston dragged himself out of the swamp and lost his way on the mountain road as he went off to find help for Endo? Or had he tried to follow Kobayashi? It was a mystery to the police as well as to Takamori and Tomoe. No one along any of the possible routes he might have taken had seen a foreigner of his description.

A golden breeze wafted in through the window of the train. As Takamori gazed at the mountain peaks crowned with billowy clouds, he suddenly had the illusion that he saw Gaston slowly climbing the mountains, there just below the highest peak. He was waving his hat at him, a smile on his horseface – the very smile they had grown so accustomed to, a foolish, timorous smile.

Takamori *san*, I'm going.'

'Where are you going, Gas?'

'Anywhere, everywhere . . . wherever there are people.'

The vision was shattered by Tomoe's voice. She was also sitting with her cheek resting in the palm of her hand, looking up at the mountains. But her imagination had taken a more practical turn than her brother's.

'Takamori, I wonder if Gaston hasn't return to Tokyo. We may find him at home when we get there.'

Takamori smiled sadly. Would she ever really understand Gaston?

'Oh, look at the egret!' A lonely egret was flying across the rice fields, and slowly and gracefully climbing into the blue sky.

'Gas *san*, goodbye,' Takamori whispered in a low voice to the bird.

More than a month had passed since Takamori and Tomoe returned to Tokyo and there had been no news of Gaston. It was a midsummer day when Takamori was visited at work by a policeman from the Marunouchi Police Station. The girl at the reception desk was concerned for him as she announced his visitor.

'Higaki *san*, I hope you are not in trouble.'

'Please don't testify against me,' Takamori answered playfully. He guessed immediately that it was something to do with Gaston. Still he was apprehensive as he opened the door to the reception room.

The detective who had received him and Tomoe when they went to the Marunouchi Police Station to pick up Gaston was sitting on a sofa with his legs stretched out in front of him.

'How do you do. Glad to see you again.'

'I'm sorry to bother you at work.' The detective was wearing black trousers and a short-sleeved white shirt. 'I came to see you about that foreigner. We still have no lead on his whereabouts. Kobayashi and Endo are under arrest, so we no longer have any business with him. But he's vanished from the face of the earth.'

'Is that so?'

'There was a report from Miyazaki Prefecture in Kyushu that a foreigner of his description had been seen there.

We're checking that out, but it looks as if it's another person.'

Disappointed, Takamori stared down at the floor. The detective picked up the tea cup the receptionist had brought him and began to slurp his tea noisily.

'We made a report of the matter to the French embassy. . . . I wondered if you might not have a clue as to his whereabouts.'

'Gaston left his luggage . . . that is to say, one old duffel bag behind at our house. Perhaps . . .'

It was agreed that the following evening the detective should come to his home and take a look at the duffel bag.

The next evening the broad-shouldered detective, in the presence of Takamori and Tomoe clumsily began to untie the strings of Gaston's bag with hands that seemed more at home in *karate*.

He pulled out of the bag patched shirts, underwear, a rusted razor, a jacket, towels; then a songbook with a torn cover; finally, one old notebook.

'It's written in a foreign language,' exclaimed the detective, discouraged. 'Can you read it?'

In the entire notebook there were to be found only two lines written in French. Foreign languages were not Takamori's forte, but Tomoe, always practical, brought out her French dictionary and sat down to decipher the lines. They were written in Gaston's abominable hand-writing and looked like worms crossing the page.

When she had finally translated the two lines, she read them aloud to her brother and the detective : 'I've failed three times to pass the entrance examination to the Mission Seminary. So I won't be able to become a missionary priest. Still I must go to Japan.'

Brother and sister looked at each other without saying a word.

Tomoe was absorbed in her typing. Her funny face with

nose slightly elevated like a cat's moved from left to right, following the words of the manuscript she was typing.

One after another manuscripts were brought to her desk for typing, and one after another she disposed of them, sending the completed text back to Mr Disanto's desk. After every half hour of typing, without fail, she remembered to put drops in her eyes and massage her fingers.

When it was close to noon, she stole a look at her watch and drew a transistor radio out of a desk drawer. She put the earplug in her ear and turned the dial to the noon stock report. As she listened, she made mental note of what stocks to buy next.

'Tomoe, I wonder if you're free this Saturday,' Osako asked in a low voice, as he pretended to be bringing her more documents to be typed. 'I have two tickets for the concert at Hibiya Hall.'

'Oh, that's wonderful! You'll take me?' she asked smiling.

Osako nodded. He was obviously well-pleased at her acceptance, as he made her a low bow.

Tomoe was confident that she would not fall in love with, much less marry, a man like Osako. He seemed to be attracted to her, but she would never admit him or anyone else at present to greater intimacy than that of good friend. If he was inclined to take her to a film or a concert, it would be very foolish of her to refuse, she thought, as long as she was free that evening.

'Did you hear anything more about that Frenchman?' asked Osako who, elated by her acceptance of the concert invitation, did not leave immediately but tried to prolong the conversation.

'If you mean Gaston, no . . . we've heard nothing. But this is working time. We'd better talk later.'

'OK.'

'Mr Disanto may see us.'

When Osako had left her, Tomoe, to re-accustom her

fingers to the keys before beginning to type again, typed the words 'Gaston Bonaparte' on her paper.

'Wonderful fool,' she thought. Where had the wonderful fool disappeared to anyway? Every so often she thought of his long horseface and his good-natured laugh, and his sleepy voice as he tried to answer her with his mouth full of macaroni. But as the days passed, these memories were becoming dimmer and dimmer.

She also thought of the day when the man of her dreams would come along. He would not be a poor, weak simpleton like Gaston, but a strong, well-built, courageous young man who would sweep her off her feet.

Takamori sat in his favourite haunt, the Otafuku Bar, with beer bottles lined up in front of him. He thought dreamily for a few moments, then scribbled something in his little notebook.

'What're you doing, Higaki?' asked his friend, Iijima, who was sitting beside him. Iijima tried to see what he had written.

'Stop that,' ordered Takamori, red-faced, as he put the book back into his pocket. It was not like him to get embarrassed like this.

'I suppose you're figuring up how much you owe us, Higaki *san*,' said the waitress sarcastically as she served him a heaped plateful of *o-den*.

Takamori smiled wryly and looked out of the cracked window at the night sky. Tomorrow would probably be fine too. A host of stars were twinkling above the narrow roofs of the bars along the street.

Suddenly he recalled the night he had stood with Gaston at their second-storey window, gazing at the stars.

Gaston has disappeared, Takamori murmured in his heart, but that's as it should be. He was a man who had to disappear. . . . Like the heroine of *The Tale of the Bamboo Cutter* he had come down from the heavens and had returned to them. This was more than mere fancy to Takamori. Somehow or other it best expressed for him the vocation of Gaston.

After he had parted from Iijima, Takamori began to walk in the direction of the station to catch his train, as he always did. But halfway to the station he had a sudden inspiration and started to retrace his steps. He had a strong desire to see the face of Chotei, whom he hadn't seen for a long time.

This was the street in Shibuya where he had caught sight of Napoleon and chased after him. The dog had probably run here and there in frantic search for Gaston. Napoleon was now dead.

Emerging from the railway underpass, he caught sight of Chotei in the dim light of his candle. The old man was bending over inspecting the hands of a woman who had come to consult him. She looked like a mother who had been worn down by a hard life. She had a bandage round her neck and a baby strapped on her back. This very evening, reflected Takamori, there were countless others like her experiencing the pain and sadness of life.

Takamori concealed himself behind a telegraph pole and waited for Chotei to be free. Gaston once hid himself behind this very pole, he whispered to himself, as he kept his eyes on the old diviner.

Gaston is still alive. One day he'll come lumbering down again from that far-off azure country to take upon his back once more the sorrow of people like these.

If you have enjoyed this book you may like to try some of the other Peter Owen paperback reprints listed below. The **Peter Owen Modern Classics** series was launched in 1998 to bring some of our internationally acclaimed authors and their works, first published by Peter Owen in hardback, to a modern readership.

To order books or a free catalogue or for further information on these or any other Peter Owen titles, please contact the **Sales Department, Peter Owen Ltd, 73 Kenway Road, London SW5 0RE, UK** tel: ++ **44 (0)20 7373 5628 or ++ 44 (0)20 7370 6093,** fax: ++ **44 (0)20 7373 6760**, e-mail: **sales@peterowen.com** or visit our website at **www.peterowen.com**

Peter Owen Modern Classics

Guillaume Apollinaire	Les Onze Mille Verges	0 7206 1100 8	£9.95
Paul Bowles	Midnight Mass	0 7206 1083 4	£9.95
Paul Bowles	Points in Time	0 7206 1137 7	£8.50
Paul Bowles	Their Heads Are Green	0 7206 1077 X	£9.95
Paul Bowles	Up Above the World	0 7206 1087 7	£9.95
Blaise Cendrars	Dan Yack	0 7206 1157 1	£9.95
Blaise Cendrars	The Confessions of Dan Yack	0 7206 1158 X	£9.95
Blaise Cendrars	To the End of the World	0 7206 1097 4	£9.95
Jean Cocteau	Le Livre Blanc	0 7206 1081 8	£8.50
Jean Cocteau	The Miscreant	0 7206 1173 3	£8.50
Colette	Duo and Le Toutounier	0 7206 1069 9	£9.95
Lawrence Durrell	Pope Joan	0 7026 1065 6	£9.95
Isabelle Eberhardt	In the Shadow of Islam	0 7026 1191 1	£9.95
Shusaku Endo	The Samurai	0 7206 1185 7	£9.95
Jean Giono	Two Riders on the Storm	0 7206 1159 8	£9.95
Hermann Hesse	Demian	0 7206 1130 X	£9.95
Hermann Hesse	Gertrude	0 7206 1169 5	£9.95
Hermann Hesse	Journey to the East	0 7206 1131 8	£8.50
Hermann Hesse	Narcissus and Goldmund	0 7206 1102 4	£12.50
Hermann Hesse	Peter Camenzind	0 7206 1168 7	£9.95

Hermann Hesse	*The Prodigy*	0 7206 1174 1	£9.95
Anna Kavan	*Asylum Piece*	0 7206 1123 7	£9.95
Anna Kavan	*The Parson*	0 7206 1140 7	£8.95
Anna Kavan	*Sleep Has His House*	0 7206 1129 6	£9.95
Anna Kavan	*Who Are You?*	0 7206 1150 4	£8.95
Yukio Mishima	*Confessions of a Mask*	0 7206 1031 1	£11.95
Anaïs Nin	*Children of the Albatross*	0 7206 1165 2	£9.95
Anaïs Nin	*Collages*	0 7206 1145 8	£9.95
Anaïs Nin	*The Four-Chambered Heart*	0 7206 1155 5	£9.95
Anaïs Nin	*Ladders to Fire*	0 7206 1162 8	£9.95
Boris Pasternak	*The Last Summer*	0 7206 1099 0	£8.50
Cesare Pavese	*The Devil in the Hills*	0 7206 1118 0	£9.95
Cesare Pavese	*The Moon and the Bonfire*	0 7206 1119 9	£9.95
Mervyn Peake	*A Book of Nonsense*	0 7206 1163 6	£7.95
Edith Piaf	*My Life*	0 7206 1111 3	£9.95
Marcel Proust	*Pleasures and Regrets*	0 7206 1110 5	£9.95
Joseph Roth	*Flight Without End*	0 7206 1068 0	£9.95
Joseph Roth	*The Silent Prophet*	0 7206 1135 0	£9.95
Joseph Roth	*Weights and Measures*	0 7206 1136 9	£9.95
Cora Sandel	*Alberta and Jacob*	0 7206 1184 9	£9.95
Natsume Soseki	*The Three-Cornered World*	0 7206 1156 3	£9.95
Bram Stoker	*Midnight Tales*	0 7206 1134 2	£9.95
Tarjei Vesaas	*The Birds*	0 7206 1143 1	£9.95
Tarjei Vesaas	*The Ice Palace*	0 7206 1122 9	£9.95
Tarjei Vesaas	*Spring Night*	0 7206 1189 X	£9.95
Noel Virtue	*The Redemption of Elsdon Bird*	0 7206 1166 0	£8.95